John Skelton

Summers and Winters at Balmawhapple

Vol. 1, Second Edition

John Skelton

Summers and Winters at Balmawhapple
Vol. 1, Second Edition

ISBN/EAN: 9783337249106

Printed in Europe, USA, Canada, Australia, Japan

Cover: Foto ©Andreas Hilbeck / pixelio.de

More available books at **www.hansebooks.com**

Summers and Winters at

Balmawhapple

MARY STUART.

From the Sketch by Janet in the Bibliothèque Nationale, Paris.

The Second Series of "Table-Talk"

Summers and Winters at Balmawhapple a Second Series of The Table-Talk of Shirley by John Skelton C.B. LL.D.

With Illustrations

Volume One

Second Edition

William Blackwood & Sons
Edinburgh and London 1897

To

A. A. S.

1867–1897.

Fides, nudaque Veritas.

THE PRELUDE.

*T*WO hundred years ago (or thereby) a Yorkshire Shirley
    crossed the Border, and settled on the banks of Loch
Leven. There his sons and grandsons continued to reside
till the other day: famous anglers when living, they now
sleep peacefully on its shores,—dreaming, it may be, of the
big trout they landed or of the bigger that they lost. A
grandson or a great-grandson, more adventurous than the
others, migrated from the inland water to the sea, and it

was thus that in *due* season I came to know Balmawhapple.[1]
Here we have no continuing city; but in Balmawhapple I
have been *content* to abide. My constancy is somewhat
singular, I admit. Our royal and ancient *burgh* may be
compared to the hive which sends off swarm after swarm.
Among sea-bred people the sea-bird's instinct is strong.
There are Balmawhapple men to be found in every corner
of the globe. The boys who *were with* me at school have
wandered away to Canada and the States, to Central Africa
and Pacific islands. One of them is an engineer on the
line that is crossing the Andes. Another is shooting ibex
in Thibet. Another has a fruit-farm in California. They
write to me at times,—letters arrive with strange stamps and
outlandish post-marks, that bring a sense of romance and
adventure into our uneventful life. But Fate, though not
unkind to me on the whole,—why should I fret, who have
been spared through it all, while so many strong men have
gone down—down even unto Hades?—has ordained that I

---

[1] *The Shirleys (I may venture to add in the modest obscurity of a foot-
note) remained persistently "English" until, marrying into a great Scottish
house (Mary Stuart was niece of Thomas and Methuen, the last Earls of
Kellie of the family of Cambo), they were able to trace their descent back
to Celtic Mormaers and the Victor of Bannockburn, and so became entirely
acclimatised, and indeed more "Scotch" than the Scots. The "Shirra"
(who married Mary Stuart sometime in the 'nineties) was the most expert
fly-fisher of his day, and came to be known far and wide as "The Shirra
of the Loch." "Will the Shirra of the Loch take a glass of wine with the
Shirra of the Forest?" was Sir Walter's greeting when they met each year
at Blair Adam.*

should stay at home. Unlike so many of our people, I have not been permitted to walk " by the long wash of Australasian seas," nor " breathe in converse seasons." I have not been a rover.

Do not mistake me. I do not complain. For even in Balmawhapple the sluggish current is sometimes interrupted, is sometimes accelerated. During the fifty years on which I can look back, the pulse of the community has sometimes beat faster than is common with, or probably good for, that somewhat feeble organ. When young Dr Diamond was found dead in his bed, with an empty bottle on the table which smelt of bitter almonds; when pretty Nellie Barton ran away with the groom ; when lawyer Jenkins, who was also the local banker, took an autumn holiday with the mid-summer rents of half the county gentlemen of the district in his pocket and forgot to return,—the usual afternoon crowd on the High Street became positively animated. And when Mark Holdfast came back from the south, where his

> *" strong and simple words,*
> *Keen to wound as sharpened swords,"*

had won him fame and fortune ; and—— But Mark must have the opening chapter to himself.

S.

CONTENTS.

BOOK ONE.

BY THE NORTH SEA.

BOOK ONE

BY THE NORTH SEA

BY THE NORTH SEA.

I.

MARK'S RETURN.

MARK HOLDFAST was one of my early friends. He was not exactly a Balmawhapple boy; but his father's house was only a few miles round the bay, and so we came to know each other. The Cleuch was rather a lonely place, — a gaunt old - fashioned house, built in the time of Anne or the first George, which overlooked the sea, and where morning and night one heard the curlews piping, and round which the sea-mews wheeled as though it had been one of their own skerries. The moorland closed round it, and on a moist autumn day the air was sweet and aromatic with the scent of the moorland, — the scent of bog-myrtle and heather. There was the breezy upland on one side, the breezy sea on the other, and such solitude

as boys and poets love. I could not go with him to
the great peat-hags on the hill where the grey goose
and the dun duck lodged; but I used to wait for him
at the smithy—Jock Tamson's smithy—just below the
lochan famous for teal, and we would saunter home
together through the autumn gloaming. Even as a
boy he was a fine shot; but it was on the water that
he was most in his element. He could swim like a
fish. He would take his boat out to sea when even
John Dun — John Dun, who once saved him from
drowning — preferred to smoke his pipe on shore. I
was often his only companion; there was a fascination
about these foolhardy doings which I could not resist.
It was the one manly excitement for which my infirmity did not unfit me: when the Daisy, close hauled
to the wind, with a double reef on her sail and the
water at her gunwale, was rushing across the bay, I
forgot that I was a cripple.

It was a hardy and independent life for a lad,—a
life that could scarcely fail to leave its mark behind.
His family, though one of the oldest in the county, had
by ill luck or ill guidance lost much of the land that
once belonged to them, and Mark was early taught to
practise thrift. They had few neighbours, as I have
said, and these were of a rank somewhat lower than
their own. They did not associate easily with country
doctors and country lawyers. My own father was
the Duke's factor,—a man with plenty of rough sense
and humour, and who was much trusted by rich and
poor. There was a long-standing acquaintance be-

tween him and the Holdfasts; and what business
they needed to be done was done by him. But even
from him they held aloof, and the friendship, such
as it was, never ripened into cordial intimacy. Each
respected the other, and there an end. The boyish
friendship between Mark and myself was accidental;
it came about without any seeking or set purpose on
either side; it would hardly have lived had it not
been that then, as always, I was a hero-worshipper,
and that my unreasoning devotion touched him. He
was very proud, and he was very shy; his instinctive
and inherited reserve was forbidding. I think the only
people who really knew him at that time save myself
were the "Buckie boys," a truculent and somewhat
disreputable race of fishermen. With them he was
popular. With them (and he often passed the night
far from land in one or other of their yawls) he un-
bent wholly; his reserve melted away, his moodiness
vanished; the picture of the nut-brown lad, tanned
up to the temples, his cheeks flushed, the wind in
his hair, the sunlight in his eyes, steering the great
herring-boat into harbour, while the rough tars looked
on, is one on which, after all these years, I like to
dwell. Young Irvine, who went to London, and is
now a R.A., painted him in his "sou'-wester" and
sailor-jacket, and it hangs to this day in the smoking-
room at the Cleuch.

When long afterwards (and yet it was not so long,
for he rose with uncommon rapidity) he came to be a
Q.C. and a leader at the Bar, his coolness was pro-

verbial. So people said; but I knew better. He kept
himself well in hand, it is true; but no discipline however severe, no effort however sustained, could change
his nature. A shy, nervous, sensitive, highly strung
temperament like his does not harden into immobility.
His self-control was certainly very complete; but, all
the same, the inner recoil—the tremor of the racer
before the start—could not always be disguised. And
the meanness, baseness, vulgarity, from which no pro-
fession is free, hurt him as a blow hurts a woman.
That sensitive shiver of disgust at the squalid effrontery
of the men who paid him would have ruined a less
capable lawyer.

When he was eighteen he went to the university.
Up to that time I had been, I fancy, almost his only
confidant. He had had as private tutor the minister
of the parish,—a fine scholar and a competent teacher,
a man, moreover, of immense energy and variously
gifted, whose services to the Church have not been
forgotten, or, to speak more correctly, are now beginning to be recognised. But Dr Evergreen was even
then well up in years; and though he and Mark
became afterwards close friends, the brilliant and
trenchant thinker, the great ecclesiastical reformer,
failed to recognise in his shy and diffident pupil a
spirit as ardent and fearless as his own. So that the
dreams and visions of what the future had in store for
him were reserved for his diary or for my private ear.
That future he had mapped out with uncommon and
almost startling lucidity.

We were sitting one afternoon in the late summer on the beach beneath the Cleuch. He had shot a brace of ducks, and his gun and the birds were lying beside him. I was occupied on a bit of crabbed Latin in an old charter; his eye wandered vaguely over sea and sky. We had been silent for some time. It was our last day together; next morning he was to leave for college.

"It has been a pleasant time," he began, speaking at first more to himself than to his companion. "I shall never quite forget it, I fancy, in all the years that are to come—nor *you*, Dick," he added, with a kindly nod. "Dick, my boy, why don't you go into the Church? When I'm Lord Chancellor I'll give you a living. But, perhaps, you don't fancy the white tie or the silk apron. Well, then, try your pen, and when I am editor of the *Times* you shall have the place of honour. I wonder which is best,—to be a great lawyer or a great writer? I mean to be both. Please don't laugh at me, Dick. I'm quite serious, as you will see by-and-by. I would hate to be a mere lawyer," he went on, "but I would hate still more to be a mere scribbler. Which do you think the more despicable —the glib pen or the glib tongue? But it is better to make history than to write it; and a man from a Temple garret may be Prime Minister before the game is played out."

So he went away to the university, — to the great world beyond the moorland. He began by using his pen, and he wrote deftly and brilliantly. He would

send me articles now and again; and I fancied that
besides being deft and dexterous I could discern something better that gave them their charm to me — a
ground - swell of passion, of emotion, which was
stronger and deeper than the easy cynicism of the
lawyer. Then almost without warning he became a
power at the Bar. He woke one morning to find himself famous. For ten or twelve years thereafter he had
the most lucrative practice among the younger men.
He was reading briefs all night; he was speaking all
day. Some great client coming straight from the great
city told us once that if he went on as he was doing he
would be on the woolsack before he was fifty. Then
there were rumours that he was to stand for the
county; "Pam" wanted to find a seat for the Solicitor
that was to be; and Mark Holdfast with his easily
won guineas had already contrived to buy back a
goodly slice of the land which in the bad times had
been parted with by his grandfather, the Admiral. It
was likely enough that he would win; a stronger
candidate could not be found. So we all said.

But it was ordered otherwise.

It was a dull day in early autumn. The wind was in
the south, and there was rain in the sky. I had been
limping along the shore, thinking of many things, but
chiefly of my old friend. I had come to the very spot
where we had parted thirty years before, when, turning
inland to cross the links to the highroad, I met him
face to face.

He was sorely changed. He had grown an old man

—an old man before his time—a man prematurely worn. He had come back to his birthplace,—could it be that he had come back only to die?

We shook hands; we looked hard at each other; in less time than it takes to write this sentence we were on the old friendly footing.

"Yes," he said, "Pam sent for me last Sunday. The great office would be vacant directly; a seat would be found for me: they would be pleased to have me in the House. It was all very flattering; no man can be more cordial or appreciative than the Chief. Then I thought I would look up Clarkson. I had felt rather queer for a week or two,—a slight difficulty in breathing, a nasty worrying pain down the left arm. Clarkson is our family doctor, you know—a very good fellow, and sharp as a needle. I told him with a jest that it was a mere matter of form—just idle curiosity—nothing more. He took out his stethoscope, listened for a few seconds, and then turned away to the window. Dick, I knew my doom before a word was spoken. 'Tell me the truth right out,' I said, as calmly as I could, though my voice sounded strangely in my ears; 'I see that you have bad news.' 'You are hurt,' he answered frankly, looking me in the face with his honest eyes; 'it is not a mortal hurt as yet, but without absolute rest you are a dead man.' It was the knock-down blow, Dick, one gets once in a lifetime. If I wanted to live six weeks—why, good-bye to the Bar. Thrust out of Paradise, banished, outlawed, where was the good of living? I took the night to consider: next morning I wrote Pam that I was going to sell my house in town and live at—Balmawhapple! Could he give me something in the Customs? He must have thought me mad. And here we are."

This was the beginning of the close friendship which has brightened my later life. These after-years indeed have been my Indian summer. Our early intimacy was renewed. He did not come alone; his wife came with him—his wife and three bright-eyed curly-headed girls. He had married Sybil Keppel for love a year or two after he was called; Sybil had been the object of his shy boyish devotion; and the slight delicate slip of a girl that I dimly remembered (the Keppels were a family of old standing and crippled means, who owned a tumble-down barrack at the other end of the parish), though she had grown meanwhile into a brilliant woman of the world, had lost none of her girlish charm. They became my dearest friends; but I cannot say that they were popular. Husband and wife were wrapt up in each other. The knowledge that he might be taken from her at any moment gave to her wifely regard a tender solicitude. The tacit apprehension that any moment he might look his last upon the sweetest face he cared to see either in this world or the next was never entirely banished. The outside public, however (ignorant of its cause), resented this unconscious and quite innocent exclusiveness. Nor can it be denied that the scorn for his fellow-mortals which he had always felt, I daresay, and which grew upon him in his retirement, was sometimes too keenly expressed. He had fallen out of the race; he had, by no fault of his own, been forced to stand aside while others pressed on to the goal—such as it was; and failure had made him caustic, possibly bitter. So Balmawhapple, when its cordial, if somewhat florid, convivialities were persistently declined, began to look askance at the new-comers. The Holdfasts were cold, proud, taciturn, and I know not what besides. I did what I could to remove the misunderstanding — with little success. Mark's abrupt retreat from public life and a great position had from the first been regarded as an unaccountable eccentricity; no one except myself knew the exact state of matters; it was given out that he had been overworked and was taking a prolonged holiday; and though the provost and bailies continued to touch their hats to him when they met on the street, there was only one house in town (save my own and the editorial sanctum of the *Tomahawk*) where he was quite at his ease, where he was cordially welcome and an honoured guest, and that was the grey old house overlooking the harbour where Miss Christian and Miss Anne—everybody knew Miss Christian and Miss Anne—had lived since they were girls.

And there were other elements of discord.

* *
*

The Bay of Balmawhapple is protected from the fierce easterly gales by two rocky headlands which run far out into the sea. The Cleuch, as we have seen, is

built at the extreme point of the one, and is a conspicuous landmark for the ships that pass along the
coast; Keppel Court, which faces it from the other side
of the bay—here a mile across—is less conspicuous.
The old tower is a ruin; and the modern mansion—
where the Keppel girls were all born—might be taken
from the outside for a mere farm-steading. Inside it
is better; the Keppels had been soldiers and travellers;
the tables were crowded with oriental bric-a-brac, the
walls with portraits of men and women,—not undis-
tinguished for valour and beauty in their day.

The "Keppel girls" were the toast of the country-
side when I was a lad. Their mother had died before
the eldest of the six daughters was in her teens; and
the breezy and beery old captain their father had left
them thereafter very much to their own devices. It
was not to be wondered at, therefore, that they should
have grown up strong, independent, and self-willed.
But wilfulness and obstinacy were their worst faults;
for, each and all, as their rustic admirers declared,
were proud as the devil, and quite able to take care
of themselves. Sybil, indeed, it was admitted — but
Sybil after all was only a cousin—had little in common
with the others: she had been delicate as a child,
and unable to take part in their rough scrambles and
rather masculine pastimes; and though she outgrew
her childish ailments, her cheek had never the plumpness, nor her voice the vigour, of the true "Keppel
girls."

Death, marriage, domestic strife, and family feuds

(for they were never so happy as when at war) had thinned their ranks. At the time of which I am writing, indeed, only two remained, the eldest and the youngest, Martha and Barbara; and the old house which had once been clamorous with boisterous girlhood had grown strangely silent. The two sisters, with a couple of rheumatic retainers, occupied the wing which looked out upon the dreary and ill-kept garden, while the wind whistled through the broken panes of the main building, and the rats ran riot.

As the years passed the characteristics of the family became in each more marked. They had few neighbours, few friends; the Court, upon its bare promontory, was very solitary except for the sea-gulls. So, for society they were thrown mainly upon themselves. Their tempers were intrinsically alike; both were exacting; but while the one was actively, the other was passively, domineering. Martha was the shriller and more vehemently feminine of the two; but Barbara's indolent obstinacy was invincible. Martha, as she advanced in life, had taken to religion; and while the one sister devoted herself altogether to the ailments of the body, the other occupied herself mainly with the maladies of the soul. Martha was evangelical and ritualistic, High Church and Low Church, meagrely Presbyterian and floridly Episcopalian by turns; and Barbara oscillated between a famous London physician and an old woman in the village who cured by conjurations and the laying on of hands.

These were the only families of any standing in the
rural part of the parish of Balmawhapple—the Holdfasts and the Keppels; for Kirkstone, though it was
hardly a mile from the Court, belonged to the next
parish — the parish of Cuddiestone.   Our county
society was thus very limited, or, as we preferred to
say, select: if you were asked to Pittendreich, you
might meet an Earl or an Ambassador; but Pittendreich was fifteen miles away as the crow flies, and
the Pittendreich people knew little of the Balmawhapple people, and cared less.   In the burgh of
Balmawhapple itself we were more fortunate: we had
not only the inevitable lawyers and doctors and
merchants and ministers, but more than one elderly
lady who had been brought up in a big country house,
and could call the best in the county "cousin."   We
were particularly proud of Miss Christian and Miss
Anne,—two inexhaustibly delightful old gentlewomen
who lived in an old house standing in its own courtyard above the harbour, who had been famous beauties
in their youth, but who had clung to each other all
their lives with the purest sisterly devotion, and had
grown by degrees into the sweetest, daintiest, spright-
liest, nattiest old maids that one could wish to meet.
The ancient ladies were my dear friends; and their
cheery drawing-room of a summer evening, with the
murmur of voices on the pier-head and of the sea
beyond coming in through the open window, with the
bright, brisk, prosperous, pugnacious Doctor (Doctor
Jackson had brought most of us into this rather bare

and bleak world) ventilating a paradox or airing an epigram,—the cheery drawing-room, where the modest "tray" appeared punctually at 9.30, was the *salon* of our very best society, and entirely charming and enjoyable to those of us who had the password. There was a vast deal of individuality in that society; the language was idiomatic, the characters strongly marked; it was good-natured upon the whole, but it spoke its mind pretty plainly; and it hated cant and dulness as it hated a Radical or a cad. They were perfect ladies and gentlemen who composed it; but I am afraid the prudes of the present day would have 'dubbed them "Bohemians," and resented a certain freedom of definition which does not find favour now.

It was for this reason, I daresay, that certain of the most eminently respectable citizens of Balmawhapple were not precisely popular with Miss Christian and Miss Anne and the inner circle of friends who had gathered round them. If they called us "Bohemians" we called them "Philistines" (or its popular equivalent for the time being); and as from the bleak hills of Judea the chosen people looked down upon the sinful Cities of the Plain, so did we regard the faction which was led by "Pike," "G. G." the butter-merchant, and other secular and ecclesiastical luminaries of the royal and ancient burgh.[1]

---

[1] There has been much controversy, I observe, as to the true site of Balmawhapple—a controversy which it would be a pity to close prematurely. The impression, however, that there are at least *two* Balmawhapples appears to be gaining ground.

Jacob Corbie (commonly called "Pike") was the pet aversion of my boyhood. He came of a family of local lawyers who had since the year One been well known in these parts for their rather unscrupulous keenness of scent and sharpness of speech; and his resemblance to a weasel or ferret — a weasel, I think, but at any rate to a class of animals where the eyes, brought into unpleasant proximity, regard each other with ill-disguised hostility — was unmistakable. Moreover, the brow was low, narrow, and sensual, and the lip-deep smile was furtive, — all which were quite in keeping with a certain unclean and slimy animalism which characterised the man. "Pike" was never at his ease; the affectation of jocose frankness which he commonly assumed was manifestly a pretence, and the impression that he had something to hide (not silver spoons exactly) was one that he never failed to leave. At the same time, it was quite clear that the man knew on which side his bread was buttered; and that his thoughts—even when in the pulpit, even when addressing a glib prayer to the Almighty, or dropping a sticky tear over a lost sheep—were steadily fixed upon the main chance. But he was a good actor, — a good second-rate actor in his way; he could feign a cordiality which he did not feel, and simulate a passion which had no true warmth; and though he was generally detected in the long-run by the quicker-witted of his persuasion, he continued to enjoy with the unobservant masses a certain equivocal popularity.

I have spoken of Corbie as if he were an ordained clergyman; but he was only one of the lay products of an evangelical revival that had swept over the district when he was keeping the books in his uncle's office. He had a share in the business, which had something to do with blubber; but he was now a sleeping partner, and merely drew (with praiseworthy punctuality) his half-yearly dividend. The rest of his time was devoted to "saving souls"; and his loose logic and flabby rhetoric were always in considerable request during the periodical fits of religious hysteria to which his countrymen are subject.

George Gilbert Gannet (or "G. G." as our busy mercantile community called him for brevity) sinned against our Bohemian code in quite another fashion. He was not only oppressively respectable, but he was dull—offensively and criminally dull. His wife was dull; his children were dull; the house was dull; the servants in the house were dull; the very dogs and cats were dull. Though the Gannets really belonged to the mercantile class—the money had been made in trade: pickled herrings and the like—both husband and wife maintained with implicit confidence that they belonged to the "county." This was the rock on which they were anchored; had it been taken away from them, they would have suffered irreparable shipwreck. So besides employing on occasion a solemn butler and a lugubrious "buttons," they drove the only carriage (except the doctor's old gig) that was kept in Balma-whapple,—a four-wheeler, lined with purple and fine

linen like the Lord Mayor's, and emblazoned all over
with griffins and unicorns, and other legendary animals.
Otherwise, the whole family — father, mother, and
daughters—were the visible incarnation of the Com-
monplace. No fire of passion, no gleam of imaginative
light, could penetrate the thick fog in which they spent
a grey, sombre, and monotonous life. Our little Bohemian doctor regarded this dismal household with a
peculiar energy of dislike. They were, he declared,
dull as ditchwater, dry as sticks, dreary as ghosts.
Even in their diseases they were incapable of invention
or originality. "Why, sir," the little man would conclude, as he trotted off on his rounds,—"why, sir, they
cannot rise above mumps!"

Corbie and "G. G." belonged to the rank and file :
the leader of the Philistines was a man of a very different calibre. David Dewar of Kirkstone, who during
the winter months became a citizen of Balmawhapple
by occupying one of the ugly aristocratic old mansions
overlooking the harbour, was as much a fanatic as
David Deans of St Leonards or John Balfour of Bur-
ley ; and, like all fanatics, he had the most perfect confidence in his own wisdom and his own integrity. His
very tricks of manner, his idiosyncrasies of gait and
gesture, proclaimed that in their owner's estimation he
was infallible as any pope. He held his chin in the air
—high in the air—and looked down on his adversary
with the superior scorn of a Westbury or a Mill. His
cold and distant condescension, his visibly contemptuous effort to adapt himself to the meanest capacity,

would have irritated the meekest of men. God Almighty to a black beetle! Yet, though his manner was
cold and impassive, fire burnt beneath. His arguments,
it is true, were worthless; for he was a fantastical
visionary; but they were urged with a red-hot intensity
of conviction that at times was not unimpressive. He
was vindictively virtuous. That steely ire, when once
kindled, was not quickly quenched. Fanaticism is intrinsically cruel, for it disregards the decent and charit-
able conventions which obtain among gentlemen, and
which make life tolerable. Even experience, which
teaches most of us to be humble, could not mellow the
laird of Kirkstone. If a client did not follow his advice,
if a friend was not convinced by his logic, he took it as
a personal insult—an insult to his own immunity from
error. And a personal insult needed to be avenged.
For the miserable dissenter from the decrees of infallible wisdom there was little peace thereafter. The
Grand Inquisitor was never satisfied until the victim
had expiated his unreasonableness at the stake. This
Radical of the Radicals was the foe of all noncon-
formity. People said that if Kirkstone was hard and
impracticable, he was honest — honest at least. He
may have been so. At any rate, we had the satisfaction
of knowing that whatever he did, however unpleasant,
was done from " the highest motives." He was bitter,
sarcastic, pitiless, cruel, supercilious from " the highest
motives." It was not perhaps altogether surprising
that this inquisitorial integrity should not have been
appreciated by the Gallios of an easy-going society;

and in spite of fair abilities David Dewar had been from
the first a persistent failure.   He could only indeed
have been an eminent success in a world from which
common-sense and prudence and sound judgment had
been banished.   Mark, who had known him pretty in-
timately at one time, did not hesitate to declare that he
was one of those dangerous lunatics whose orbits are
incalculable.   Kirkstone was certainly more or less
crazy at irregular intervals; but there was method in
his madness, and, happily or unhappily, he was too
sane to be shut up.

David Dewar had spent the best part of his life in
the United States, and he had returned on the death of
an uncle who had left him the old Dewar Mansion-
house that overlooked the harbour, and a few acres in
the parish of Cuddiestone.   He had brought little or
nothing back with him from New England except the
nasal twang of the Yankee, a bitter contempt for mon-
archical institutions all over the world, and a profound
belief in—David Dewar.

There was thus plenty of explosive materials about.
" Mark was standing on the brink of a volcano; he was
sitting on the roof of a powder magazine; he might be
drawn in, he might be blown up, at any moment."
These were the doctor's similes when one day he spoke
to me of the matter rather urgently : for the doctor, like
myself, though he belonged ostensibly to neither of our
factions, was a bit of a hero-worshipper, and Mark had
been his hero, as he had in a more personal and intimate way been mine.   The similes were perhaps a little

mixed, but they represented a substantial truth; for the foes of our own household are the most bitter and un-scrupulous, and Corbies, Keppels, and Dewars were either by birth or marriage closely allied with the Hold-fasts. "Mark hasn't the remotest idea that they hate him," the doctor added. "I must get Dr Evergreen to speak to him. But why don't you warn him your-self? There's that clever cat, Martha Keppel, hates him like poison; Mrs G. G.'s malicious tittle-tattle is all over the place; Corbie knows that Holdfast wouldn't touch him with a pair of tongs; and what daft Davie Dewar, who is as mad as a March hare, will or will not do under any conceivable circumstances, God only knows!" And the worthy doctor, perspiring profusely, started on the daily round which he so immensely en-joyed. I saw him moping the bald pate—the bald pate that rose like a dome over the inquisitive eyes and the solid gold spectacles—all down the High Street.

I had almost omitted to mention that Dr Evergreen, Mark's old tutor, the senior minister of our collegiate church, was still alive. The earthly tabernacle indeed had wasted away, had become perilously delicate and transparent, as if its owner were already clothed with that spiritual body of which the apostle speaks; but the unclouded intellect was alert and luminous as ever. He resided at what was called "the Old Manse,"—a quaint, pleasant, old-fashioned house upon the outskirts of the town, sheltered from the wild winds of winter by the high walls and the thick hedges (often white in storm-time with driven spray) of the cosy garden in

which, like Topsy, it had "growed." All Balmawhapple loved Dr Evergreen. He had by this time
indeed almost entirely withdrawn from public life;
but the noble and venerable figure was familiar to
all of us. In these later years he had grown very
lonely; the children he idolised had one by one been
taken from him to a distant heaven (a heaven, alas!
in which he did not entirely believe); yet the sunset
light on the worn face—the after-glow—was full of
sweetness; and he had emerged from the waves of
controversy and strife with the heart of a child, and
a spirit that had been tempered as by fire.

The battle was already won—it had been a stiff fight,
though the ultimate issue was never doubtful—but he
had not doffed his armour, nor would he while he was
able to bear it; for he was one of those who hold, with
a great poet of our time (as the editor of the *Tomahawk*
remarked in his obituary notice), that the energy of life
may be kept on after the grave, but not begun—

> "And he who flagged not in the earthly strife,
>   From strength to strength advancing—only he,
>   His soul well knit, and all his battles won,
>   Mounts, and that hardly, to eternal life."

Nor must I forget the *Tomahawk*, for the *Tomahawk*
was a power in Balmawhapple, and the *Tomahawk* did
not love the Philistines. The *Tomahawk* cost a penny,
and was published on Saturday,—on Saturday as a
rule, though, if the editor happened to be "otherwise engaged," it sometimes failed to appear till the
middle of the following week.

Pat Salamander, the editor of Balmawhapple's sole literary organ, had seen a good deal of Mark in the early years when the young barrister was still writing leading articles for the daily papers, and Mark always retained a kindly remembrance of the frank and friendly intercourse of that rather skittish Bohemia. Pat had drifted about the world a good deal, and it was probably owing to Mark's good offices that he had finally settled down in the editorial sanctum of the Balmawhapple *Tomahawk*, and become our *censor morum*. Except Pat, the *Tomahawk* had no regular staff, and it trusted for its occasional diversions—*De omnibus rebus et quibusdam aliis*—mainly to amateurs. It was in the Poet's Corner of the *Tomahawk* that Dobbs—Dante Gabriel Dobbs, of whom we shall hear anon—first wooed his modest muse.

Thus though the forces of the Philistines were formidable, the chosen people in Balmawhapple were able to hold their own, especially when reinforced by their allies from St Abb's. Of the Homeric battle which was waged by the contending factions over Hector's body we shall hear anon. But, as becomes an orderly and veracious chronicler, I am going to begin at the beginning, and the stories that in the meantime I purpose to relate will take us a long way back—to primitive Balmawhapple and Holdfasts of historic record. By easy gradations — stepping nimbly but cautiously from century to century, and leaving behind us as we move the evil figures of an ugly past,

"Waving each a bloody sword,
    For the service of their Lord !"—

we shall by-and-by return to the men and women who
meet us in the street, and whose lives are bound up
with our own.

I choose instinctively a humble arena. History
transacts itself on the grand scale in Courts and
Camps; but in every nook and corner of the land,
age after age, men and women were living their own
more or less uneventful lives, while they listened to
the echoes from the great world outside. Mark and
I tried hard to live that old Balmawhapple life over
again; it was our favourite occupation for many years
(the audience growing as the years wore on)—the
Table-Talk of many a Winter Night. In this book
that TABLE-TALK is reproduced in forms for which
I am solely responsible. But in each case behind
the literary presentation there is a solid basis of fact;
I have taken the narrative from records which are
still accessible, and easily to be deciphered by experts.
If in the earlier pages I have mainly followed the
fortunes of a single house, it is because in the Holdfast charter-chest the documents from which I
borrow, — "convey, the wise it call," — are for the
most part lodged.

II.

QUEEN MARY'S HOLDFAST.

THE Holdfast charter-chest is one of the institutions of Balmawhapple. When it was sent in
to our office on the occasion of a famous lawsuit,
the whole community turned out to inspect this
masterpiece of a medieval artist. The fineness and
intricacy of the decorative ironwork on lock and hinge
and handle are only rivalled by the dexterous adjust-
ment of the crowd of figures on the panels of carven
oak. The incidents represented on the worm-eaten
panels are taken from the old miracle - plays and
moralities which served to amuse and edify the
people in what Charles Kingsley has called "the
milky youth of this great English land," — Joseph
of Arimathea, and the long-bearded Eastern sages,
and the devil himself with horns and tail and cloven
hoof. Rude snatches of verse in archaic characters
are deftly inserted here and there, to aid the unlearned
spectator in following the action of the play. A
compendious history of the world from the time when
Adam and Eve in the Garden of Eden "stabunt nudi,

et non verecundabuntur"! To Mark and myself,
when boys, the exterior of the Holdfast charter-chest
was as good as a story-book, and later on we found
that when the lid was unlocked the contents were
by no means so dry and musty as they looked. Even
in the mere title-deeds the name of some long-
forgotten Muriel, or Eufame, or Alyne, or Agatha,
or Alicia, or Veronica, or Clare, or Ursula, came
like a flash of light out of the past. There were,
moreover, records of the fifteenth and sixteenth
century Holdfasts, written by themselves in quaint
little note-books of the time, which in spite of a certain
grandiose gravity and stately deliberation were eagerly
perused by us. We knew that the Holdfasts could
wield their swords; it now appeared that more than
one of the house had been as clever with the pen.
But the story we liked best was the story of a girl
who had lived as maiden and wife and mother through
the wild times that followed the flight of Mary, who
had been taken as a child to hear Knox preach in
the great church in the High Street, and who in
extreme old age heard in her northern home of that
tragedy on the scaffold at Whitehall which revived
the memory of the still more cruel tragedy at Fotheringhay. I had a copy made once, and Mark says that
I may use it if I like. This is the story of Lilias
Maitland and Gilbert Holdfast, as written out by
Amias his brother, with some such slight modern-
ising of archaic phrases and obsolete modes of speech
as will make it intelligible to the reader of to-day.

I.

WE were twins—Gilbert and I—born in the year of our Lord
1560. We had lived together in the old house that our
grandfather had built about the time of Flodden ever since
we could remember. Ravenscleuch it was called (more
commonly "The Cleuch" for brevity), a simple square tower,
with narrow slits which served for windows in the upper flats,
and a strong oaken door below. Such towers are common
all over Scotland; they are the homes of the gentry and
lesser barons; and though not to be compared with Lething-
ton or Craigmillar, or the vast castle that the Chancellor
is building beside the Water of Lauder, they are fairly comfortable; ours is at least, especially in the summer-time, when
we take the air on the flat roof, and look across the estuary
of the Whapple to the hunting-lodge which belongs to the
king himself, and the rough moorland park where, as the
twilight falls, the bittern booms and the stags bellow.

Ravenscleuch stands high, and the view from the leads
embraces all the country round about. Far away to the
east there is the sea itself; then the white line of breakers
along the bar; then the landlocked bay, noisy with screaming
terns and black with water-fowl; then the sandhills clothed
with yellow bent on either side of the estuary, which gradually narrows until it reaches the reef of rock on which the
Cleuch is built; then the great park on the farther shore,
golden in spring with the broom, purple in autumn with the
heather, the turrets of the lodge half hidden by the group of
giant firs which shelter it from the sea; then, on our side of
the stream, dotted over the level carse, some half-dozen
weather-beaten keeps, with battlements and pepper-boxes
like our own; then right under our feet the huts of a few
poverty-stricken fishermen clustered round the ruins of the
abbey, which had been swept by "the fiery besom" a month
or two before we were born. The abbey of Balmawhapple
had been famous in its day; but it was among the first that
the iconoclasts wrecked; and the community which it had

sheltered for five hundred years had been broken up, and
driven into a world with which they were unfamiliar. The
kirk of the Reformation was a low barn-like building, which,
with the manse, stood in what had once been the orchard of
the monastery. But the fertile fields which the monks had
industriously tilled had been allowed to run to waste, and the
whole monastic domain was in the meantime little better than
a wilderness. This vast pile of ruin was our favourite play-
ground when boys. It had a fascination for us which we did
not try to explain, though we rather avoided it after dusk,
when the owls began to hoot, and the shadows cast by the
moon took bodily shape, and moved in ghostly procession
along the ruined aisle. It was here that the old lords of
the district had been buried—Holdfasts, Maitlands, and
Grays; but the carven slabs, on which knight and lady
rested, had been cracked and blackened by the action of
the fire, and epitaphs in stately Latin were no longer
decipherable.

Our nearest neighbours (with the exception of the Reverend
Peter Gibson, who occupied the manse) were the Maitlands
of that Ilk, who lived at Balmain, a mile or so up the river.
Still farther inland, at the Cadger's Pot, where the salt water
ceases to mingle with the fresh, there is Greystone—a seat
of the Master of Gray, as the eldest son of the peer of that
name is called among us, according to our Scottish usage.
There was a bridge across the Whapple within a few hundred
yards of Greystone,—a venerable bridge, which had been
built by the first James, when one of his train, crossing at the
ford to Earlshall—the royal hunting-lodge—had been carried
away by the flooded water and drowned.

There were only the two of us,—Gilbert and Amias Holdfast. Our mother died when we were infants; she had been
the close friend of the Dowager-Queen, Marie of Lorraine,
who had been loath to part with her favourite maid to Sir
Martin Holdfast; for our father, she knew, had been infected
with the heresies of his namesake, and it seemed probable,
should civil war break out, that he would cast in his lot with
"the congregation of Jesus Christ," as the followers of Knox

and the Lord James were pleased to call themselves. But his wife, as Knox sorrowfully complained, was more dear to him than his religion; and when the fierce band of iconoclasts swept down upon Edinburgh, he retired to the Cleuch, and declined to take any active part in the conflict with the dying queen. Marie of Lorraine breathed her last on the day that we were born; and from the double shock our mother never recovered. There was a vein of fanatical intemperance in our father's character; so long as he was allied with Knox he was persuaded that he belonged to the elect; and the deep gloom that settled upon him when his young wife had bidden him a tender, tearful farewell, was due in no small measure to the conviction that, for mere carnal gratification, he had forfeited his spiritual birthright. He lived for eight or ten years; but the shadows never lifted. Prayer and penance were in vain; night and day he was assailed by visionary fiends who would not relent; and even when Knox solemnly assured him that his sin had been blotted out, and that his name was registered in the book of life, he refused to be comforted. I cannot tell how he had come to persuade himself that he was guilty of the sin against the Holy Ghost; but the vision of a jealous God, who hated the creatures He had made with more than mortal bitterness, haunted him to the end.

The gloom that had settled upon the Cleuch during my father's widowhood was not dispelled by his death. The two bewildered little fellows who crept noiselessly about the darkened rooms until the neighbours came and bore the black coffin to the niche in the abbey vault, which had been hastily prepared for its reception, could hardly have been left more lonely and friendless had they been gipsy-born. There was the clergyman, to be sure—the Reverend Peter Gibson —who paid us an occasional visit; but he was tedious and pedantic, and his clumsy efforts at cheerfulness rather added to our depression. Gilbert, who was my senior by an hour, and consequently entitled to all the privileges of primogeniture, would abruptly disappear whenever he heard the strident voice on the stair; and but for an uneasy conviction on my

part that the good man really wished us well, I would have
followed the example that was set me. An hour afterwards
I would find Gilbert on the roof, gazing wistfully and dreamily
into space.

For Gilbert was a dreamer, and in these visionary hours,
when he escaped from the harsh environment of our ordinary
life into an ideal kingdom, he was comparatively content. I
was too matter-of-fact to follow him; and left behind, could
only sit down by the dusty roadside and cry myself to sleep.
There were compensations, however. Meg our ancient nurse,
and Mathy our pompous major-domo, never thought of troubling Gilbert with the financial anxieties of the household; I
was their confidant, and I was flattered by the preference.
We were taught to ride and fish and shoot by the keeper;
and our education otherwise was not entirely neglected. A
lean and lanky divinity student from the College of St Mary's
was engaged by Mr Gibson to introduce us to the *Etymologie*
of Lilius and Hunter's *Nomenclatura ;* and though he was shy
and nervous, and hardly capable of controlling a couple of
able-bodied lads, who were growing out of their jackets, we
made fair progress in the "humanities." Then there was a
store of curious old poems and romances on a shelf in the
great hall ;—*Lancilot de Laik*, printed at Rouen in 1488, as
well as the *Morte d'Arthur* of Sir Thomas Mallory, printed
by Mr William Caxton in 1485, and the strange story of
Ogier, King of Denmark, who, going to the Court of Charle-
magne, was enslaved by the fairy Morgana in her palace at
Avallon, where, while the shades of King Arthur and the
Knights of the Round Table passed before him as in a
dream, the magic ring she had placed on his finger kept him
from growing old, and *Le Livre de la Diablerie* and the
Garden of Pleasance, and the poems of Ronsard and Clement
Marot, and Mr George Buchanan's translation of the Psalms,
with the elegant dedication to the Northern Nymph he had
not yet begun to revile,—in all of which, but mainly in the
romances, we read diligently. The life was sombre enough,
but healthy, as an open-air life must be, and, as the years went
by, not altogether unhappy.

It was Lilias Maitland, however, who first shot a streak of radiant light through the more or less murky clouds that clung persistently to the Cleuch.

We had been out in our light skiff after wild-fowl on the half-frozen mere. The winter sun had set, but the western sky was still ablaze with light; a pale pure light such as comes before a bitter frost. There was the pallid ghost of a moon overhead; it had taken the place of the ruddy orb that had left us, and seemed indeed altogether more in keeping with the chaste serenity and solemnity of an ice-bound world. We were waiting on the other side of the water, just below Earlshall, for the evening flight of the ducks as they came down from the inland swamps to the sea. Save for the occasional croak of a water-rail among the reeds, or the pensive plaint of a plover, the silence round us was absolute. Only high up in the frosty ether we could hear the beat of wings.

There is a low belt of wood along the margin of the water, hazel, birch, seedling oaks. Lying on our oars, we were suddenly startled by the sound of voices within a few yards of where we lay. "John, what are we to do?" were the only words we could clearly distinguish before, through a break in the wood, the speaker appeared.

She was a girl of six or seven. She wore a rough dark-blue riding-coat, and a cap of the same colour with a black-cock's feather. The rough rustic dress heightened by contrast the dainty, high-bred, delicate beauty of the face. There was the faintest glow of colour on the cheeks, and a streak of gold through the auburn hair. There might be a suggestion of mockery about the mouth; but the brow was broad and ample, and the tranquil brown eyes were honest as the day. The general effect was of extreme purity; the dainty child might have been one of Dian's pages. The blackcock-feather, indeed, was fastened to her cap by a silver buckle representing the crescent moon; it was only the crest of the house, but it might have been taken, might have been assumed, as the symbol of vestal consecration. I do not mean to say that all this was visible to us then; we found it out later; at least

Gilbert did; for Gilbert was a poet, and could pay pretty compliments that somehow never occurred to me.

She was leading a pony that had fallen dead lame, and she was accompanied by a portly Jehu who was riding a spare and long-legged Rosinante. He had a pair of heavy pistols, such as servants carry, stuck in his belt; and coming unexpectedly upon us in the fading light, he mechanically laid his hand upon them. The twilight had no doubt magnified us into bandits or "broken men" (as they say) from the neighbouring highlands—into poachers at least who had ventured, or were about to venture, into the royal preserves. The alarm was confined to John; for the little lady, observing the movement, said deliberately, "Don't you see they are boys?—mere boys?" she added after a pause, with a touch of scorn in her voice. And then she hailed us. It appeared that Donald, her moorland pony, had quite unnecessarily put his foot into a rabbit-scrape. He had not exactly broken his leg (as he deserved), but he had strained it so severely that he could only hirple along at the rate of a mile an hour. They had come for a canter in the royal park over the smooth turf that had never been turned by the plough; and though Balmain was less than a mile as the crow flies from where we were, the distance by road (which went round by the bridge above Greystone) was at least six or eight times as far. It would be dark long before they could get home,—"and mother," she said, "will think I am lost." What was to be done?

Our skiff was a mere cockleshell; but Gilbert, with a low bow that might have become a finished courtier,—it came to him by nature,—suggested that she might do us the honour to accompany us. We would take her across in half an hour; the groom could lead the horses round by the bridge; and so no harm would be done.

She thanked us as a queen might have thanked a loyal subject, and graciously accepted the offer. Handing Donald over to Jehu, she stepped, or rather essayed to step, into the boat. But the tide was ebbing, and the stones were slippery with sea-weed; and, after a demure and dignified rebuke, she was pleased to allow Gilbert to take her in his arms and lift her over the gunwale. She settled herself in the stern, and, before we had reached the other side, had melted into friendly sociability. "I am Lady Lilias Maitland," she said, drawing herself up, after we had explained about the Cleuch, "and I don't know that mother will let me know you boys; but if she does, you may call me Lil. We only came home last week—mother and I; and now we are going to stay. So it will be rather nice to have you about—if mother does not mind."

It was thus that our acquaintance began.

Mary Stuart had been to Lady Maitland what Marie of Lorraine had been to our mother,—"the dearest queen in all the world," to use the words of poor Francis Throckmorton after he had been on the rack. ("Now have I disclosed the secrets of her who was the dearest queen to me in the world.") The pathetic intensity of the devotion which the imprisoned queen inspired would have dignified any cause; and it may be said, quite truly, that there were few men or women who had known her in close intimacy who would not have laid down their lives for her. Lady Maitland was no exception to the rule; she had given up her brilliant husband, her brave boys,—they had fallen in that devil's dance, led by Morton, which is known as the "Douglas wars"; her own life she would have resigned without a murmur; and even Lilias—even Lilias in the last extremity would have been silently sacrificed. The craze, the *hysterica passio*, which seized whole families when Mary Stuart's fortunes were in the balance, is even yet—when many years have passed—incapable of rational explanation. It need hardly surprise us, then, that grim zealots like Knox should have attributed "the enchantment whereby men are bewitched" to the direct interposition of an Evil Power.

It was no wonder that Gilbert the dreamer should have been fascinated by our charming neighbours. Lady Maitland was the ideal gentlewoman; and Lilias, with a more intangible and delicate beauty, was as high-bred and high-spirited as her mother. *Mater pulchra, filia pulchrior?*

Hardly so. For my own part, I used at times to think the mother even fairer than the child. Something of the blue, no doubt, had faded out of eyes which had survived so much; but what they had lost in brilliancy they had gained in sweetness and seriousness. Her carriage was regal; and a passion of enthusiasm, a passion of pity, kept her young.

She had known our mother when they were girls; and during the years that followed our little adventure on the river, she made herself—what shall I say?—a second mother, yea, more than a second mother, to the friendless and solitary lads. Balmain became to us another home; Lilias a dearer sister. We were much together; angling, riding, boating, "Lil," at least, never failed us. We seldom ventured indeed beyond the circle of hills that enclosed the level carse. We had been warned to be cautious. Morton was Regent; and Morton, who did not love the Maitlands, was as cruel as he was unscrupulous. Had he known that Lady Maitland continued to correspond with Mary in her English jail—that many of Mary's secrets were in her keeping—it might have gone hard with the woman he had helped to make a widow.

Once indeed we caught a glimpse of him on the river—a powerful, slovenly, blear-eyed, red-bearded man. He had brought the little king to Earlshall that spring; the child had been ailing, and it was thought that our sea-breezes might suit him better than doctor's drugs. To do the Regent justice, it must be admitted that he cast his line deftly; the flies fell lightly upon the water; even Gilbert was forced to admit that there was no more skilful angler in the Carse. We were lying among the bracken as he passed up the river alone, and he did not notice us. One might have fancied, seeing him then, that he was a simple fisherman and nothing more, so absorbed was he in the sport. I believe the "dark and dangerous Douglas" was bad to the core, detestable from almost every point of view; yet the man who could stroll up the river-side where deadly foes might lurk in every bush, with only a trout-rod in his hand, and forget his ambition and his evil deeds in the passion of the chase, must have had some redeeming traits.

But Gilbert would listen to no plea on his behalf. Morton had been the deadliest enemy of Mary Stuart; that was now enough for Gilbert. For Gilbert had been entirely won over to the Queen's side. Lady Maitland had enlisted a new recruit for her mistress; and Gilbert's devotion to the cause was hardly inferior to her own. Even Lil could be satirical at times; when the spirit of mischief moved her (as it did on occasion), she would ventilate the most outrageous heresies about John Knox and the Lord James. Lil's was a character not easily read. Her irony, I believe, was only skin-deep; at heart she was a fierce partisan. But she hid her passion under a mask of mockery; or it might possibly be more correct to say that a vein of mockery lay alongside a vein of visionary exaltation. Gilbert, on the other hand, made no pretence of concealment; his grave absorption, his almost ascetic devotion to the idea that had taken possession of him, was visible to all the world. The Catholic does not pay a more devout homage to the Virgin-Mother than Gilbert paid to his tutelary saint.

None of us, indeed, even the most prosaic, were able to resist the fair enchantress of Lady Maitland's reminiscences. The talk at Balmain was of Mary Stuart, and of Mary Stuart only. *O dea certe!* It was a topic of which we never wearied. We came to know the brilliant girl who had suffered such foul wrong as if we had seen her face to face. On high days and holidays Lady Maitland would bring down the locket which Mary Stuart had given her when they parted at Dunbar. Within was a miniature (painted by Janet, if I am not mistaken, while Mary was living with her grandmother at Joinville), the miniature of a young girl in a heavy conventual garb, such as Antoinette de Bourbon may have worn during her thirty years of widowhood. The sombre dress of the cloister emphasised the gay and delicate beauty of the face, the peach-like bloom on the velvet cheeks, the covert smile that lurked in eye and lip. It was one of those faces about which grown men go crazy; if a lad lost his head over it, one cannot wonder much.

Lady Maitland, you may be sure, would listen to no word

against her queen.   She treated the charges that Morton had manufactured, and that Elizabeth had circulated, with absolute incredulity.   Mary was honest as the day.   She was at once the queenliest and the homeliest of women who have worn a crown.   The trappings of state, the gewgaws of royalty, were gladly laid aside by her.   She had no patrician exclusiveness. She had the true eye which sees the true metal.   If a man were brave and honest, a woman modest and sincere, she took them to her heart.   She was supremely faithful.   But her nice sense of the becoming was quickly offended by boorish inde-corum or mean servility.   Half the nobles at Court were boors who could not write their names ; the rest were rotten to the core.   These were the men who had conspired against her,— these, and Knox, to whom the saintliest of Catholic women would have been no better than a Jesebel.   Knox, though ferociously intolerant, was frankly sincere ; the others were profoundly corrupt, and in Elizabeth's pay.   Every day a new calumny was invented.   The innocent girl of eighteen was a mature Machiavelli.   Her harmless merry-makings were the orgies of a Messalina.   Her craft was devilish, and she revelled in abominable wickedness.   The nation did not believe them ; and more than once the conspiracy was foiled.   But Knox and Cecil were persistently hostile ; and, with Morton's aid, they robbed her of her crown, and tried to rob her of her good name.   "It was base, base.   They had themselves consented to Darnley's murder; they had themselves thrust her into Bothwell's arms—Bothwell whom she loathed !   A Jesebel indeed !   A wicked woman !   Do not believe them.   She was, she is, pure as the snow.   But alas !" Lady Maitland would conclude, "our Mary is a Stuart ; and her father, who died of a broken heart, is the only Stuart who died in his bed !"

"But, mother dear," Lil would say—Lil was sixteen now, only sixteen, but a cruelly accomplished coquette—"don't tell us, please, that our dear queen is a saint.   It would take away half the charm if she wasn't just the least morsel wicked like ourselves.   I wouldn't want her to do anything very bad ; but just confess now that she would have dearly liked to box

Knox's ears when he prayed for her as—what was it he said?
—as a thrall and bondwoman of Satan, because she didn't go
to bed at ten! And then the uncomely skipping at your innocent merry-makings—did he mean that she danced badly?
—only I daresay he wasn't much of a judge except of a Scotch
jig—what do you say to that, my lady?"

Lilias was only a girl; but she was as mortally ashamed of
her tears as if she had been a man. The grave Gilbert was
partly distressed and partly fascinated by her mocking sallies;
had he been able to watch her critically, he would have discovered (as I did) that laughter is not seldom akin to tears.
But he could not criticise her coldly. That Gilbert loved her
from the first day he took her, as a child, in his arms, I never
doubted; but neither man nor woman could tell what she felt
for Gilbert—especially when the Master of Gray was with us.

I have said little about the Master as yet; I suppose the
serpent was bound to get into Eden; but the innocent beasts
would no doubt have been well pleased could he have been
kept out.

Paddy, as they called him, had been occasionally at Greystone when a child—with a French nurse, who had taught
him many dainty French oaths, and broken snatches of French
ditties that were not particularly edifying. The old lord his
father and his lady mother had been an ill-matched pair; they
had led a cat-and-dog life for a year or two, and then she had
been cast off like an old coat. Lady Maitland took pity upon
the neglected boy, and did what she could to make his life a
little less hopelessly forlorn. She was a good woman; I have
never known a better. But, in spite of his brave looks, none
of us cared for the Master; only for Lil he had a curious
attraction—the sort of attraction which the rattlesnake has for
the bird. To do him justice, he was a superb boy—a tiger
cub such as Veronese would have delighted to paint. I have
never indeed seen a child more insolently handsome. As he
grew up, people said that he should have been a girl,—the
beauty was too feminine for a man. Yet he was not timid as
a girl might have been. I remember as if it were yesterday
a herd of our wild cattle charging down the moor upon Lilias

and her mother. The Master had only a light riding-switch
in his hand, but he stood his ground, and hit the foremost
bull a smarting blow over the eyes. The brute bellowed and
pawed the turf, but turned, and the rest followed him. Not
timid certainly, but cruel and crafty. So Gilbert maintained.
But Gilbert, who loathed him as he loathed a viper, was possibly unreasonable. Gilbert had found him one day taking
young birds from the nest, and deliberately putting their eyes
out with a red-hot piece of wire; and when he had cuffed his
ears, the Master, with the snarl of a baby wolf, had flown
upon him, and bitten him to the bone. This, however, might
have been accidental; for those who saw only the candid blue
eyes and a smile as honeyed as Delilah's, declared that a cruel
and crafty cherub was as impossible as a centaur or a griffin.

He went to France while still a lad, and we did not see him
again for several years. But at intervals a bright, clever, dexterous letter came from him—it was to Lady Maitland he
wrote—in which he played adroitly upon her devotion to the
captive queen. The Duke of Guise had made him his confidant; his dear and noble friend Philip Sidney had been won
over; letters—grateful letters—had come to him from Mary
herself; if all went well she would be a free woman before the
year was out. There were mysterious hints of a great Catholic
crusade, led by the Duke and officered by the veterans of
Spain. Tears of thankfulness came into Lady Maitland's eyes
as she read; Lilias, with a mocking glance at Gilbert, would
declare that there was no accounting for the prejudices of
home-bred squires; but Gilbert was not moved. He remained
incredulous; his gloomy suspicions grew in force; the boy
was the father of the man,—the boy had been cruel and crafty
and corrupt,—the man would be capable of any mischief, of
any treachery. Of that conviction neither the tears of the
mother, nor the gibes of the daughter, could disabuse him.

But even Gilbert was disarmed when the Master returned.
He was so frank, so friendly, so confidential. He had devoted himself to Mary's service. He had been selected to
organise the Scottish loyalists, and to bring James round to
his mother. He had been at Stirling, and the king was

already plastic in his hands.   It might be well, however, that
Lady Maitland should see him; James was passionately fond
of the chase, and was coming to Earlshall to try the new dogs
that the French king had sent him from Fontainebleau; Lady
Maitland's recollections of Holyrood would be welcome, and
her fidelity to the mother might fire the rather sluggish sense
of filial duty in the son.

The brow was open; the eye was candid; and, as I have
said, even Gilbert was disarmed.   I fancied, however, that the
curiously contradictory Lilias was not satisfied.   Some false
note jarred upon her finer sense.   She made no palpable show
of her distrust (if distrust him she did); but I could see that
she was on her guard, and that she watched him with a vigil-
ance that did not tire.   She was a curious girl; and I do not
pretend to have fathomed her moods.

I think it was owing to Lilias that Lady Maitland was more
reserved with the Master than she would otherwise have been.
A good deal, however, had been said during the first days of
frank and cordial intimacy after his return, which perhaps had
better have been left unsaid (for scraps of paper carefully
hidden away in the lining of a cloak or the scabbard of a
sword, on which microscopical symbols in invisible ink had
been carefully engrossed, still came to Our Lady from Tutbury or Chartley); and we could only hope that nothing had
escaped which, if a traitor was among us, would be fatally
compromising.

Meantime there was much stir at Earlshall, for the young
king had come.   Morton had been in his bloody grave for
five years, though his head from the prick on the gable of the
Tolbooth still grinned at the passers-by (yet some have said
that it had been taken down by the Lord Angus after a dinner
he gave the king); poor Esmé Stuart, who, I have heard, was
more sinned against than sinning, had gone back to France
to die; and the men who were now the most powerful at the
Court of Holyrood had little to recommend them (saving their
good looks and their soldierly bearing) to prince or people.
The Ochiltree Stuarts—James, who had been made Earl of
Arran, and his brother the Colonel—in spite of a thin veneer

of Parisian polish, were sordid ruffians at heart; mercenaries
to whom the slums of Europe were better known than its
colleges or churches. The aged John Knox had married
their fifteen-year-old sister,—a scandalous marriage which the
brothers had made the theme of many a ribald jest. They
feared neither God nor man; their cynical disregard of the
decencies of life had everywhere excited a keen recoil; and
James himself, who was inordinately vain, was growing weary
of favourites who treated him with scant respect. It was at
this moment that Patrick Gray, lovely as a Hebe, audacious
as a Phaethon, unscrupulous as a Machiavel, came to the
front. He rose, mushroom-like, in a night; it was thought
that he would sink as suddenly. The preachers denounced
him as a "young, insolent, scornful boy," and freely criticised
from the pulpit what our Mr Gibson called "his impudencie,
and custom to lee." Arran, who had helped him to rise, now
turned against him, and Arran's enmity was as the blight of
pestilence; even the violent attachment of the young king, to
whom he had become indispensable, would hardly have prevented him from going the gait that Cochrane and Rizzio had
gone. But this was a boy who was craftier than the oldest
courtier, and who never lost his head or his temper.

II.

Our quiet neighbourhood was rather scandalised by the life
that the Court led at Earlshall. I am afraid that the privilege
of being occasionally accosted by the king himself did not fan
our loyalty into a clearer flame; royalty indeed never assumed
a more grotesque disguise than in the person of James; his
stutter, his goggle-eyes, his loose sprawling limbs, his ungainly
gait, his flushed and bloodshot face, were apter to breed
laughter than to win reverence. He had, however, the most
unlimited and unqualified belief in himself. He was a master
of logic, and a dungeon of learning. There was no mystery,
divine or human, which he could not solve. He was the head
of the Church as well as the head of the State. The ministers,

who held that in spiritual matters they were supreme and subject to no temporal jurisdiction, were summoned to Holyrood
or Falkland, and soundly scolded by this egregious schoolboy, who was employing his leisure in a commentary on the
Apocalypse. If they were obstinate they were sent to jail,
where they were herded in noisome cells with Highland
caterans and Border thieves.

It was indirectly through the conflict between the preachers
and the Court, which was at this time at its height, that I
came to see something of the interior of the royal hunting-
lodge. Our old friend, Mr James Gibson, had taken no active
part in the struggle; he was sheltered by his obscurity; and
the good man had been, moreover, too much occupied in
getting his stipend modified, and in repairing the dilapidations
of manse and glebe, to have much time for doctrinal discussions on the enormity of tulchan bishops or the limits of
spiritual independence. But his spirit though peaceful was
stout, and when thoroughly roused the little man was as com-
bative as Mr Andrew Melville or Mr James Lawson. Reports
of the evil life led at the Lodge, and the bad example set to
his parishioners, had come to his ears; and I daresay Arran,
and the Colonel, and the new Earl of Bothwell (to say nothing
of the Master, who had been a thorn in his side all along),
were not a whit better than they were represented in Lek-
pravik's broadsheets. Mr Gibson went home in a fit of
righteous indignation, and composed a discourse upon the
profane mockers of God's Word, under fifteen heads, which
he preached in the parish kirk on the following Sunday. The
Master of Gray was the sole tenant of the Earlshall pew; he
had become of late a very "frank Protestant," and sang the
new metrical version of the Psalms by David Wedderburn
with as much fervour as if they had been "gude and godly
ballates"; and he listened with respectful gravity to the de-
nunciations of "Jesebel" and her lord. "Jesebel" was my
Lady Arran (who had been my Lady March, and had got a
divorce from her first husband on a shameful plea), and if
any Scottish woman deserved the name, she did. But the
preacher went on to arraign the courtiers one and all,—they

were goats of the flock and not true sheep, false professors and
not true Christians, perjured men and not faithful people,
promise-breakers, merciless tyrants, and false backsliders; and
the king himself and his issue, if he continued in that crooked
course, would be rooted out like Jeroboam. This was the
exordium; and then, under one or other of the fifteen heads,
the preacher proceeded to show *how* they were goats and not
true sheep, perjured men and not faithful people, and so on.

The Master's face was impassive, but I could not help
thinking, as I looked at him, of the tiger-cat about to spring.
The beauty was unmistakable; but there was a stealthiness in
its lithe grace, and the claws, though hidden, were not far
under the fur.

I walked home with Mr Gibson, who was in a state of
nervous exaltation. He had done his duty; but now that
the excitement of composition and delivery had been followed
by the languor of accomplishment, he had begun to doubt
whether he had been well advised. I certainly shared his
doubts; and, before we parted, casually suggested that he might
find it convenient to be called away by urgent business to the
other side of the Tweed.

My warning did not come too soon; for early next morning
a messenger arrived with a missive from the Chancellor requiring Gilbert and Amias Holdfast to bring the Reverend Peter
Gibson before his Majesty's Council.

The message was by no means welcome to me, for I thought
it not unlikely that inconvenient inquiries as to the cause of
Gilbert's absence from home (of which more presently) might
be put to me. When I went down to the manse I found considerable difficulty in gaining admittance, for the minister had
gathered some of his flock around him—burly fishermen from
the village—and had made up his mind to stand a siege,—
resisting the minions of the Court, as he said, even unto the
death. After some hesitation he agreed to accompany me to
Earlshall; and we were quickly afloat, with four of his body-
guard at the oars.

It was a lovely day of early summer,—the late oaks and ashes
were just bursting into leaf, and the birds were piping merrily,

while a soft west wind rustled the leaves and moved along the water. As we crossed the river, we met the Balmain boat anchored in mid-channel; Lilias was on board dressed in the loose fishing-garb which became her so well, and she beckoned to us. She had apparently guessed our errand, for leaning over the side to disengage her line (as it seemed) she whispered in my ear, "Beware of the Master. We are being watched;" and then aloud to Mr Gibson with significant emphasis, "The breeze is fair, Mr Gibson—why, you might be in Berwick by sundown." Then we ran the boat ashore, walked up to the Lodge, and were at once ushered into the great hall where the Council were sitting. My companion had pretty well recovered himself by this time; and he informed me that he had resolved to speak as the Spirit of God would move him. I knew pretty well what this meant. He had obviously arrived at the conclusion that it was as well to be hanged for a sheep as a lamb; or as the English say, in for a penny in for a pound.

It was a curious scene. Three or four men in the prime of life, handsome and stalwart, sat at the end of a long table. They had finished breakfast; but the table was still heaped with the *débris*—a flagon of claret, an earthenware jug of beer, bowls of oatmeal porridge, a round of beef, dainty French rolls, a sea-trout fresh from the salt water. There had been, one could guess, a late sitting the night before, and the revellers were only recovering from their debauch. And these —I said to myself—these were the men who governed Scotland!

Engaged in noisy and even boisterous talk, they formed an animated group. But there was to my ear something sinister in their merriment. Their laughter, it seemed to me, was furtive and menacing—a sombre mirth void of any true gaiety. The hangman when he relaxes after an "engagement" may take his pleasure in this fashion.

One member of the group, who seemed from native irritability unable to sit still, was on his feet. He moved restlessly about—his loose ungainly limbs jerking spasmodically as he moved. The St Vitus' dance from which he obviously suffered was unpleasant to witness. His dress was slovenly; his

speech was confused,—the language, from the rush of words
to the mouth, being frequently unintelligible; the goggle-eyes,
as he turned to stare at us, seemed starting from his head.
"And as for you, Francie," he was saying, addressing the Earl
of Bothwell, who was lolling indolently in a huge oaken chair,
"you are an unmitigated reprobate. I wonder sometimes
why I made you an earl; the Bothwells have aye been a sair
trouble to the Royal family. Do you mean to tell me to my
face, you leein' knave, that I complained to Cuddy Armorar
with tears in my eyes that they were saying that I was Davie's
son?" ("Solomon, the son of David," said the Master under
his breath, while the Colonel, who, according to his enemies,
had been originally "a cloutter of old shoes," gave a hoarse
chuckle.) "And wha in the deevil's name may this be?" he
stuttered, turning suddenly upon the usher who was waiting to
introduce us.

"The Reverend James Gibson and Master Amias Holdfast," he continued, when the man had mentioned our names;
"and what may Mr Gibson and Master Holdfast want wi'
me?"

The Master of Gray interposed, "Mr *Gilbert* Holdfast and
his brother were instructed to bring the Reverend Mr Gibson
before your Majesty's Council this morning."

"Of course they were; and what has come of Mr Gilbert
that he does not comply with the command of his sovereign?"
he asked testily.

I had been prepared for the question, and I answered that
my brother had been suddenly called to Edinburgh before the
summons arrived.

"Edinburgh," quoth the king, "is not the place for a young
lad who has not been weel grounded in the philosophies of
Aristotle, and he had best return with all convenient speed.
I have heard somewhat of this Gilbert Holdfast, though I do
not at present precisely remember the particular occasion, and
I would advise him as a friend to walk warily." Then, turning to Mr Gibson, "And this is the smaicke who discourses
on Jesebel and Jeroboam!" And snapping his fingers in his
reverence's face ("clanking with his finger and his thowme,"

as his habit is), he resumed his uneasy walk. "Let him sit down, and I will confer with him presently."

"Will your Majesty examine him at once?" Arran inquired. "Mr Randolphe writes that he is to be with us this afternoon, and will bring the huntsmen that have been sent from England with Sir Henry Wotton."

"What says he? what says he?" exclaimed the mercurial king; and when the letter was handed to him, he ran his eyes over it till he came to the passage to which the Chancellor had alluded, and read it aloud: "I have sent the king two hunting men, verie good and skilful, with one footman that can hoop, hollow, and cry, that all the trees in Falkland will quake for fear. Pray the King's Majesty to be merciful to the poor bucks; but let him spare and look well to himself."

"'Tis very considerate of Mr Randolphe, to be sure, and we shall not forget his civility,—though how with a toom purse, Mr Chancellor, we are to reward our friends and well-wishers, passes all understanding. But what means he by warning us to look well to ourselves?"

"I heard a bruit this morning that the ill-disposed preachers had been stirring up the rascally multitude against your Highness," Gray remarked. "Possibly Mr Gibson may be better informed."

"Bring him up, bring him up, and we will ourselves show him wherein he hath been ill advised. So, Mr Gibson, they tell me that you and your brethren in Christ are miscontent with our rule. Of what complain you?"

Mr Gibson. "Persecution, sir."

The King. "Persecution! persecution! what call ye persecution? Can ye define it?"

Mr Gibson. "Shortly, sir, it is a troubling of the saints of God for professing a good cause; and mainly, for Christ's sake."

The King (*sharply*). "Say ye that ye were persecuted for Christ's sake? Who was your persecutor?"

Mr Gibson. "Captain James Stuart."

The King. "The man you unmannerly call so is as good in religion as yourself; for if he were as good in all other things as in religion, he had not been evil. And if ye had called him so before the Parliament, being one of my earls, I had said ye were a leein' knave."

Mr Gibson. "Your Majesty may call me what you please; but he was never other to me and to all good men but an enemy to God and His truth, and one in whom there is no goodness."

The King (to the Chancellor). "Haud your peace, my lord; we will manage him ourselves. (*To Mr Gibson.*) What was your text when ye named these names,—Captain James, Colonel William, and Lady Jesabell?"

Mr Gibson. "Out of the twenty-seventh psalm, 'The Lord is my light.'"

The King. "What moved ye to take that text?"

Mr Gibson. "The Spirit of God, sir."

The King (ironically). "The Spirit of God! The Spirit of God! The Spirit of God!"

Mr Gibson. "Yes, sir; the Spirit of God, that teacheth all men, chiefly at extraordinary times, putteth the text in the heart which serveth best."

The King. "What doctrine gathered ye there, and how brought ye in their names?"

Mr Gibson. "After this manner: David, speaking there in the person of Christ, compareth the Kirk of God to an immovable stone, that whosoever did rise against the same in any age, to the dust they fell. This I proved by Scripture, by history, and by experience without the country and within the country; and so came to the last that had fallen before this stone; and, having occasion to speak of our present Kirk, I said I thought it had been Captain James, Colonel William, and Lady Jesabell that had alone persecuted the same; but I now saw it was the king himself because he pressed forward in that cursed course they had begun."

The King (in great anger). "What! call ye me a persecutor?"

Mr Gibson. "Yes, sir; so long as ye maintain their wicked acts against God and the liberty of His Kirk, ye are a persecutor."

The King. "Call ye me Jeroboam?"

Mr Gibson. "Having occasion to speak of Jeroboam, I said that as Jeroboam, for leading the people of Israel from the laws of the house of Judah, and from the true worship of God, to follow idolatry, was rooted out, he and all his posterity, so should the King, if he continued in that cursed course, be rooted out and conclude his race."

The King. "Said ye that?"

Mr Gibson. "Yes, sir."

The King. "There is no king in Christendom would have suffered the things I have suffered."

Mr Gibson. "I would not have ye like any other king in Europe. What are they but murderers of the saints of God?"

The King. "I am Catholic King of Scotland, and may choose any that I like best to be in company with me; and I like them best that are with me for the present. If I cannot choose my company, Mr Barebones, I should not wear the lion in my arms but rather a sheep."

Mr Gibson. "I say again, for we maun damn sin in whatsoever person it has place, that ye are surrounded by evil company, and that ye are in greater danger now than when ye were rocked in your cradle. If ye love not them that hate the Lord, as the prophet said to Jehosephat, it may yet be well with your grace; but if ye company with harlots and murderers——"

But this was more than the king could stomach. "Away with the loon, the smaicke, the seditious knave," he shouted, as the blood mounted to his head and his breath failed him for anger. "Let him cool his heels in the Tolbooth. See that a warrant is made out, Francie, and we will sign it with our own royal hand."

The Master met us as, once clear of the Council chamber, we hurried down to the shore. "Get the babbling old fool out of the way," he said, in a low voice, "or it will go hard with him." The boat was waiting; our men were ready; in half an hour we had landed below the manse. "Wait, my lads," I said, turning to the crew, and then to the minister,

"Miss Maitland was right. There is a fair wind for Berwick. You have not a moment to lose."

An hour afterwards the officers of the law arrived; but by that time the boat was outside the bar, and rapidly rounding the farthest headland. The Master had accompanied the messengers. "So our brother in Christ," he said, "has found discretion the better part of valour. Good. Possibly he has gone to join Gilbert at—at—shall we say—Tutbury?"

I looked him in the face. "Patrick Gray," I said, "you are playing a double part. I pity the woman—queen or no queen—who puts her trust in you."

"Truly," he answered, with a sneer. "Why, man, I am constancy itself. Don't you know the motto of our house—'Anchor, fast Anchor'? Good day — I am going to — Balmain."

And with a mocking salute he had turned his horse and was gone—to try his luck with Lilias, might it be?

III.

It was quite true that Gilbert had gone, and gone secretly. A travelling pedlar had arrived at Balmain, and while he was disposing of his wares he had, unobserved by the rest, slipped a note into Lady Maitland's hand. It came from the captive queen. A plot to rescue her had been formed. The arrangements for a convoy and relays of horses as far as Northumberland had been completed; but the Scottish part of the enterprise had been confided to the Master of Gray, and within the past few days grave doubts of his fidelity had arisen. A letter from him to Elizabeth, in which he seemed anxious to enter her service, had been intercepted by Mary's friends on the Border. Burleigh had been heard to commend the Master's ability to discover *le pot aux roses* if he listed to speak plain language. Knowing that he was suspected, Gray had written an insolent letter to Mary, complaining that he had been libelled by a prattling knave who had received a thousand rose nobles from the Queen of England, and vowing that while he lived, and could discern the shadow from the verity, he would never again lift his hand on her behalf. It was feared that this truculent letter had only been written to cover his treachery. In these circumstances it had become imperative that some one on whom absolute reliance could be reposed should take the Master's place, and, if at all practicable, obtain by hook or by crook a secret interview with the queen. Lady Maitland had told her mistress of Gilbert's passionate devotion,—would Gilbert come?

This was the subject which, during the evening preceding Mr Gibson's memorable discourse, had been eagerly discussed at Balmain. Lilias, with appealing eyes, had urged him to go; her mother, now that the crisis had arrived, was rather disposed to hold back. It had been a fatal service to so many; must another young life be spent, another victim sacrificed? Gilbert himself was resolute to go. To him no Crusade against the Turk, or for the Sepulchre, could be holier. He said little; Gilbert was never demonstrative; but his grave enthusiasm did not need the aid of words. At length, when he would hear of no delay, Lilias rose hurriedly, crossed the room to where he sat in the twilight, took his head between her hands, and kissed him on the forehead. None of us were surprised: none of us felt that there was any immodesty in the act. It was a kiss of consecration. Then with eyes on fire she fled from the room.

After this, and in the end, Lady Maitland could not but acquiesce. "Go, then," she said, as she gave him a parting blessing. "The service is full of peril; but it is true that our bitterest enemies are gone to their account. Of the assassins of David all are dead,—save the Laird of Faudin, and that brutal lord of whom our dear lady was wont to say that she felt his cold dagger pass by her cheeks. That worst outrage at least has not remained unavenged."

We started at midnight. I walked with him across the moonlight moors that rise steeply behind the Cleuch. The track crosses the Lammerlaw, and when we reached the watershed where the cairn stands, we parted. Ere I got home I saw a streak of light on the eastern heaven, and as I entered the house the sea was trembling in the dawn with that shiver of awakening life which an Italian poet, whose verse is loved by Lilias, has truly called the "*tremola della marina.*"

For some time thereafter it was mainly through Gilbert's letters to Lilias that we learnt what was doing in the great world beyond our hills.

But long before any word came from Gilbert, we had been duly assured of Mr Gibson's safety. His letter—it had been written at Berwick—was rather apologetic in its tone; in his dreams, it might be, he had looked forward to being not only a witness but a martyr for the truth; but he had meanly, as he felt, preferred a whole skin to the glory of testifying at the Luckenbooths; and he was driven to Holy Writ for a rather lame vindication.

"The moving cause," he wrote, "was the express commandment of our Master, Christ, saying, 'When they persecute you in one city, flee into another;' the practice of which commandment we find in the most dear servants of God; as in Jacob, from the face of his brother Esau; in David, Elias, Paul, yea, and in Christ Himself. But one might say to me, Call ye the execution of justice persecution? Ye were summoned to underlie the law, according to justice, which cannot be called persecution. I answer, I call not the due execution of justice (which all godly men ought to entertain) persecution; but I call the pursuit of an innocent man under the form of execution of justice (when nothing less than justice is meant to him) a most crafty and mighty kind of persecution. And this kind of persecution was not invented of late years by Satan against the servants of God. For Daniel, that faithful man of God, as we may read, was cast in the lions' den because he had transgressed the act and council made by the king; Elias was put to flight because he was thought a troubler of Israel; Christ, our Master, was condemned to death as a seditious mover of the subjects against Cæsar. And though it doth not become me to boast as one who putteth off his armour, yet I say assuredly that the devil and his angels shall not prevail, but with all the workers of iniquity shall be cast into hell.

"You will have heard, perchance, that an Erastian assembly of bloody tulchans and mewches of the archbishop hath condemned my sermon and suspended me from the office and function of the ministry. The true servants of God who are banished by the wicked action of the king assure me that the sentence is of none effect. A good friend writes me from Edinburgh that worthy Mr Robert Bruce, my old bed-fellow at the college of St Salvator, was admonished in his dream the night before, not to be present at the pronouncing of the sentence. He thought he heard these words following: 'Ne intersis condemnationi servi Dei.'

"It is spoken here that Captain James and the Colonel were fain to have made a breach in the amity betwixt the Crowns. At the least, it is commonly reported that a common scold, called Kate the Witch, was hired with a new plaid and six pounds in money, not only to rail against the ministry, but also set in the entry of the king's palace to revile her Majesty's ambassador, Sir Francis Walsingham—a deed more worthy of punishment to the hirer than to the hireling—and she herself confessed, when liberally entertained in prison, that the Colonel, who, they say, was a clouter of old shoes, gave the money and Captain James the plaid. Profane mockers of all religion, more fit to be the executioners of a Nero, they shall reap what they have sown."

From the bundle of old letters religiously preserved by Lilias, I am permitted to extract such of those that came to us during that unhappy year (when our dearest queen was cruelly slain by wicked men) as will serve to interest and inform the reader who may hereafter have access to this brief and unpretending record. They were for the most part written in England by Gilbert Holdfast to Lilias Maitland; they have been yellowed by age and wet with many tears.

* * *

"Lilias, I have seen her. She is very worn, very sad, but the high spirit has not been broken by years of suffering, and even to-day she is every inch a queen. I understand now what poor Francis Throckmorton meant when he said of his dearest queen that though her voice is soft as running water at night, there is no shadow of fear in her eyes. I was disguised as a mendicant when she came out closely guarded; the crowd of sturdy beggars who were waiting at the gate clamoured for alms; there were tears on her cheek when, turning to them, she said with a great sob in her voice, 'All has been taken from me; I am a beggar as well as you.' Then I caught her eye, and as she bent down to straighten her habit, I managed somehow to whisper in her ear that the rescue had been fixed for Friday at midnight. She looked me full in the face, paused a moment as if to revolve what I had said, and then smiled at me through her tears, a watery wintery smile, as of one who had long since bidden farewell to joy. Then I got back to the inn on the great North road, where Hamilton and Ferniehurst were waiting."

* *
*

"We have had a grievous fright. The inn was full when we arrived, and the landlord (who is understood to be well affected to the queen) could only give me a bedcloset that opens into the public room. The inner door between the rooms is locked, and is concealed besides by a piece of old tapestry representing the people of Israel as they passed through the Red Sea. I had noticed a mean-looking fellow, with a squint in his keen, ferret-like eyes, and an ugly sneer on his thin bloodless lips, hanging about the house. Whenever I saw him he was poring over papers, which he used hastily to thrust into his doublet when interrupted. There was clearly some mystery about the man; but till lately I paid little heed to his shuffling ways. Last night, however, after I had gone to bed (being worn out by the long tramp), the great bell in the courtyard clanged (which intimates that a party of travellers have arrived); and in a few minutes I heard voices in earnest speech in the next room. I was drowsy, and did not at first catch the sense of the words; but as the silence in the house deepened they became more clearly defined.

"'Yes, my lord, her health is better. She drove in the park yesterday. I was near her: she gave me a sharp suspicious look. I had a smiling countenance, but I said to myself (your worship knows the line),

"Cum tibi dicit Ave. Sicut ab hoste cave."'

"'Never mind your learning, man,' the other speaker interposed, 'but tell me what you have found to make you look so devilishly attractive. You were to attend her very heart in her next, you said; have you done so? Has she given us the chance for which we have waited so long?'

"'I had hoped she would have spoken more plainly; but the cipher is complicated and deceptive; and there may be more in it than meets the eye. I daresay, however—with a little judicious manipulation—we may manage.'

"'Take care, Philipps, for God's sake, take care. I am willing to run some risk; but mind that your decipher will be scanned by some of the keenest eyes in England—not over friendly to ourselves.'

"'Oh, your worship, I am not afraid. They cannot produce the originals, and I will answer for the copy. And besides, a dozen words will serve. She approves of the rescue; she approves of the landing; if she doesn't exactly say that Elizabeth should go *ad Patres*, she certainly means it."

"'Philipps, you are a cunning dog, and—yes—tell me— what makes you hate her so?'

"I could not hear the reply; the other speaker resumed—

"'I had expected to meet the Master of Gray to-night; but it seems that he is detained at Court. He warns us of one Gilbert Holdfast of the Cleuch, who, with Ferniehurst and Claud Hamilton, have been despatched by the Scottish rebels to bring their queen to the Border. Keep your eyes open; you may come across him. Yet stay; it may be wiser to leave the young fool at large; Gray knows all; he has been as frank as we could wish; the Lady of the Castle will get to heaven before she gets to Scotland. Ah, Philipps, that blow between the head and the shoulders—it hath sovereign virtue! And now, adieu—I must be in London to-morrow. When

Mary Stuart is in a better world, you will not be forgotten by your grateful mistress.'

"When I saw the landlord next morning, I said to him casually that he had had late guests last night. 'Late guests?' he replied, looking round. 'Hardly guests,—they only stopped one hour to bait their horses,—the Secretary was in haste to reach the Court.' 'It *was* Walsingham, then,' I exclaimed. 'Hush, sir, hush!' he answered again, lowering his voice; 'least said, soonest mended.' And then addressing Philipps, who had stealthily descended the stair: 'A fine morning, your honour—going for a stroll?'"

* * *

"Of course the rescue miscarried; a double-dyed scoundrel had deceived us all. Our small troop of horse was hidden in the Aston woods; I went on alone. The night was pitch-dark; there was thunder in the air; at intervals for a second a glare of lightning dispelled the darkness. More than once I fancied that I heard footsteps; the tramp of horse, it might be; but I had waited fully an hour—it was close on midnight—before any one appeared. Then it was only a boy—a mere child (I knew him by sight—it was the keeper's son), with a scrap of paper in his hand, wet with the rain. 'I was bidden give you this,' he said; 'father would have brought it, but the soldiers are round the Lodge.' Then came a long, bright, wavering flash, by which I read the words—they were written in French—'All is lost: save yourselves'; and then, giving the boy a silver piece, I felt my way back along the road. The rain came down in torrents; the lightning seemed to search the woods. You may fancy how we felt—men who knew that a foul trick had been played—and how we cursed the traitor."

* * *

"They have tried and condemned her—Lilias, they have ventured to condemn an anointed queen. The curs who have yelped at her, have dared to bite. She bore herself like a queen—even her enemies admit as much. What tears she shed were for her friends, not for herself. 'Alas!' she said once very pitifully, 'how much has the noble house of Howard suffered for my sake!' It is nowhere believed that she is guilty: she is the victim of a miserable trick, contrived by Walsingham himself—so they report, and I can partly testify. And now, Lilias, your mother must go to the king; his mother's life is in his hands; they will not venture to execute her if he summon every Scotsman to arms. She must tell him the truth; tell him that if in this supreme, this awful moment, he fails to save her, fails to move earth and heaven on her behalf, he will be shamed for ever. But she must go at once, else it will be too late."

* * *

It is almost impossible to realise at this day the thrill of anger, of indignation, of horror which passed over Scotland when it was known that the Scottish queen had been condemned by an English court. The wave of passion carried all before it—all except James himself and the Master of Gray. Had the king refused to act, as he seemed at first inclined to do, I believe that his crown would have been in peril. When the news was received, the Court was at Earlshall, so that our dear lady was saved the long and arduous journey to the capital. Her request for a private interview with the king was at once granted with almost flattering readiness. James, however, was in his most testy and querulous mood, by no means inclined to listen to any remonstrance that did not suit his whim. He was at the moment, indeed, the victim of a ridiculous monomania, which possibly accounted for his irritability. He was determined not to be outdone by a subject; and as the Laird of Dun had been at work for two nights running, James had not gone to bed for three. He was writing a sonnet, dictating a speech, reading a despatch, discussing the points of another couple of buckhounds that had lately come from Elizabeth, putting a finishing touch to his commentary on the Apocalypse, when Lady Maitland entered.

"My dear lady," he said, "I am very busy, as you may observe, but you are not interrupting me. Most people can only attend to one thing at a time; I am able to overtake four or five with comfort, and when hard pressed can manage a round dozen. There is not another king in Christendom can do the like. This is sad news, my lady," he went on, as his face flushed and his stammer sensibly increased with his embarrassment; "our dearest mother has been ill advised; her rascally servants are much to blame; a good hanging would mend their manners. I cannot say that she has used us well; if it be true that she has renounced her title to the succession to the Spanish king in respect of our firm attachment to the true Evangel, she hath not shown that confidence in us which we had a right to expect. I have advised our cousin of England, indeed, that it might not be amiss to keep her in seclusion for a season,—a joint government, you see, is a utopian imagination, and our dearest mother cannot be burdened at her age with the cares of State; but to take her life —that is another matter, as the Master says. Don't you think so, my lady?"

It was with difficulty that Lady Maitland controlled her indignation. "Oh, my liege," she exclaimed between her sobs, "it is shameful, infamous, incredible. All Europe will protest against an intolerable outrage. For *you*, sir, there is only one honourable road. Send round the fiery cross. Call your subjects to arms. Appeal to the God in whose name kings are anointed, and by whose authority they rule. Be sure that if the Queen of England will not listen to reason she will yield to force."

"My dear lady," the king replied, visibly embarrassed, "we must try reason first. Our good cousin is a wise and Protestant princess, although her views on the Apocalypse are by no means to be commended. We may rest assured that she will not permit our dearest mother to suffer an inconvenience, I may say an indignity, that will reflect discredit on ourselves. But our Council have already resolved to despatch a solemn embassy to the English Court, and the Master of Gray is now preparing to set out."

"The Master of Gray!" Lady Maitland exclaimed, in a tone of genuine horror. "Oh, my liege, any one but the Master. He is her bitter enemy; he is working for her death; send the Master, and you send her to the scaffold."

"Madam," the king, now gravely displeased, replied, "we are aware that certain calumnies, which have been traced to a neighbour of your own now in England, have been circulated against a noble gentleman who has ever been faithful to us. You will do well to discredit them and their author. Pardon me, madam,—our Council is about to meet."

He had been stumping back and forward while he talked, and now, touching his hat (much the worse for wear) to Lady Maitland, who had not recovered from her consternation, he abruptly disappeared.

It was the evening of the same day. Lilias was sitting by the shore, gazing dreamily at the incoming tide. Then shivering slightly, as if the wind had grown suddenly chill, she looked round; the Master stood beside her.

"I leave for England to-night," he began; "but I hear that you and your mother regard my mission with disfavour. The Master of Gray is a black sheep! Believe me, it was not of my seeking; whatever happens, I shall be blamed; but the king insists, and go I must."

"I would give much to believe that what we have been told of you—you who were once a dear friend—is false," she replied. "But can you deny that you have deserted the queen, who has been good to you since you were a boy?"

"Desertion, my fair cousin, is a foul word. It may be true that I have been forced to recognise that it is for the good of our country that Mary Stuart should not be permitted to return. What then? Am I to be deterred from doing what is for the public welfare by private and personal scruples?"

"Do not mock me, Mr Gray. The time has come for plain speaking, and speak I must. You say that desertion is an ugly word; but there are worse behind. It is openly alleged that you have not only deserted but betrayed the queen; that you have revealed her most secret thoughts to her deadliest enemy; that but for you she would now be free. O Patrick

Gray," she cried, clasping her hands, "tell me that you have
not been so base !"

"Lilias, you are unreasonable. You speak as a schoolgirl
speaks, ignorant of the larger and graver interests which appeal
to the statesman and the patriot. Mary Stuart is impossible.
Mary Stuart means civil war, the Pope, the Inquisition. There
is no safety for those whom Mary Stuart hates if she escape
from her English prison——"

"That is what it comes to at the last. Patrick, I see it
now. You have betrayed her, and you are in mortal dread of
the punishment that will follow ! But our mistress is generous
—she forgets and forgives. Had she been less ready to forgive, indeed, she might yet be queen. Even my mother, however, has wellnigh ceased to hope that she will be restored.
Guarded as she is, escape is impossible. She is ill. She is
dying. Will nothing but her violent and shameful death
satisfy your rancour and your ambition ? O Patrick, I im-
plore you on my knees, think of your honour, think of your
duty, think of what posterity will say when it learns, as learn
it will, that you have sold your fair repute, your eternal salvation, for thirty pieces of silver."

She fell on her knees before him, sobbing as if her heart
would break.

"Lilias," he answered, coldly as it seemed, but there was
subdued passion in his voice, "this is summer madness.
What care I for posterity? Posthumous fame is but the
shadow of a shade. The rewards of the Hereafter are the
dreams of fools. When I am dead, let them speak of me as
they will. When life is gone, all is gone to me. I seek a less
visionary recompense." Here he paused ; she had turned her
head away ; she was drying her eyes. Then he went on, but
the mockery had died out of his voice. "Lilias, it may be
that you are right. I am what I am ; what I shall be in the
years that are coming, God knows. You are formed of nobler
stuff ; the man who wins you may well be proud ; there is no
station, however high, which you would not grace. Lilias, I
have loved you all along." Her tears were dry, and she looked
him in the face. "It has been a duel between us ; why should

we not agree to a truce, or rather, to lifelong amity ? Say that
you will be my wife ; and, Lilias—Lilias, on my honour—the
queen's life is safe.   Elizabeth will not dare to refuse ; our
appeal will be backed by arguments which even the Queen of
England cannot refute.   Lilias, is it to be ? "

"It would be a shameful bargain," she replied slowly, after
a pause, drawing herself up to her full height, and turning
away.   "Only yesterday I heard that you were betrothed.
Would you betray this Marie Stuart as you have betrayed the
other ? Life itself may be too dearly bought.   Think you our
gracious mistress would accept the sacrifice you have been
good enough to propose ? Sir, she would spurn the mercenary
and recreant knight who will not do for honour what he will
do for pay, as—as—I spurn him.   Do your worst, sir ; to your
victim, to your blameless victim, it will prove, it may be, the
truest service you can render.   She wears the martyr's crown,
while Judas—yes," she added, as she turned away for the last
time, " Judas will go to his own place."

His face was bloodless with rage ; his eyes blazed, as the
tiger's blazes ere it springs.   But he only said in the softest,
sweetest, and most dulcet purr, "My fair virago, you have
signed her death-warrant."

IV.

THE letters that came from Gilbert during the months that
followed were not calculated to allay our anxiety.

* * *

"Since the rescue failed, I have thought it fittest to abide
mainly in London, where, as the houses are many, and the
people swarm in the streets, it is easier for me to remain unknown.   Francis Howard, a cousin of his Grace of Norfolk,
is of the royal household, and well affected to our queen.
He opines that Elizabeth will not venture to put her publicly
to death, but will either secretly practise against her, or else

by severity in prison make an end of her life. Our queen is very feeble, but beareth herself bravely. It is rumoured that if she will ask pardon of Elizabeth her life will be spared ; but this I believe not. She will ask no pardon of man or woman, but will commit her soul to the mercy of the Almighty. Her keepers are unmannerly churls ; Amias Paulet sits covered in her presence (even in the case of a simple gentlewoman no true gentleman would be guilty of like discourtesy), and hath violently removed her cloth of state. She hath put in its place the pictures of our Lord's Passion, which hath increased his choler. Her chaplain has been taken from her, and Paulet, who is a bitter sectary and a precise Puritan, hath told her insolently that he himself will act as her priest. The Secretary Walsingham, her great enemy, is stirring the people against her,—the hue and cry in all the ports and country places is, that the Papists have landed, and that London is on fire. Since I wrote the above, Francis Howard hath told me that his mistress is minded to spare our queen's life, and will do so without fail if the King of Scotland declares plainly that her execution will break the amity."

"There is an evil change at the palace. Howard hath been secretly informed that it is the Scottish ambassadors (a shameful fact if it be true) who have stirred up his mistress against the queen our sovereign. Patrick Gray has come, and, they say, hath resolved the Secretary that James would have his mother 'put off,' and is not willing that any mildness should be shown unto her. Lilias, he is a villain, and if we chance to meet it will go hard with one of us. His perfidy is known unto many, and should he pass on his return through the parts of Yorkshire which are Catholic, he is like to be recompensed for his evil dealing."

"Howard hath told me all. Gray hath had a secret conference with the English queen. The king, his master, he said, in very truth desired that the execution should go forward; seeing that so long as his mother lived his own place was insecure; and that neither England, nor Scotland, nor the amity were safe unless she was removed. It was the dead only who did not bite—*Mortui non mordent*. Howard himself being in attendance, heard the Master's words—*Mortui non mordent*. The English queen now goeth about with a Latin apothegm in her mouth, which is to the effect that if you would not be stricken you must strike. *Aut fer, aut feri; ne feriare, feri*. The ambassadors, Howard adds, had thereafter a formal audience of his mistress. The Secretary and the Lord Leicester were present. Much earnest persuasion (as it appeared) was used by the Master; but the English queen, having previously been advised in private by him, would not listen to their memorial. Gray would have had her believe that if our mistress renounced her state and title to the succession to her son, she would cease to be a danger —the son coming in the mother's place. The queen declared that that would put herself in more evil case than before, using these despiteful words,—'Is it so? then, by God's passion, that were to cut my own throat; because, my Lord of Gray, for a duchy or earldom to yourself, you or such as you would cause some of your desperate knaves kill me. No, my God,' she added, 'he will never be in that place!' Sir Robert then craved that our queen's life might be spared for eight days, so that the king might be advised; but she answered with another great oath—'Not for an hour'; and so stormed and left them."

* * *

"Lilias, dearest Lilias, I know not what I write. The queen is dead: I have seen her die. I was present at Fotheringhay when the axe fell, and a gloomy fanatic, with her bleeding body at his feet, said 'Amen.' I saw it with these eyes, and yet I cannot believe that it is true. That the proud

and beautiful woman, who was yesterday without a peer, should
be now a headless corpse, covered with a bloody cloth, seems
entirely incredible.   Lilias, your mother has loved her since
they were girls; but all that went before is mean in comparison with the end.   No martyr ever went to heaven with
a more willing mind.   When she came out of her chamber
with the radiance of death upon her joyful face, there was not
a man in the crowd who did not feel that he was everlastingly
shamed.   In a happier age a thousand swords would have
leapt from their scabbards ere that gracious head had been
profaned.   Lilias, I cannot write more; the scene haunts me,
will haunt me while I live.   But I thank God that her high
spirit did not fail her, and that, confident in the justice of God
and of a future age, she died as a queen should die.   Of the
miserable hound who has been, directly or indirectly, the
cause of her death, I dare not speak; among the noble army
of martyrs which our dear mistress has joined, his presence
would be profanation.   But the time will come——"

There had been a wild burst of anger when it was known
that our queen had been condemned; when it was known
that she had been put to death, the nation was aghast.   Had
there been a great soldier among us, every man capable of
bearing arms would have been across the Border in a week;
and the nation, whether it won or lost, would have slaked the
thirst for blood which at times it cannot control.   Fortunately,
as we can see now, we had no captain who could lead us to
victory or to defeat; and in the stony despair of righting the
wrong which follows a tragedy which cannot be repaired on
this side the grave, we sat still until the moment for action
had passed.

Elizabeth's noisy protestations of innocence were received
with grim derision, and James's simulated sorrow deceived no
one but himself.   Neither Elizabeth nor James could well be
brought to book; but it was necessary, to allay the public
passion, that a victim should be found.

It was at this moment that the Master of Gray, who had hitherto been the coolest of players, lost his head. He quailed before the universal detestation which, rightly or wrongly, met him on his return.

The fate of Arran could be traced directly, so his friends averred, to the intrigues of the Master with the banished lords. Ordinary prudence would have suggested to a far shallower brain than his that the unscrupulous brother of the fallen Chancellor was the last man to whom dangerous secrets could be safely intrusted. But it would seem that when a man of profound craft loses his balance he goes further astray than the most blundering fool. Mortification and resentment were probably at work—passions which for the moment escaped all politic restraint; and though the web which he spun was a wide one, and though many flies were to be caught in its meshes, yet I think the moving motive of the whole conspiracy was his bitter animosity to the Secretary of State—John Maitland—who had often thwarted him, who was now all-powerful at Court, and who was the head of the family from whom, as he fancied, he had received a deadly insult. It is only in this way that I can account for the fantastic scheme of revenge which he meditated, and which with fatuous frankness he communicated to the Colonel,—that "cloutter of old shoes" against whom Mr Gibson (who, by the way, had been permitted to return to his flock when the Chancellor was dismissed) had so vigorously declaimed. The change in the Master's manner was plainly visible to the least observant; even the English ambassador had occasion to deplore the "hasty wrath and passionate dealing" of one whose temper had been hitherto imperturbable. There were, in short, all the signs of the disordered mind with which the gods afflict the man whose perdition is assured.

It was in the great room at Earlshall, where I had first seen the king, that the mine exploded. James had been very good to us of late (it was probably the reaction from his unreasonable resentment); and more than once, on returning from the hunt, he had called at Balmain and the Cleuch. He had offered me indeed a small place in connection with the

Council which I had not yet definitely refused; and it was in virtue of this provisional appointment that I happened to be present at the meeting which I am about to describe.

The Council had disposed of its ordinary business, and was ready to adjourn. The king had presided, and Bothwell, Secretary Maitland, and the Master of Gray were among the members present. The Master had been more than usually irritable and cynical, and his polished shafts had been discharged all round: even the vain and good-natured monarch had not been permitted to escape. "The Master must have got out of bed on his wrong side," Bothwell whispered to Maitland. To which the Secretary had blandly replied, "It is the spleen, my lord,—the east wind bites shrewdly to-day."

At this moment the Colonel, who had sent to request an audience, was ushered in.

"This is an unlooked-for pleasure, Colonel Stuart," the king observed, with marked coldness. "We thought that you were at a distance from our Court. May I ask what your errand may be? Our horses are at the gate, and we ourselves are nearly as impatient as the dogs, who seem inclined to take part in our Council."

"My liege lord," Stuart answered coolly, "I shall detain you a moment only. But reports have reached me which I feel bound to communicate without delay to your Highness— reports of a treasonable conspiracy against the Secretary of State and other members of this Honourable Council. I trust in God, sir, that it is not directed against your Highness's own person. But of that I have no certain knowledge."

"What, sir! a treasonable conspiracy possibly directed against ourselves!" James, palpably discomposed, exclaimed. "Are Cuddy Armorar and our men-at-arms at hand?" he added hastily, looking to the door.

"Had we not better learn some further particulars?" the Secretary interposed. "The people are still in a rash and unreasonable mood, and many injurious reports are afloat. They venture to say that our resident at the English Court has now slain the mother, as—pardon me, your Highness—he slew the father. Daily libels indeed are set up in the open street.

Only yesterday I saw on the door of the Tolbooth a scurrilous lampoon upon her Majesty of England, whom they ventured to call a 'murdering Jesebel.'"

"And to whom they have insolently offered a Scottish chain, as they call it," Bothwell added,—"that is, a cord of hemp tied halterwise."

"We must discover the authors of libels that may disturb the amity," James said, resuming the seat from which he had risen. Then turning to the Colonel,—"Speak out, man. What ails you? If there is treason in contemplation, there must be traitors abroad. It is your part as a leal subject to hide nothing from your prince. Whom do you accuse?"

The Colonel paused a moment, and then answered with the studied and technical elaboration of a legal indictment,— "Patrick—commonly called—the Master of Gray."

There was again a painful pause, while James looked with keen scrutiny at his favourite.

The Master sprang to his feet. "This is *your* plot," he said, turning fiercely upon the Secretary. "A bully can only repeat what he is taught; it is in your school, Mr Secretary, that the Sticker has learnt his lesson. This is not the first time by many that you have slandered me, and by God——"

The truculent "cloutter of old shoes" did not approve, apparently, of being called "the Sticker" (the nickname by which he was known among the common people), and laid his hand on his sword, which he partly drew. "Hoots, my lords, hoots!" cried the king, who hated the sight of cold steel. "Colonel, if you touch your sword, you are guilty of the treason you impute. Can it be true, Patrick?" he continued, turning to Gray, "that you have plotted against us and our Council?"

"Never against my most generous master," Gray exclaimed. "But that I have good cause to reckon with the Lord of Thirlstane, he will himself admit."

"You hear what he says, Sir John? What cause of offence have you given him?"

The Earl of Bothwell interposed. "May it please you, sir, there is a little trifle of an epigram which you may not have seen, though it has flown like wildfire through the Court. If

the Master has a sharp tongue, the Secretary has a sharper
pen.   I can give your Highness the copy, if it has not been
mislaid."   Opening his pocket-book, he took from it a slip of
paper on which some Latin lines were written, and handed it
to the king.

These were the lines :—

> " Sis Paris an Graius dubito ; pulchelle, videris
> Esse, Paris, forma, marte et amore pari.
> Fax etiam patriæ, nec fato, aut omine differs ;
> Græca tamen Graium te docet esse fides."

As he ran his eyes over the lines, James broke into a fit of
hoarse laughter.

" Hoots, Sir John, this is too bitter, too bitter by far ; we
ourselves could have given it a nicer edge, and the scholarly
turn of the true epigram of antiquity.   Our Secretary wants
the *suaviter in modo* whereof we are masters ; and yet, Patrick,
the *Paris* and the *Pulchelle* are not altogether amiss ; nor yet
the *Græca tamen Graium*, though there be over-much of the
verbal play than altogether suits the severer taste of the pupil
of Buchanan—God rest his soul !—who hath been nourished
upon the masterpieces of our Augustan age.   Now, my lords,
we will put a happy ending to this untoward comedy of errors,
and, as you say yourself, Patrick, let byganes be byganes, and
fair-play in time to come."

Gray had begun with an affectation of courtly deference,—
" Whatever your Highness is pleased to propose "—when he
was again interrupted.

It was Gilbert—my brother—who entered.   His face was
pale as death ; his eyes were sunk and hollow ; he looked like
the messenger of Fate.   It was obvious that he had been fear-
fully ill, and that he had risen from a sick-bed to discharge the
solemn trust that had been committed to him.

The Master started.   Had the sword of the Avenging Angel
been suddenly unsheathed before his eyes he could hardly have
been more unmanned.

The apparition, for such it seemed, stalked up to the head
of the table where James sat.

"*Mortui non mordent*," it said, in a ghostly whisper. There was no need for more; each one of us knew too well to what the ominous words referred, and against whom they were directed. "*Mortui non mordent.*"

But, as he spoke, Gilbert's strength failed, and he fell prostrate on the floor.

* * *

Every Scotsman, however little acquainted with the secret history of the time, has heard the sequel. Gray was tried and condemned. It has been said by contemporary writers that he was not executed in respect of the intercession of the Lord Hamilton. I fear the true explanation must be looked for elsewhere than in the public records. I have good reason to believe that the Master had a letter in his possession (addressed to him when on his English embassy) which was fatally compromising for others than himself. It would be found from it (so it was reported) that Gray had acted in strict conformity with the secret instructions which he had received from the king. This letter he had prudently deposited with a friend in England; it was enclosed in a sealed cover which was only to be opened if Gray was executed.[1]

His life was spared; but what at one time promised to be a great career was brought to an unlamented close. His ambition was nipped in the bud. His sin had found him out. He wandered across Europe—a soured and sullen man; until years afterwards, in a spirit of contemptuous toleration, the Scottish Government permitted him to return. "To what base uses may we come, Horatio," one William Shakespeare, an English play-actor, has lately written; and the baleful career of the Master furnished a theme that the rich and animated invective of the Calvinistic pulpit has turned to good account. Mr Gibson in particular has used his old enemy as the text of

---

[1] Mr Froude, writing me in February 1893, remarks: "You have filled out the figure of the Master of Gray—I daresay correctly. I could never make him out very clearly." Though the Master strongly impressed his contemporaries, he is, it must be admitted, an enigmatical and ambiguous figure.

many a discourse (protracted into a twentieth or thirtieth head;
for the good man's sermons grew long as he grew old), in which
it was conclusively shown that Erastian prelates and tulchan
bishops, to whom conscience was an idle word, and God a
nursery bogle, would go where Gray had gone.

How Gilbert was brought back to life by the tender ministra-
tions of a ministering angel, is a story of which his grandchildren
do not readily tire.   I cannot truly say that the shadow which
had fallen upon them was ever entirely lifted; but such happiness as was possible to a great Scottish landowner and his
lady in a troubled age, when men had ceased to believe as
their fathers believed, and to worship as their fathers wor-
shipped, was known to "Gilbert Holdfast and Lilias his
wife."

Note by the Transcriber.—Of that later and sunnier life, we
gain through this musty pile of papers only a partial and
transient glimpse.   In a letter from Gilbert to Lady Maitland,
written some six or eight years after the execution of Mary,
this passage occurs :—

"Little Will is very well, I thank God: he drinketh every
day to Lady Grandmother; rideth to her often and yet within
the Court; and if he have any spice cake I tell him Lady
Grandmother is come and will see him, which he then will
either quickly hide or quickly eat, and then asks where Lady
Danmode is?"

III.

THE DEVIL TO PAY.

BALMAWHAPPLE was still in its civic infancy when the seventeenth century was young. These were hard years for Scotland. The king had gone south; the nobles had followed suit; and in the remoter districts the moral and spiritual supremacy of the successors of Knox had become a grinding tyranny. One superstition had made way for another. Any show of religious independence, of intellectual curiosity, was sourly repressed. The ministers, indeed, were everywhere omnipotent. The kirk - session was more powerful than the secular tribunals; and from the excommunication of Presbytery and Synod there was no appeal. The clown who had used profane language, the girl whose frailty had been exposed, the urchin who gathered " grosers " in time of sermon, had to do penance in face of the congregation — often for hours, sometimes for days. Great county families like the Holdfasts resented the dictatorial inquisition of the Church Courts; but they were comparatively powerless, and even when holding the office of Judge-Ordinary were unable to save their dependants from the vengeance of ecclesiastical fanaticism. It was often as much as they could do to save themselves; and the high-born dame that Will Holdfast married—she was one of the great Catholic house of Huntly — was forced to ask pardon on her knees. It is to be feared that too many of the ministers of religion really *enjoyed* the power to bind and to loose that had been vested in them by law or usage; they inflicted pains and penalties with a light heart; they were cruel as well as ignorant and bigoted. Will Holdfast can hardly be regarded as a witness whose testimony is unimpeachable; and it may be that the opinions which he formed were coloured by the prejudices of his order, and by his close connection with more than one of the culprits against whom the clerical *anathema maranatha* had been recorded; but after every allowance is made, his notes of certain incidents which occurred at Balmawhapple in the year of grace 1620 may be taken as substantially accurate. Mark assures me that I may print them without any fear of reprisals; and as judge, jury, and victim have been dust for two hundred years, there is little risk at least of an action for defamation. So here are Will's notes, Will Holdfast, the eldest son of the Gilbert, who, as you may remember, saw Mary Stuart die.

I.

Nobody knew how old Lisbeth was. She had been in the Maitland family long before any of us were born; she had been our mother's nurse as well as our own. We loved her; yet she was never exactly a lovable woman; and our love was mingled with fear. Until we were able, indeed, to shift for ourselves, her fidelity was absolute, her devotion unremitting; and she would, I have no doubt, have laid down her life for us gladly. But as one after the other we grew up, her attitude changed. Imperceptibly but surely a wall of separation rose between us. Even her solicitude had been austere; whenever she permitted her thoughts to wander away from the work in hand, a frown would settle upon her face. Possibly there were bitter memories in the background; her only son, we knew, had been drowned at sea; and the catastrophe, which had been brought about by the recklessness of his mate, had been neither forgotten nor forgiven. It was curious, however, how her tenderness waned or appeared to wane (if it did wane) whenever we came to man's or woman's estate. We used to tease her at times, no doubt, and possibly the frivolities of youth hurt her more than we knew or cared. Her Calvinism had been learnt in a gloomy school: for every idle word God would bring us into judgment. Then, though our mother was a Maitland, our father was a Holdfast; and among the godly the Holdfasts were "suspect." The conviction that we did not belong to the elect, that we were outside the pale of those who had washed their robes in the blood of the Lamb, did not become actively aggressive while we were in the cradle or at her knee. The tricks of infants were as the tricks of kittens, to which no moral code applied. But with responsible beings it was otherwise; and whenever we arrived at years of discretion, as the saying is, it seemed to be borne in upon her, with a force that she could not resist, that we were numbered with the reprobate.

My brother Angus, who went to Paris to study at the famous medical school of the university, used to tell us that Lisbeth was mad. There was madness in her eye; and her theology, he said, was the concrete form it assumed. But there was something more, he added—a bodily as well as a mental taint; and he recommended that she should be closely watched. A convulsive fit, of the nature of epilepsy, might attack her at any moment; and, if alone, she would die before assistance could be obtained.

This was the view of science, however; and science, as it is called, has as yet made small way in Balmawhapple. Angus treated the popular judgment with characteristic contempt; but few of us, or of our neighbours, had risen to his standing-point; and by the popular judgment—not at first, nor for long, but with redoubled energy at the end—it was definitively settled that Lisbeth More was a witch.

For a good many years now she had led a solitary life. We had built a cottage for her among the sandhills of the Whapple, where the rabbits burrow and the sheldrakes breed. The plaint of the whaup is almost the only sound that disturbs the summer silence: of a winter night, however, the moonlight water up to the cottage door is alive with wild-fowl—the wild-fowl that are shy of men. So she had no friends or neighbours; and till her niece Betty came to stay with her, when her strength failed, she had lived absolutely alone. In these circumstances it was little wonder that her hold on the life round about her had slackened, and that she should have seen visions and dreamt dreams. The fishers returning from the Dogger Bank in the early twilight (while the stars grew faint before the dawn) had heard as they glided past screams of demoniac mirth or (it might be) of demoniac despair — had seen a woman, or the figure of a woman, with clasped hands and bowed head, wrestling with invisible enemies as she paced restlessly along the beach. The reek of burning brimstone which is known to attend the visits of the Prince of Darkness had been distinctly perceived by more than one of them. Little Betty was very loyal to her aunt; when Angus was away Betty was the one freethinker in the parish; and Betty treated the ugly and malevolent rumours with supreme scorn; but in spite of Betty's protests, the fact that Lisbeth was a witch, who held illicit interviews with the Evil One, could no longer be concealed. The general feeling was that the time had come when minister and session must take prompt action.

My brother Angus, indeed, continued to ridicule the whole affair. "Well done, Betty!" he said to me one day. "That trim little lass has all the sense of the parish in her head. She is constantly with Lisbeth, and she knows that the poor old doited body is clean crazy. Why, in the name of all that's rational, are Master Knox and his brothers in Christ so keen against witches? There was the Witch of Endor, to be sure; but she was quite out of date long before their blessed Reformation. The fairies no doubt were in vogue under the old *régime*; but I would a deal rather have to do with the Queen of Elfame than with a parcel of dirty half-witted old wives; and whatever else they might be, if we are to believe the Bishop, the good people were at least good Catholics." And he went away to see a patient, humming to himself some rhymes which had been made by a witty prelate:—

> "When Tom came home from labour,
>   And Ciss to milking rose,
> Then merrily went the tabour,
>   And nimbly went their toes.
>
> By which we note the fairies
>   Were of the old profession;
> Their songs were *Ave Maries;*
>   Their dances were procession."

And indeed I am partly inclined to agree with Angus; at least I fancy sometimes that it is because the preachers are persuaded that the charms and invocations used by the witches had a Catholic parentage that they are so bitter against them. And rightly so, most of us will add, no doubt.

Yet I am not certain that the tide of popular feeling would have risen as it did had it not been for the Reverend David

Dickson. The Reverend David Dickson was the assistant and successor of the Reverend Peter Gibson (whom we had known as children), and he was much esteemed as a powerful preacher of the Gospel throughout the Merkland. But there was much godly jealousy between him and the minister of Cuddiestane, the Reverend Ebenezer Macfulzie, who was cousin in the tenth degree to John Knox himself, and esteemed accordingly by the more precise Protestants. The rivalry had latterly grown somewhat keener than was seemly. There were rumours indeed (which had been traced as far as Cuddiestane) that the incumbent of Balmawhapple was not sound in the essentials, but addicted to pagan and papistical literature. So it behoved him to silence the evil reports of the ungodly ; and when he was given to understand on credible testimony that at the Inquisition of Witches which was about to be held, Cuddiestane would provide no fewer than *three*, he perceived that the honour of Balmawhapple and his own repute for piety and penetration were at stake. I really believe that he would have preferred to leave Lisbeth to die in her bed, or by her fireside (for he was naturally a kindly man) ; but the pretensions of Cuddiestane (where witches had been hitherto suspiciously rare) were not to be tolerated ; and it was decided, with only one dissenting voice, that Lisbeth should be cited to appear and answer before the session,—*quam primum*, as the clerk added. Cuddiestane would thus be driven to admit that Balmawhapple was still a fruitful field in the vineyard, and that it could yield as goodly a harvest as in its best days.

It was Betty who brought the citation to Angus. Her indignation had been succeeded by alarm ; and she had, as it appeared, real cause for anxiety—"Granny," as she called Lisbeth, having of late laboured under the delusion that she was demoniacally "possessed."

The event which had finally persuaded the old woman that she was in league with the Evil One had occurred not long before. Rab the Ranter was one of the vagabond people who call themselves Ægyptians, and had gone about the country with minstrels, sangsters, tale-tellers, and other idle and masterful beggars, practising jugalarie, fast-and-lous, and other unlawful games. Even in the wild community to which he belonged, Rab was regarded as insanely vindictive and ferocious, and he had been convicted more than once of monstrous and abominable crimes. But he was a polished ruffian; and had it not been for the cruel sneer on his lips and the wicked cast in his eye, he might have passed, as he sometimes did indeed, for one gently born. He had been banished again and again. He had been scourged. He had been branded with red-hot irons. His ears had been nailed to the Tron and then cut off. But he had never been hanged, and indeed he seemed to bear a charmed life. The Devil had been good to his own, it was said.

Possibly a popular superstition had contributed to the impunity he enjoyed. The common people believed then, as they still do, that the body of a man who is guilty of unspeakable wickedness is inhabited by a devil. They hold that if the devil is driven out he will seek elsewhere another lodging; and that the surest way to drive him out is to hang the man in whom he lodges. But if the effect of hanging is simply to give another (man or woman) into the keeping of an evil spirit, and if it is quite uncertain into whom the evil spirit may prefer to enter, is it not more prudent to leave him in the abode which he presently occupies? This mode of reasoning may be faulty, but it was not without force, and Rab had profited by it.

But he had come to the end of his tether, and a week or two before the day when Lisbeth was cited, he had mounted for the last time the ladder on the Gallows hill. By an unhappy fatality the old woman had been passing at the time; and, dazed though she was, the unusual assemblage had attracted her attention. Rab had fixed his evil eye upon her as she paused, and with a villainous sneer had addressed some mocking words to her, which were understood to imply that he left her his interest in the fiend as a bequest or legacy which she was to use to the best advantage.

The shock was too much for Lisbeth's shattered nerves, and she fell down in one of those fits to which she had latterly become subject. It need not surprise us if, as she writhed convulsively upon the ground, the ignorant spectators should have fancied that they actually observed the foul fiend enter into her.

I am afraid that Angus's advocacy (that Lisbeth should have shared in the delusion, as her niece sorrowfully admitted, only proved, he declared, that her insanity had taken an acute turn) did the old woman no good. The scorn which he could not conceal was not calculated to conciliate; and our interview with Mr Dickson—we asked him to dinner, and drank his health in a bumper of claret that had been brought from France in The Gift of God, the year of the king's marriage—was far from satisfactory. Though his heart was not in the business, he would not listen to our remonstrances, and words ran high (between him and Angus) before we parted.

The *quæstio vexata* was gradually approached, and we found him at first not unreasonable.

"The law," he said, "punishes with severity the strolling vagabonds who feign to have knowledge of charming, prophecy, and similar abused sciences. The fantastical imaginations of those addicted to witchcraft are of like evil effect, and must be not less strictly repressed."

"Then you do not think," I said, "that they have veritable communication with the enemy of mankind?"

"Many of them have confessed that they have——"

"But only after their memories have been refreshed by the pilniewinkies, the caschilaws, and the boots," Angus interposed.

"Pardon me, I have known many cases in which the admission was voluntary. They gloried in their shame."

"Vanity, diseased vanity, assumes many disguises," the man of science replied. "Nor can it be alleged that what they do is invariably hurtful. Most of them, on the contrary, from their knowledge of herbs and simples are skilful in the cure of disease."

"But they pretend to cure by charms and conjurations, and the silly people who haunt them are misled by what they are told."

"Faith, we know, can move mountains. Even in the schools we require the faith of the patient as well as the skill of the leech. Miracles of healing," he added, after a pause, "have before now been ascribed to Beelzebub."

This was too much for our reverend friend. "I hold no communion with scoffers and blasphemers who are prepared to ridicule the mysteries of our holy religion," he exclaimed, as he rose hurriedly from his seat. "The session will hear of this," he went on, turning to Angus. "The spirit of unbelief is abroad. Sir, I do not believe that you believe in the Devil!"

"My good sir," Angus answered, with provoking suavity, "do not leave us under a false impression. I should be loath indeed to surrender my belief in One who is so eminently serviceable to your cloth. And yet," he added, with a shrug, "I am whiles inclined to agree with a vernacular writer of high authority who maintains that there is sma' need for a deevil in a warld where there are deceitfu' hearts and leein' tongues."

After this any hope of truce had to be abandoned. It must thenceforth, we knew, be war to the knife.

II.

THE session-house was a low wooden shed on the north side of the church; and it was inconveniently crowded when we arrived. The minister sat at the head of the long table which occupied the centre of the room; his elders, the men who composed the session, were placed on either side. They were for the most part farmers—quiet, shrewd, douce, as the Balmawhappians mainly are; but they had come straight from the plough, and they brought with them the fresh smell of the newly turned earth. The local schoolmaster acted as clerk of session, and he was reading the minutes of the immediately preceding meeting when we entered,—room having been made for us near the end of the table where Lisbeth and her niece were seated. There was a lamp beside the minister which threw a dim light upon the strong grave faces at the other end; the rest of the room was in darkness. The sense of gloom was oppressive, and the raven-like croak of the clerk's harsh monotonous voice seemed exactly to suit the surroundings.

This (or words to this effect) was what he read :—

"The said day it is ordainit that a new pair of stocks be made for the punishment of stubborn and unruly delinquents. It is also ordainit that those who harbour papists or witches, who are present at fights, who do not communicate, who drink during divine service, who let on of bonfires, who do not attend the examinations on Sabbath afternoon, be excommunicate or required to satisfy as adulterers.

"The said day it is ordainit that Patrick Wilson for drinking after cockcrow stand in sackcloth two Sabbaths at the kirk-door, and be fined four merks ; and that George Thomson and Elspit Gray be fined four merks of penalty, and sit on the stool of repentance two Sabbaths, for drinking during divine service.

"The said day George Gordon is cited to appear for profaning the Sabbath day by gathering grosers in time of sermon.

"The said day Grizzel Murrison is ordainit to mak her public repentance barefooted, twenty-six Sabbaths at the kirk-door, first betwixt the second and third bells, and thereafter upon the stool of repentance.

"The said day it is ordered that intimation be made from the pulpit that none of the parishioners receive Margaret Charles, who was lately parted with child in the parish of Cuddiestane.

"The said day Archibald Russell, presenting himself to be contractit, and being ignorant of the Ten Commandments, is ordainit to pay forty shillings to the poor, and to learn them before he is married.

"The said day Alexander Cairnie, in Tilliochie, was delaitit for brak of Sabbath in bearing ane sheep upon his back from the pasture to his own house. The said Alexander compeirit and declairit that it was of necessity for saving the beast's life in time of storm. Was rebukit for the same, and admonished not to do the like."

Tilliochie's case was the last, and while the minute was being attested as correct, Angus whispered to me that there was an earlier decision, which had obviously ceased to be regarded as a precedent in the ecclesiastical courts :—" And He took him, and healed him, and let him go: and answered them, saying, Which of you shall have an ass or an ox fallen into a pit, and will not straightway pull him out on the Sabbath-day?"

The minutes having been duly approved, the Moderator (as the chairman is called) rose and stated that the first business of the present meeting was to inquire into a *fama clamosa*. It was alleged that a parishioner, well known to them all, had been guilty of the mortal sin of witchcraft, and they had met to obtain, if possible, a free confession from the culprit, according to the practice of the ecclesiastical courts. Then, looking steadily at Lisbeth, he asked her if she was prepared to confess that she had had dealings with the Devil ? The old woman, roused for a moment from her stupor, mumbled (and yet the answer was distinctly heard through the room), " It's ower true, it's ower true."

That was all; but Betty, who half supported her aunt in her arms, looked at Angus. " Will you no' speak for her and for me ? " she said, with an air of pitiful entreaty. Angus rose, and observing that surely more was needed than the avowal of an aged woman, who was labouring under a deadly disease, and whose wits were gone, insisted that some evidence at least should be led. The request was too reasonable to be entirely disregarded, and two or three of the audience were invited to relate what they had witnessed. Jock Tamson, the smith, had been present at Rab's hanging, and had seen Lisbeth's convulsive struggle when the fiend took possession of her. Mrs Tamson and her neighbours had applied to her on various occasions for advice, and she had given them potions that had cured them with miraculous and unprofessional rapidity. One of them had seen her in the dawing gathering the herbs of which they were compounded. Another had found her sitting in a field of green corn before sunrising, and on being asked what she was doing, she had replied, " I have been peeling the blades of the corn ; I find it will be a dear year for us a',—the blade of the corn grows withershins (that is, against the course of the sun); when it grows sungates (that is, with the sun), it will be a cheap year." Another on the Eve of St John had helped her to gather the deadly fern-seed, which on that night only is visible to mortal eye. The evidence, to say the least, was not very conclusive.

It was in vain, however, that Angus ridiculed the contention that these nocturnal rambles clearly indicated that she was in pursuit of unlawful knowledge, and assured them, as a physician, that a convulsive seizure of an epileptic nature was quite consistent with innocence. Mr Dickson, in a few weighty words, reminded the session that the unfortunate woman had openly confessed that she had entered the service of Satan, and advised them to disregard the atheistical plea that all the symptoms which had hitherto been associated with demoniacal possession could be ascribed to natural causes. So on her own confession Lisbeth, as a witch, was remitted to the Commission.

Lisbeth, in the same dazed, half-conscious state, was removed from the session-house, and lifted into the cart which we had sent with her, by Angus and Betty. None of the neighbours would assist; was she not, on her own confession, a woman accurst? Angus led the moorland pony; Betty walked beside her aunt. There is a road all the way to the links (the others being mere tracks); *that*, at least, we owe to the old monks. The motion and the fresh air seemed to revive the old woman, and ere they reached the cottage she was talking eagerly to herself—in strong trenchant words, such as she was wont to use before her mind went.

"Ye ken, sirs, that my mither was burnt for a witch (by the gude Lord James in his last progress through Fife), and her mither afore her. It's a sair burden for an auld wife like me. The feythers have eaten sour grapes, and the bairns' teeth are set on edge. Yet the Lord Himsel' hath declared that we wull not be judged for the evil done in the auld time. 'As I live, saith the Lord God, ye shall not have occasion any more to use this proverb in Israel. Behold, all souls are mine; as the soul of the father, so also the soul of the son is mine: the soul that sinneth, it shall die.' But I wudna

lippen; I was ay prood; I was uplifted by the conceit that
I belanged to the elect. But indeed, cummers, we maun
stan' or fa' on our ain feet at the last. 'The soul that sinneth,
it shall die.' And so for my sins I was made over to the
power of evil, and delivered into his hand.

> "'Like to ane bird tane in a net,
> The whilk the fowler for her set,
> Sa is our life weel win awa'.'

He cam' at me like a roarin' lion, like a roarin' lion seeking
his prey. And I cud not resist, though I bethought me of
the gude and godly and comfortable promises of David's
psalm in James Wedderburn's version;" and then she sang
in a weak quavering voice the well-known verse,—

> "The net is broken in pieces small,
> And we are savit fra their shame,
> Our hope was ay and ever sall
> Be in the Lord, and in His name,
> The whilk hes creat hevin so hie,
> And made the eird so marveilouslie,
> And all the ferlies of the same."

Betty walked silently beside her aunt, looking neither to
right nor left; the tears had dried on her cheeks, and her
face was set and hard. "Let them wirry us baith," she said
under her breath; "it's a cruel warld."

Poor Betty!

III.

THE exploits of the Commission that sat at Aberugie that
year have not yet been forgotten. They burnt more than
one hundred witches—not counting the wizards and warlocks.
Their industry was indefatigable, and was attended with remarkable success. But the field was so wide that they were
unable to overtake it, and sub-commissioners were despatched
to the outlying districts. These got through a very creditable
amount of work; all along the coast, from the Moray Firth

to Berwick, the reek of tar-barrels and fagots darkened the air.   Passing mariners from France and Flanders had seen no such sight before,—except possibly during the season of " muirburn."

It was rather difficult to understand why so many foolish and evil-disposed old women should have been indicted together.   One can understand a nervous panic pervading a whole community ; men and women, in unreasoning and uncontrollable alarm, frightened out of their wits.   But, except in one or two instances, there was no sign of any personal animosity ; on the contrary, in most cases there appeared to be a friendly understanding between the witch and her neighbours ; and " Old Lucky " or " Mother Bunkle " was not unfrequently a not unpopular functionary in the parish,—holding her own against the parson and the laird.   And I believe, as I have said before, that, but for the preachers (who felt possibly that the tussle with Satan was a matter of life and death for themselves), there would have been few prosecutions.

The sub-commission that sat at Balmawhapple (in the big room of the old Holdfast Arms) consisted of three clerical and three lay members, and was presided over by the sheriff of the shire.   An advocate from the county town had been sent to see that convictions were duly obtained ; but, indeed, his services might have been dispensed with, for the zeal of the commissioners did not require encouragement, and most of the old women—there were ten in all—had been prompt to confess their misdeeds.

I was a spectator only ; my name might have been included in the Commission had I desired ; but Angus had persuaded me to abstain from taking any active part in the proceedings.

"The ministers will vote to convict," he urged, "and Boghall and Tap-a-tourie will go with them ; so that you could do no good—even if the shirra were friendly."

I don't think I shall ever forget—live as long as I may—the miserable row of wretched creatures who faced us.   But with the exception of Angus and myself, and an English gentleman who was our guest, every one in the room appeared to regard the terrible ceremony with the most callous and stolid indifference. How was that cruel lust for innocent blood to be explained? The question puzzles me now as it puzzled me then.

A prayer by the Reverend Ebenezer Macfulzie, in which the Lord was implored to ratify in heaven the sentences that His ministers on earth were about to pronounce, having come to a close, the assize was opened, and the first case was called by the macer, who, having ascertained that the accused was present, proceeded to read the indictment or "dittay."

The first case was that of Alison Dick, who was accused (as indeed they all were) of contravening the eighteenth chapter of Deuteronomy, as well as the seventy-second Act of the ninth Parliament of Queen Mary. Alison had been thrown into the Loch of Lindores with her thumbs tied, *and had floated*, which was *prima facie* evidence at least that she was in league with Satan. She was accused, moreover, of taking off and laying on diseases—the consent of the dog or cat on whom they were laid not having been obtained; and she had told Agnes Finnie that she would "gar the Devill tak' a bite of her." Though it was clear that Alison Dick did not deserve to live, yet, as she had made a free confession, the court, it was intimated by the sheriff, would deal mercifully with her—she should be wirried (or strangled) first, and then burnt. Alison, when she heard the sentence, contentedly bobbed her head,—which was her equivalent for a curtsey.

Old Lucky Wishart did not fare so well. She had, it appeared, made a wax figure of the king, and it had been seen melting away like ane burning candle, fortunately without any evil effects to him of whom even the Devil himself was forced to confess, *Il est un homme de Dieu*. She had gone at midnight to the thief's gallows to cut some choice morsels for the brew she was compounding, and she had been seen with other witches at the Cross of Muirstone above Kinnell, where they had danced reels and jigs while the Devil played the pipes. A pricker of witches declared that Lucky bore the Devil's mark; that he had driven a pin into it, and that she did not bleed. Her fingers had been in the pilniewinks, her legs had been crushed to pulp, a rope had been twisted round her head, heavy weights had been laid on her stomach, and yet she would not confess. For her malignant contumacy she was allowed no grace. Her sentence was that she be taken straight to the stake, and there burnt incontinently.

Most of the witches who undertook to cure disease had, it came out, apart from the freemasonry of the craft, charms or conjurations of their own. Bessie Boyd's curt formula was (the patient in the meantime having partaken of her hellish liquor), "Gif thou wilt live, live; gif thou wilt die, die;" but at other times she would repeat the lines which betrayed their Catholic origin :—

> " All kinds of ills that ever may be,
> In Christ's name I conjure ye;
> I conjure ye, baith mair and less,
> With all the virtues of the Mess ;
> Furth of the flesh and of the bane,
> And in the erd and in the stane,
> I conjure ye in God's name."

Isobel Gowdie cured, or pretended to cure, the "heart-fever"; her patients, kneeling before her, repeated after her the invocation to "the nine maidens that died in the boor-tree in the Ladywell Bank," and then were appointed on nine successive mornings to eat the wayburn leaf; while Gielie Duncan, who was a sort of horse-doctor, employed the charm which, from time immemorial, has been noted for its singular efficacy in curing sprains and bruises :—

> " Our Lord forth raide,
> His foal's foot slaide ;
> Our Lord down-lighted,
> His foal's foot righted,
> Saying: Flesh to flesh, blood to blood, and bane to bane,
> In our Lord His name."

It appeared from Gielie's examination that the Devil had come to her as a gentleman in black, and asked her whether she was a poor woman, to which she had replied that she was ;

and that thereupon the Devil, in the shape of a gentleman, had said that if she would grant him one request, she should never want for meat, drink, nor clothes; whereupon she exclaimed, "In the name of God, what is it that I shall do?" upon which the gentleman in black (or rather, the Devil) vanished clean away from her. The sheriff was not satisfied with her explanation, and proceeded to cross-examine her.

The Sheriff. "In what shape or colour was the Devil?"

Gielie. "In black, like a bullock."

The Sheriff. "Did you never see the Devil but this time?"

Gielie. "Ay, once before. I was gathering sticks, and he came to me and said, 'This poor woman hath a great burden,' and would help to ease me of it; and I said, 'The Lord has enabled me to carry it so far, and I hope I shall be able to carry it further.'"

The Sheriff. "Did the Devil never promise you anything?"

Gielie. "No, never."

The Sheriff. "Then you served a very bad master, who gave you nothing. But maybe you will see him again shortly, when he will be better disposed," he concluded with grim irony, as he signed the order for her execution.

Angus had said once that he preferred the old Catholic fairies to the new Protestant witches; but there was one case —that of Grissel Jaffrey—which seemed to show that the stories of Elfame were still current among the vulgar. Grissel's familiar was not the Devil, but Tam Reid, who fell at Pinkie on the Black Saturday. Tam had promised her, she said, baith household gear and kye gif she wad deny her Christendom and the faith she took at the font-stane. Tam, it appeared, had been all these years in Elfame, where many others made their abode—the king that died at Flodden and Thomas Rhymer among the rest. More than once the good wights from Elfame who accompanied Tam had desired her company, and when she refused they would vanish incontinent,— an hideous ugly sough of wind following them as they partit. The elves or female fays would ride upon white palfreys, with the queen at their head, and they bore candles and swords, which, more closely examined in the daylight, proved to be nothing except dead grass and straes. Gangin' once afield, she added, to tether her horse at Restalrig Loch, there came a company of riders by that made such a din as if heaven and eard had gone together; and incontinent with a hideous rumble they rade straight into the loch and vanished. Tam told her it was the gude wights that were riding in middle eard.

Grissel was found guilty of sorcery and other evil arts, and the Commission ordered that she should be tortured with hot irons first and then burnt. The severity of the sentence was no doubt intended to deter others from listening to the fables of fairyland which had been everywhere popular before the May-day sports had been interdicted by the Reformed clergy: so Angus at least suggested.

Of all the witches who were examined during the day, Barbara Napier was the most communicative. She had been very intimate with Satan for many years, and had discovered him under various disguises. She had attended many witch-dances,—sometimes riding over the sea on a corn-sieve, sometimes on a corn-straw. To put her steed in motion she had merely to cry, "Horse and hattock in the Devil's name!" when it would fly away as thistle-down flies before the wind. The Devil, who would often take the likeness of a black dog that yowled at those who passed, would appoint the place of meeting, and then vanish. The kirk of North Berwick was a favourite rendezvous, and many a time twenty or thirty witches might be seen, by those who ventured abroad, riding on their corn-straws across the Forth. There, in the likeness of a man with a red cap and a rump to his tail, they found the Devil, and the wicked orgies would begin. But before they danced he would make a discourse to them in manner of a sermon, his favourite text being, "Manie goe to the mercat, but all buy not." He found fault with those who had been indolent in ill-doing; those who had been busy he called his beloved, and promised they should want for nothing. Then playing upon a trump he watched them dance, and those whose devilish antics had pleased him most were allowed to kiss his toe. The dance would last till long past midnight; but before the first cock crew they had mounted their corn-stalks and were sailing home.

Barbara's narrative was listened to with breathless interest; and when she had finished there was a deep sigh of relief. Even Angus was impressed; if we should ever have another Dunbar among us, he said to me, what a play he might make of the half-mad, half-clad hussies dancing with might and main to the skirl of the pipes!

The afternoon had worn away, and the appetite for horrors had been wellnigh sated, when Lisbeth More was called. She had had another fit, and was now obviously moribund. Betty, who essayed to say a word for her aunt, was peremptorily silenced. Where there had been a formal confession formally recorded, there was no need for further argument. So she was told, when, white with indignation, she had burst out against the travesty of justice. Besides, the short winter daylight was on the wane, and the judges had become impatient of delay. A foregone conclusion had no need to wait on argument. They had been latterly sentencing the culprits in batches; and they were not going to spend the few minutes that remained on one old woman who was already at death's door. A rather amusing incident, however (at least to those behind the scenes), occurred while the clerk was writing out the judgment of the court. The minister of Cuddiestane interposed. This was a case, he said, in which the culprit had no title to be burnt alive. She was not a first-class witch, and could not be treated as such. She must be *wirried* first. Our friend Mr Dickson was on the horns of a dilemma. He was not a cruel man, and death by strangulation, he knew, was speedier and more merciful than death by burning; but, if he gave way, Cuddiestane, with its three first-class witches, would entirely eclipse Balmawhapple. It is undoubtedly to his credit, as Angus admitted, that, in spite of the provocation, he held his tongue.

Next morning the sun rose upon a fine, clear, cold winter day. The snow lay thick upon the ground; every object was a dazzling white, except the sea and the black line of stakes, with their tar-barrels and piles of fagots, that had been erected along the beach during the night.

But the baron-bailie was wroth. It had been ordered by the court that the executions should take place within the burgh where the assize was held. Thus the whole cost had to be defrayed by the civic and ecclesiastical authorities of the parish; and the cost of burning ten old women would be heavy; for even the bodies of the two who were to be strangled had afterwards to be reduced to ashes,—the belief that to save the soul it was necessary to burn the body not being confined to Spanish inquisitors.

"The expense is just terrible," the bailie confided to the junior magistrate. "What authority has the court to saddle Balmawhapple with the cost of towes and tar-barrels for Cuddiestane? Cuddiestane should burn its ain witches."

"But think o' the honour and glory, bailie!"

"Think on an assessment o' saxpence in the pund! It'll come to that and mair. Here's the account o' the broch's disbursements when Chirsty Bell was brunt. *Imprimis*, for ten loads of coals, three punds sax and eightpence Scots; item, for a tar-barrel, fourteen shillings; item, for towes, sax shillings, forby the charges of the executioner: four-and-thirty punds Scots *in summa*, of whilk one-half, nae doobt, was recovered from the session."

"Aweel! aweel!" responded his colleague. "It'll be a fine ploy for the bairns!"

The condemned met their doom with astonishing placidity. The children romped noisily around while the irons were being heated; the girls from the burgh stood and gossiped with the country hinds: it was bitter cold, and more than one of the old women, it was noticed, sat with stolid composure, warming her hands at the fire that was about to consume her. Then the executioner came round with the "towes," and tied them up, one by one; the barrels were lighted; the flames curled round the bodies of the helpless victims, as the smoke drifted out to sea; some of them, through the crackling of the fagots, could be heard praying (or cursing?—it was reported afterwards that they repeated the Lord's Prayer backwards); while a devilish chuckle, that made the blood of the spectators curdle, was the only response. The Devil had been paid his dues, and he was possibly well pleased.

Lisbeth was the only one of the actors who failed to attend, and she was not much missed. She and Betty had been placed for the night, through Angus's interposition, in a barn belonging to one of our tenants. When the door was opened in the morning it was found to be empty. The explanation commonly accepted was, that the Devil had carried off the witch—soul and body—during the night. What became of Betty they did not care to inquire (when last seen she had been supporting her aunt's head upon her lap): many years afterwards I met her in London (where they do not burn the witches, though there are many), in the service of a great noble related to ourselves. Her hair was grey, but she held herself as erect as in the old days, though the shrewd brown eyes were softer and less watchfully defiant than of yore. In the Holdfast burial-ground, within the ruins of the venerable Abbey, there is a plain slab on which is written, *"Here lies Elizabeth More."* By-and-by it came to be surmised (not merely surmised, but openly asserted) that she had died during the night, and that one or more of the family she had served so well (according to her lights) had given her Christian burial. Possibly Angus and Betty could have told.

IV.

OUT OF THE DARK.

I HAVE diligently perused the records of the Holdfasts during the century that followed the famous
Inquisition of 1620; and Mark has occupied a wet
afternoon now and again in putting them in order;
but it cannot be said that they rise at any time into
the dignity of history or romance. The Holdfasts had
been austerely loyal for more than one generation;
but as the Court faction became more arbitrary they
began to incline to the Covenanting side. Will's
eldest son (he was a Hugh) married a daughter of
Forbes of Waterton, who brought the scriptural
phraseology of that family into her husband's house,
and who left behind her a vast mass of clandestine
correspondence, which she held with those of her
own persuasion during the hard years after the
Restoration; letters with disguised addresses, "For
the Lady Park," with earnest entreaties to "read and
burn," with initialed signature only as "L. D.,"—
"L. D." representing, Mark tells me, a certain Lilias

Dunbar; a charming devotee, it would appear, who
no doubt found, as other fair saints have found more
recently, a pleasant outlet for her warm feelings in
a little pretty fanaticism, rendered then all the more
piquant and exciting by the danger, mystery, and
intrigue it involved.

The second Gilbert, son of the aforesaid Hugh,
lived well into the eighteenth century, and married
Miss Betsy Peterkin, whose brother, the Doctor, was
a man of science and letters, and an active member
of the Royal Society. Gilbert's mother had been all
her life delicate and sickly; and her accounts with
the village apothecary for "tussilago flowers, maiden-
hair, mouse-ear, horse-tail, John's wort, penny-royal,
Althea-root, white lily-root," and other obsolete simples, are still extant. His father combined the *bon-
vivant* and the *littérateur*. He added in one year
four hundred volumes to the library; his household
accounts are scribbled over with scraps from the
Odyssey; he had a great respect for Mr Addison's
opinions; and he corresponded with Professor Black-
well of Aberdeen, who wrote him in reply hearty,
lively, sagacious epistles, bristling with French, Latin,
and Greek inscriptions. On the other hand, he was
rebuked by the Synod for sitting over his wine at a
county convivial meeting until two o'clock on Sunday
morning; and he and his brother the Colonel, during
a two days' carouse in the little tavern at the mouth
of the Whapple, drank "2 gills of brandy, 8 pints of
ale, and 57 bottles of claret." Clever Lord Lovat,

writing a letter of condolence to the son, pronounces
the father "an honour to mankind"; and to Mark
and myself, much meditating over the latter exploit,
he loomed large and portentous, a son of Anak, a
giant before the Flood. Of Hanoverian politics, the
old laird continued to stand well with both parties.
Prince Charles dined with him shortly before the
battle of Culloden. "You have had my *cousin* with
you," said Cumberland, who came next day.

Gilbert, during whose reign the Cleuch was re-
built, inherited his father's literary tastes, if not his
convivial. He was a good Græcian, and corresponded
with Dr Moir about the great Scottish edition of
Homer. When Dr Peterkin is at the Cleuch, the
itinerant postman, who arrives pretty regularly now,
carries letters thitherward from all parts of the kingdom. From caustic Lord Kames, from the self-
taught astronomer, Ferguson of Glasgow, from David
Hume, Harry Erskine, Gilbert Eliot — letters dis-
coursing of love, war, literature, philosophy, the
'Review,' the Royal Society, and Johnson's Dic-
tionary. Gilbert Eliot, who writes in an amusing
tone of mock solemnity, relates how the author of
Douglas has descended from the dignity of the drama
to the polemics of the General Assembly; and how
David Hume wanders disconsolately about a huge
library, and is resolved to let the world come to its
senses before he honours it with another volume. For
the rest, the laird encloses, builds, gardens, shoots,
and fishes during the day; dines out at two or three;

and of an evening in the drawing-room—the drawing-room has been in use for a good many years now—there are his books, his music, his wife sewing and knitting, and writing letters (she writes like a sensible woman, but spells abominably), his boys' lessons, and his little daughter Betsy, who plays on the spinet, though her uncle, the Doctor, prefers "the gutarre, or mandolino, as it is called by the London ladies," and is addicted to "cutting paper," a mysterious female occupation of the past, which he considers innocent but trifling, and is especially fond of sliding with her brothers on the ice, but gives it up when he suggests that it may bring her into "unlucky falls and situations."

This little Betsy ultimately (her brothers dying without issue) becomes Lady of the Cleuch, and grows quite grand and demure. She is a prime favourite with the Duke and his famous Duchess Jean, who is still well remembered among us for her plain-speaking, her eccentric habits, and her kind heart. Mistress Betsy, like the rest of her family, is addicted to literature. Old Lord Kames, gallant and bewigged, fantastic, and yet sparkling with fine sense, vivacity, and *bonhomie*, visits her ladyship sometimes on his way to the Northern Circuit, and brings her the latest intelligence from Edinburgh about the literary men who live there, and the popular new burletta *Serva Padrona*, in which the celebrated Italian singer, whom they ask to supper after the play and talk to in Latin, has made such a sensation. She reads Mr Harvey's

Contemplations on Night, The Whole Duty of Man,
Walpole's *Memoirs,* Dr Johnson's *Poems,* Spence's
Sermons, and raves about *The Man of Feeling,* which
Henry Mackenzie sends her in sheets as it goes
through the press. Henry is her cousin and earliest
correspondent, and his letters are the letters of the
superbly polite gentleman of the old school, who bends
benignly over his fair correspondent and kisses the tips
of her rosy fingers. When he comes down to visit her
at the Cleuch, they dedicate walks to "melancholy,"
and write fantastic inscriptions, whereof Henry can-
didly owns that "they are little more than *mere* poetry
after all." Besides this, her ladyship, being a literary
lady, keeps a private Diary of her own, in which she
discourses to herself as if she were walking on stilts.
One wonders if in these charming morocco-bound and
silver-clasped volumes of our own time, into which
it is "death for any male thing but to peep," the
owners talk much about "the best of parents," "the
responses of an agreeable conversation," and "the
little circumstances which are of import to the bosom
of tenderness,"—as Mistress Betsy was in the habit
of doing about the year of grace 1770?

There is little or nothing in all this, I fear, that will
interest the rapid reader of to-day. But one sketch
left by our friend Dobbs (of whom more anon) has not
been hitherto published; it is a narrative of certain
events which took place in Balmawhapple and its
neighbourhood while Culloden was still a living
memory. The story had been used, I take it, to

illustrate the old conflict between good and evil,
between day and night; and to do Dobbs justice,
the little frivolities of style, the little eccentricities
of sentiment in which he indulged, did not extend
into the domain of ethics. *Out of the Dark* was acci-
dentally discovered in the office of the *Tomahawk* when
the editor's sanctum was being scrubbed during his absence on "urgent business" at Tibbie Shiel's; and as
it is the only document in my possession that throws
any light upon the Balmawhapple of last century, the
reader, I make no doubt, will be glad to have it. The
fame of Lala's gold pieces still lingers in the burgh,
and the truth of the main incidents is attested by a
parcel of papers in the Holdfast charter-chest which I
have seen.

I.

St Abbs is, or was, the rival of Balmawhapple. Balmawhapple indeed regards the pretensions of St Abbs as the
ox in the fable regarded the frog's. The population of
Balmawhapple is twice as great; it sends thirty big ships
to the Greenland seas, whereas St Abbs has only one; the
herring-boats that fish from Balmawhapple are numbered by
hundreds, those from St Abbs by tens. But then St Abbs
has a real live Earl; and St Abbs is so close to the Earl's
seat that a day seldom passes without some of the family or
domestics from Cardono being seen at the Erskine Arms or
elsewhere in town.

The best consolation that we have is that his lordship is
not only Earl of St Abbs but Viscount Balmawhapple; and
Viscount Balmawhapple is the courtesy title assumed by the
eldest son when there is a son. So that St Abbs cannot be

held to have an exclusive or vested interest in the Earl; some part, at least, of his lordship belongs to us.

At present (that is, be it understood, at the time of which I am writing—1775, let us say) there is no elder son—only a daughter, in fact; and this is a constant source of discomfort to lord and lady alike, for the title is limited to heirs-male, and on the Earl's death goes to a distant Mar or Marshal or Menteith, who does not care to add to a dignity which was in existence before Robert Bruce was born, the more modern honours of St Abbs. It was a younger member of the great house who stood by James VI. in the Gowrie House at Perth who was the first Viscount; for they were Viscounts of Balmawhapple before they were Earls of St Abbs,—which, indeed, is another feather in our cap.

Yet another feather we had; for all Balmawhapple knew that the Earl's only sister, Penelope Erskine (long before her brother was like to be a peer; for there had been at one time a dozen good lives at least between him and the title), had married Adam Holdfast, the laird of Ballallan, who had been bred to the Bar, and who now held the dignified office of Sheriff of the county. The "Shirra" continued to live at the old house of Ballallan—it is now a mere ruin overgrown by ivy—which was just outside the burgh boundary of Balmawhapple, and a couple of miles from the Cleuch, where Adam, a younger son, had been born. It was a hospitable house—none more so in all the country-side; the front door stood open from morning till night, as if inviting all who passed to enter; and, on the weekly market-day, gentle and simple from far and near were proud to be numbered among the guests. The lands of Ballallan were not extensive, and the official salary was the merest pittance; but "Aunt Penelope" was a famous manager, and £100 a-year in those days went further than £1000 goes now.

Cardono is built upon the rocks, and overlooks the sea. The view from the bay-window of my lady's boudoir where husband and wife are sitting this winter afternoon is almost too vast for domestic comfort: that boundless plain of waters, that illimitable heaven, overpower the imagination. Once in a

way it were well; but day and night to listen to the sob of
the waves and the moaning of the wind from this aerial perch
is a fearful joy—a joy that is near akin to pain. The perpetual strain, indeed, is too severe for sober bliss. A man
may live up to a flower-pot or a teapot if he tries very hard;
but too much is required of him when he is invited to live up
to the sea.

They were pleasant and simple people, and (in spite of the
close vicinity of their awe-inspiring neighbour—to whom, indeed, they had become used) they led a pleasant and simple
life. They had been brought together originally in the
strangest fashion, and they used often to speculate what
would have happened if a certain East Indiaman had not
foundered one stormy night off the coast of Moray, a hundred
miles to the north of where they were sitting.

"But for that we would never have met," said the Earl.

"Marriages are made in heaven, my dear," was the lady's
reply, as a bright smile lightened up her handsome face;
"and Providence, we may hope, would have found some
other way to bring ours about."

At this moment the door opened, and a rather pretty girl
of eight or ten, with fair unconfined ringlets drifting behind
her, burst into the room. The rain was lashing the window-
panes by this time, and the shadows of the winter twilight
were falling upon the sea.

"I have been telling nurse *the* story, mother, but she says
I have got it wrong," the girl exclaimed, breathlessly, as the
ruddy firelight fell upon her chubby cheeks. "Please,
mother, tell me it again."

"Your father knows it by heart, child, and he is the best
of story-tellers," said my lady, glancing rather mischievously
at her husband.

"Such a story-teller!" said the little woman, with a slight
lisp, that rather added to the insinuating sweetness of the
address. It was one of those voices in which we seem to
feel the caress. Men like to be coaxed into doing what they
wish to do by just such a voice. "Oh, such a story-teller!" she
said, with an arch little laugh, as she climbed on to his knee.

VOL. I.   G

"Well, it's the very night for the story," said the good-
natured Earl, as the windows rattled in the rising gale.   "It
was just on such a night that the East Indiaman went down."

So he began *the* story,—the *coincidences* of which are wellnigh past belief.   Yet it is attested by credible witnesses,
some of whom I have spoken to as a boy.

"It was soon after the '45," the Earl began.   "Our people
had been mostly 'out,' and some of them never came back.
My grandfather, the Black Earl, as they called him, was
abroad at the time of the rising—which was lucky as it
happened, for he was a fierce Jacobite, and would doubtless
have been one of the first to join the Prince.   He was wild
when he heard afterwards that the Prince, on his way north,
had lodged for a night or two with the then laird of Troup—
Simon Gordon.   The bairn has never been at the Tor, Anne,
—we must take her there some day.   The rocks at Tor of
Troup, Nell, are higher than ours, and the house itself is built
like a hawk's nest on a shelf that overhangs the sea.   If you
have a steady head and can look over the parapet, you will
see a straggling village of fishers' huts, and a church that they
say is older than Iona.   Then the sharp saw-like teeth of the
reefs run right out to sea, and the ship that scrapes them
when the wind is inshore goes straight to the bottom.   They
rip her up—like the tusks of a wild boar.   Well, Nell, one
night not long after Culloden such a gale got up, and the
laird was wakened—he slept in the tower where they kept
a light burning from dusk to dawn—by the minute-guns of a
vessel obviously in sore distress, which he heard now and
again through the fury of the storm.   Of course no ship in
that sea could live through the night, and before the laird and
his people reached the shore the guns had ceased, and the
vessel was in fragments.   Not a soul escaped except one little
girl whose crib was miraculously washed far up the bay, and
stranded upon the beach.   The baby was sleeping the sleep
that babies sleep, and when they woke her up she had no
consciousness that anything was amiss, but laughed and
babbled as if on her mother's knee.   The word 'Kit' was
worked in blue-silk thread on her night-dress, but there was

nothing else to show to whom she belonged, and the laird took her into his house and heart, and brought her up with his own little girls, who were called—what do you think?"

"I know," said Nell, gravely; "Anne and Joanna."

"Two very plain girls," continued the Earl, "with red hair and freckled cheeks."

Nell put her hand upon his mouth and stopped him.

"Mother is just bee-u-ti-ful," she said, carefully accenting each syllable.

"Well, Nell, if you won't believe me, mother must tell you the rest."

The Countess put her spinning-wheel aside, and took up the running, Nell standing at her knee.

"Indeed, Nell, nobody would believe a word of it who didn't know it was true. Kit grew and flourished till she was quite a big girl—bigger than your little mother, bigger than your aunt Joanna—but such a dear sweet girl that everybody loved her. Father, indeed, made so much of her that we grew quite jealous at times."

"You hear, Nell," said the Earl, pulling her curls. "Wasn't that naughty?"

"No," said the little hero-worshipper; "mother couldn't be naughty if she tried. It was only in fun," she added to explain the situation.

"Then when Kit was eighteen, what do you think happened?" This was Nell's opportunity.

"Another great storm got up, and another ship was wrecked below the house, and when grandpapa went down again he found the poor people on the rocks, and he took them up to the Tor, and gave them tea and brandy and bread-and-butter; and next morning one of them said—What did he say, mother?" Here Nell paused, out of breath.

"He was as fine a gentleman as any of us ever saw; and though he spoke with a slightly foreign accent, no one could doubt that he was English. We girls came running into the breakfast-room a little late."

"Mind that, Nelly—that's the point." Nelly shook her

curls, but did not deign to reply to the interruption. "Go on, mother."

"And no sooner had he cast eyes on Kit, who had grown a great girl as I told you, than he said as if to himself, but so that we all could hear, 'Why, that's our little Kit.' And who do you think the fine gentleman was?"

"Kit's own uncle, of course," Nell replied, as if such a meeting were to be looked for any day.

"It was indeed her own uncle; though we all thought it more wonderful than you do, Nell, that they should have been brought together after so many years in this strange fashion. His sister, he told us, and her only child, had left Madras on her husband's death in the summer of the year that the Indiaman went down at the Tor, and they had never been heard of since. They never thought of coming to us to inquire: the vessel was bound for London, and it had been driven five hundred miles out of its course. Kit, though she came in time to love her uncle right well, had of course quite forgotten him, and could not bear to part from us. So we promised—Joanna and I—to go with them to Gottenburg, where he had settled after his brother's death, and was now one of the leading merchants. And when we got to Gottenburg, Nell, whom should we meet but two young Scotch lads, who were either already partners or about to be partners in the business. Tom was the elder brother, Methuen the younger. They were saucy boys, and at last they teased us so that—would you believe it, Nell?—I married the one and Joanna the other."

Nell gave a great sigh of satisfaction. "And that was the end," she said, as the nurse entered to take her to bed.

II.

Penelope Erskine had married our "Shirra"—Mr Holdfast of Ballallan—long before her niece Nell was born; and their eldest son—Ralph—had gone away to India when the child was yet in the cradle. India was then on the other side of

the world; unwieldy Indiamen, commanded by the cadets of
great Scotch houses, came and went by the Cape: if the
winds were unfavourable the voyage might last for a year;
when they came back they brought with them gems of
unknown value, strings of pearls, priceless shawls, blue bowls
of Nankin china, and much else that was rare and wonderful
to fathers and mothers and sisters who had never crossed the
Tweed. India was still a land of romance; still governed
by its native princes, except where the merchant-princes of
England had begun to build up an empire greater than the
Mogul's; a land through which men made their way at peril
of their lives, and from whose obscure and malign enchant-
ments they rarely escaped quite unharmed in body or soul.

Within that enchanted mist—the veil that Central India
drew around her—Ralph Holdfast had disappeared as utterly
as if he had been swallowed up by the sea. Not a scrap
came from him for years. To the peaceful household at
Ballallan he was as one long dead. Even the rumours that
he held high office at a native court, where he had discarded
the creed of Christ for the creed of Islam, and where, in his
crowded seraglio, he held worse than heathen carnival, had
died out too.

But one spring morning a letter bearing the Calcutta stamp
was delivered at Ballallan. It was read aloud by the Sheriff,
who was now a widower, before he went to court. It came
from the head of a well-known East India house which traded
among the sacred towns on the Upper Ganges,—towns at
that time as remote and unsubstantial as those in ancient
fable. Their agent had been met at Agra, or Benares, or
Delhi, or Oudh by an envoy from a state that preserved a
jealous isolation, and which for many years no foreigner had
been permitted to enter, who had delivered to him an ebony
chest or cabinet securely corded and sealed, and scrawled
all over with hieroglyphics in an unknown tongue, and a
dark-eyed tawny girl-child (with her native nurse), who wore
round her neck a filigree chain of gold, delicate and fragile
seemingly (but a strong man could not break it), to which
was attached the seal which had been used to secure the

cabinet, and a scrap of parchment on which was written, "I bequeath all to my daughter Lala.—Ralph Holdfast, the younger of Ballallan."

The letter went on to say that the little girl had been brought down to Calcutta, where the chest had been opened, and its contents lodged in the firm's secret safe; for there could be no doubt that their value was immense—£50,000 at the least, according to the rough estimate of the expert they had employed. The child and the chest itself would be sent on to Scotland by the next ship that sailed for Leith. The child, though very dark, seemed strong and healthy; but the writer regretted to add that the native nurse had died on the voyage from Benares. They had consequently been unable to obtain any information as to Ralph Holdfast or his surroundings: the fact, however, that he had sent his daughter and the treasure he had amassed out of the State appeared to indicate that he considered his position, and possibly his life, insecure.

I may say here that what became of Ralph in that outer (or inner) darkness was never known: the scrap of writing attached to Lala's chain was the last that was received from him. He may have been strangled by the Rajah or poisoned by one of his many wives, or he may have died in the odour of sanctity as a dancing dervish or priest of Brahma at a good old age. When the State was annexed by the English fifty years afterwards inquiries were made; but no one, it appeared, had ever heard of Ralph Holdfast. He had probably been known to the natives by another name.

So out of that Cimmerian darkness Lala arrived at Balma-whapple one summer morning when the "Shirra" and his daughter Mailie were still at breakfast—a small, scraggy, olive-skinned, black-eyed girl (her round black eyes turning slowly from one to the other, like a doll's, shall I say? or a heathen idol's?), with a mysterious ebony chest as big as a herring-barrel, filled to the brim with gold pieces which had been coined in the mints of the East any time during the last thousand years. They took her in; they tried to make her one of themselves; the chest was deposited in the strong-room of the National Bank; but it cannot be said that the suspicions these worthy, if somewhat primitive, people entertained when she first came among them were ever entirely allayed. Was she indeed what she pretended to be? or was she not rather an imp, a goblin, the offspring of some horrid Indian jugglery or devilry, who had assumed a human shape, but in whose wake evil would surely follow? And the gold pieces which had served so many masters, which had passed through so many dusky hands, which had been used, doubtless, in so many infamous bargains, and which had been the curse of numberless generations,—would they remain solid in the bank's safe, or would they not rather turn into worthless rags, and waste away like withered leaves?

"It's a bad business altogether," the old laird muttered many times when he was left alone with this inscrutable heathen baby, and the great round doll's eyes would slowly revolve until with sinister deliberation they settled upon his own.

These fancies, as the baby grew up to girlhood, as the girl grew up to womanhood, gradually lost their force. The people round about, who had rather avoided the child whose fierce temper was, as it seemed, ungovernable, and who was yet so imperturbably mischievous and malicious, forgot their first impressions. The gaunt little Indian baby was developing into a really splendid woman, and the chest of gold pieces was still intact. The chest itself, that is; for its contents had been gradually disposed of to the great traders in London, where the coins of immemorial dynasties fetched fancy prices; and more than the estimated £50,000 had been safely invested in Lala Holdfast's name. The cabinet itself had been removed to her bedroom, and in it she kept, besides her chain and her seal (on which an Arabic charm was engraved), a string of precious stones which had been found underneath the gold, hidden away in a drawer of which she only had divined the secret. Lala thus became a personage of vast importance as she approached a marriageable age. A match like this was not to be met with every day within a hundred miles of Balmawhapple.

III.

RALPH HOLDFAST'S younger brother Jim (for there was one other son, and a daughter "Mailie," who, by-and-by, married another Holdfast—one of the south country Holdfasts of whom we have heard elsewhere) had, after he left the University of Edinburgh, lived mainly with his uncle, the Earl, at Cardono. Although an ardent sportsman, a dashing rider, a keen golfer, a dead shot, an angler who could wile the trout from pool or shallow when no one else could, he was an excellent man of business, and had the almost exclusive management of the Earl's extensive estates in three counties. He and Nell Erskine had been thrown constantly together, and, in the close association of cousinship and mutual tastes, love had been born. Both in mind and body the resemblance between them was close. Blue-eyed and fair-haired, their souls were as candid and limpid as their eyes. The healthy outdoor life suited them both; for both, the simple songs of their own people, as well as the more intricate melodies of the old English poets, had a perennial fascination. Nell had a pure voice, dulcet as a flute,—everything about her, indeed, was pure; *that* was the first and last impression. She was simple as a lark, fresh as a new-blown daisy. One had to seek in woodland and meadow-land for appropriate similes, —in woodland and meadow-land while the dew is yet on the grass.

It was not surprising, perhaps, that between Nell and Lala a tacit antipathy should have grown up. This pale flower of the North might to some eyes have seemed insipid beside the tropical splendour of the other. But there must have been something more than rivalry—something impish and uncanny in Lala herself—to account for the mortal aversion with which Nell regarded her. When her dusky, dark-eyed, black-haired cousin came into the room, it made her actually shiver, as we shiver in the Pontine marshes before an attack of malaria. "That woman blights me," she had said once, half in jest, to her lover.

The mischief of it was that, when Lala was present, a mist of misunderstanding seemed unaccountably to rise up between her and Jim. How it happened no one could exactly tell. Jim did not love Lala any more than Nell did; but Lala had a curious faculty of making people see as she liked. The mesmeric force had not then been fairly recognised by science: had it been, Lala's influence might possibly have been attributed to the baneful attraction of a purely physical agency. It was impossible to idealise any one when this merciless realist was present: somehow she made the finer virtues look mean, as the east wind takes the colour out of the landscape. This oriental enigma was to Nell as bitter and biting as the east wind itself—and not to Nell only. It seemed as if, born without conscience herself, Lala had resolved to reduce every one with whom she was brought into contact to her own level.

Nell as she grew up had parted with not a few of her childish attractions. Her cheeks had ceased to be as rosy as golden pippins; the plump little maiden, as round and solid as a dumpling, had shot up into a tall and graceful, but rather spare and statuesque, girl. There was an exquisite but perilous fragility about her figure which might have excited alarm had it not been for her ready laugh, her constant activity, her unwearied interest in high and low, in story and song, in beast and bird. It was hard to believe that in one so full of buoyant life the seeds of death had been sown. Her daughter, indeed, was close upon twenty before the Countess began to get seriously alarmed. The girl was feverish, could not sleep at nights, was apt to take cold on the slightest provocation; her cheeks, except when painfully flushed, were perfectly colourless; her hands had grown delicate and transparent as alabaster. Jim—her mainstay in the old time—was often away now; when they met he was silent and embarrassed—and so was she. He had no idea, indeed, how ill she was; the hectic flush which his coming provoked blinded him to the truth.

But one day—one of the softest days of the dying summer —his eyes were opened. They were paddling about the bay below the castle. It was a windless calm; not a ripple broke upon the rock. The towers of the castle were half hidden in the warm mist that rose from the water; the flag on the old keep, that was as old as the Comyns, did not stir. All at once, as if by magic, the wall of separation which had risen up between the lovers was broken down. I do not profess to explain how this came about: no word was spoken, but both were simultaneously aware that any estrangement there had been was over and done with. He was lying on his oars; Nell came close up and nestled beside him where he sat,— the action was wistful and pathetic. He put his arm about her; she had grown painfully thin and emaciated, and tears were slowly trickling down her cheeks; a great wave of pity and tenderness and remorse and hopelessness passed over him.

"Jim, dear Jim, I am dying! Neither mother nor the doctor will listen to what I say; but I know better."

"Dying? O Nell!" he said, drawing her closer to his side. She lay in his arm like a tired but contented child.

"It is good, very good, Jim, to know that you love me dearly,—that even the evil eye cannot hurt our love. For, Jim, that woman has the evil eye: I am wasting away because she has poisoned my life."

He tried to disabuse her mind of the delusion, as he deemed it; but his reassuring words were of no avail. "No, Jim, she is one of those deadly blights that God sends to punish us for our sins. But so long as I have you with me, the pain does not hurt much."

What could he say? "The sense of tears in mortal things" is poignant when the young die. But when it is the girl on whom we have lavished all the love in our hearts who is summoned away, what can we do but, with bowed head, pray God to be pitiful?

Meanwhile the black-eyed Lala had other fish to fry. Many fresh-run salmon were in her net. You do not like the metaphor? let me vary it, then, and say that her web was full of flies, who were first sucked dry and then hoisted over-board. But the biggest and noisiest blue-bottle, the finest gallant of them all, was the young laird of Ardlaw. He was by nature lavish and ostentatious; but he was one of the wealthiest commoners in the county; and people said that he could afford to pay for his follies. He was mad about Lala. She dazed and dazzled him, and for her part she found the young fellow an eligible wooer. His reckless audacity suited her mood; his fresh laugh, his comely person, his animal courage and powerful physique, appealed for the moment with an irresistible attraction to the sensuous instincts of this oriental sultana. So, in an evil day for the vain and foolish but honest lad, she consented to become his wife.

It was the most splendid wedding that had ever been seen in Balmawhapple. The bride blazed with jewels; her necklace of precious stones alone was worth a king's ransom. The "Shirra" gave her away; the Catholic and Apostolic Church consecrated the union; the ships in harbour, back from Greenland seas, hoisted their colours; the post-boys, in pink jackets and top-boots, cracked their whips; amid the cheers of the populace they took the highroad to the south.

But there are certain unions that even the prayers of an ordained priest cannot purify; and some of those present had an uneasy consciousness that they had been assisting at such a witch's carnival as Faust attended.

While Balmawhapple rejoiced, gloom settled upon St Abbs. Poor Nell's prevision had been too true. The doctor, indeed, would not listen to any suggestion of evil eye or occult oriental jugglery; the girl's lungs had been always more or less affected, he declared; the hectic fever of disease had manifested itself to his professional experience from her childhood in sparkling eye and chubby cheek. But that somehow she had been blighted in the bloom of her youth was all that those who loved her cared to know; nor did they inquire too curiously, then or afterwards, from whence the blight had come. For my own part, in these obscure affections of the brain, I sometimes fancy that credulity is true wisdom; and that the evil eye, inherited from ancestors who had tried every form of devilry, is often more deadly than henbane.

A pure bride lying on her maiden bed with eyes closed and hands folded; a father and mother sorely stricken, but still humbly hoping that Death has been good to her; the lover with tearless eyes taking a last farewell,—it is a picture from which we do not shrink, because, though beyond measure pitiful, there is in it nothing tawdry or vile or wicked. They will lay her gently in kindred dust; the sea will make its moan as of old; one by one they will come to her where she lies—father, mother, lover. For this lover was one of the constant sort who keep steadily at work till they are old men, but—do not forget.

There was a scared look in young Ardlaw's eyes, when he came back from his triumphal honeymoon, which his friends did not like. He was not one of the cowards who try to drive a spectre away by drink, and so end in delirium tremens. But he became still more recklessly lavish; his extravagance knew no bounds; he drove his four-in-hand about the county with his splendid sultana at his side; he spurned all restraint; the broad acres of Ardlaw, and Lala's gold pieces and precious stones, melted rapidly away,—the latter so rapidly, indeed, that the original conviction that they were mere elusive counterfeits seemed to have come true.

They lived on till they were old and penniless, maintained on a pittance that Lord St Abbs had left them, and the meagre profits of a squalid lodging-house in Balmawhapple. The husband died before I was born; but I still remember her vaguely —a skinny and peevish old woman, in whom all that remained of her once splendid beauty were the doll's eyes and the black blood. Outsiders declared that her temper was simply fiendish; but the grey, stern, and emaciated woman who nursed her— the one daughter who had survived—maintained a dogged and absolute silence. Explain it how we may, however, this malign incarnation of an evil past had in point of fact infected everything she touched, and even her own children could not escape the blight.

At the same time, it must be frankly admitted that the most

industrious gossip in Balmawhapple never ventured to allege that this woman had broken any express commandment of God or man. She had scrupulously observed the decencies of society; had listened to scores of sermons; had subscribed to hosts of charities; and her "good works" was a theme of which, had any local newspaper existed, much would have been made by the judicious penny-a-liner. Yet her track had been marked, like Attila's, by devastation. Lovers estranged; household peace destroyed; a duel fought for an idle word; a soldier false to his colours; a moon-struck boy with an ugly gash in his throat,—of her as of another sorceress it might have been written—

> "The children born of thee are sword and fire,
> Red ruin and the breaking up of laws."

Since she lost the Earl, St Abbs has gone down in the world, and even her own people confess that any allusion to the historic rivalry with Balmawhapple is now ill-timed. Where the carcass is, there the carrion-crows gather together; and the growing prosperity of Balmawhapple is attested by the pervading odour of herrings in every stage of nastiness, and the intolerable stench of boiling blubber. Whereas the air of St Abbs since its harbour has silted up, and its one whaler was lost in the ice-pack, is not a whiff better than mere country air.

V.

IN THE YEAR ONE:

THE STORY OF THE CROOKIT MEG.

THERE are Holdfasts outside the parish of Balma-whapple; and those who have read a certain volume of essays in romance may remember Martin and Stephen,—Martin who loved May Marvel, and Stephen who was cast out of the Church of Christ by Brass and Butterwell for heresy. Both Martin and Stephen have been gathered to their fathers, and the place that knew them knows them no more. *R. I. P.* But I am told that the reminiscences of another branch of the Holdfasts, which originally appeared in the *Tomahawk*, is no longer to be had for love or money, and I have been entreated to tell the story again for the benefit of the generation which has grown up since it was written. I am loath to part with the homely friends of fifty years ago, and if I could only succeed in making them visible to younger eyes, I should feel that I had not wholly failed. We have nothing like them now; and yet they did not

seem strange to us at the time.　Balmawhapple was
very cheery in those days; I don't think there were
quite so many "fads" going, and men and women
were less serious than they are now.　It is perhaps as
well that they are gone ; the Temperance people would
have been scandalised by the Provost's punch-bowl,
which, if I am not mistaken, was known far and wide
as the Bullers-of-Buchan (and indeed it was wellnigh
as deep); and I am afraid a free-thinking and whist-
loving Doctor of Divinity would have run a grievous
risk of being deposed by the ecclesiastical courts for
habits unbefitting a minister of the Kirk.

This then is my Balmawhapple story of the year
One—severely abridged.

I.

It was the year One—the first year of a century which has
passed the Psalmist's threescore-and-ten.　Seventy and odd
years have played sad havoc with most of us ; the new-born
babes who were then sleeping quietly in their cradles are now
mainly under the turf, sleeping a sounder sleep—if it be a
sleep that rounds our little life.　Oblivion scattereth her poppies.　These monotonously returning springs and summers
and autumns are frozen into a winter from which there is
no recovery.　Their harvests are all gathered in, and death
has reaped the reapers.

Throughout that district of Scotland which (according to
the Gaelic derivation of the name) lies in the bend of the
ocean, and more particularly in the seaport of Balmawhapple
—the "Broch" being then, as now, the capital of a remote
and secluded community—there was manifested on the first
day of October, in the year One, a certain measure of restrained excitement,—an excitement as keen, indeed, as these

reticent people ever permit themselves to manifest.   There
were wars and rumours of war.   The Deluge was rising over
Europe.   It had come to be felt on all sides that the an-
tagonism between the rival forces was too vital to admit of
any compromise.   That wild flood of hate and fury and revenge needed to spend itself before any thought of peace
could be entertained.   The triflers and critics were brushed
out of the way.   The clever young gentlemen of the 'Anti-
Jacobin' laid their pens aside.   Pitt alone—Pitt, who had
divined from the first that the contest, the merciless contest
between the old ideas and the new, must be fought out to
the bitter end—Pitt among the statesmen of Europe was left
almost by himself,—and Pitt's heart was breaking.

But the excitement at the Broch was not due to any of the
misadventures which at that moment were vexing the soul of
the Great Minister.   They were seafaring people.   The roads
to the south were barely passable.   The official who carried
the post-bags came twice or thrice a-week, and the news he
brought was about a fortnight old.   They were practically
cut off from the outer world.   A French privateer, indeed,
had once entered the bay; but the guns of the battery on
the Ronheads had been quickly manned, and a few round-
shot had induced her to seek a safer anchorage.   The people
had waited up all night, with clumsy old muskets under their
arms, on the chance of the return of her boats; but when
the morning broke only a white cloud of canvas was visible
on the horizon.   The stout, ruddy, weather-beaten farmers
and fishermen returned to their usual work, and had not
again been disturbed.   So that the echoes of the fierce conflict outside were barely heard by them.   The stories of great
victories, which were carried week after week over the land
a year or two later, when the lion (or the devil) was at
length fairly roused, had not yet begun to arrive.   It was, in
short, the news that the Jan Mayen was in the offing that had
brought the whole seafaring population of the district to the
pier at Port Henry on the 1st of October 1801.

The Jan Mayen, a schooner of a hundred tons, was then
the only whaler hailing from a seaport which now sends thirty

great ships to the Arctic seas. Some far-sighted merchant-citizen of the day had taken it into his head that a vast mine of wealth lay away to the nor'ard, beyond the Man of Hoy and the Stones of Stennis. The Dutch had a fleet in these seas among the seals and whales and icebergs, which year after year came back to the Scheldt loaded with ample store of blubber and whalebone and sealskins. The Dutch had grown rich in this adventurous industry: were not the Balmawhapple seamen as plucky, and the Balmawhapple traders as keen at a bargain, as any Dutchman? So the Jan Mayen had been built and fitted out; the shares had been taken up eagerly by all sorts and conditions of men in the burgh and the surrounding districts; there had been a series of surprisingly successful years; and this morning, for the fifth time, the Jan Mayen was again in the offing.

It was one of those lovely October days which they used to have in Scotland before the east wind was invented. A brisk breeze, indeed, was blowing from the north, and the Jan Mayen, with all her sails spread, came sweeping swiftly towards the harbour mouth. Nearer and nearer the good ship, with so many of the "burgh's bairns" on her deck, and so much of the burgh's wealth in her hold, approached the shore; and the demure elation of these undemonstrative Scots became actually audible when it was seen that "a garland" hung from the topmost spar of the mainmast. "A full ship, lads," said an old tar cheerily to the crowd, as he shut up his glass, from the top of the herring-barrel which he had mounted. "A full ship!"

The crowd was essentially a representative one. Fishermen, farm-labourers, shopkeepers, lawyers, merchants, doctors, ministers—no class in the community was unrepresented. There was Dr Caldcail, who prosed in the Muckle Kirk, and the Reverend Neil Brock, who ministered in a backyard to the Original Reformed Particular Anti-Burghers; there was Captain Knock, of the coastguard, and Corbie, the burgh lawyer (or "liar," as they call that functionary in these parts); and—most interested of all—there were the wives and sisters and sweethearts of the crew who manned the gallant little craft.

Just as the men of the Jan Mayen had lowered the main-sail, just as the last "tack" to enable her to clear the reef outside the harbour mouth had been completed, a young man with a dare-devil look in his face, and riding, with an air of reckless abandon, a half-broken colt of the native breed, then commonly used in the remoter districts of the north, galloped down to the beach. He threw a half-scornful, half-defiant greeting to the crowd, which fell back as he pushed his way through it to the pier-head. "It's that wild lad, Harry Hacket," said Corbie to the provost of the burgh, who stood beside him. "What deil's errand brings him here?"

Then ropes were caught, the foresail loosed, the ship brought up and made fast to the pier; the crew swarmed on shore, and the landsmen swarmed on board; there were tears and laughter and cordial greetings, the eager embrace for the husband, the shyer welcome for the lover. The gallant old ship looked finely weather-beaten; the treasures of the hail and the snow had been poured out upon her, and her stout sides had been torn by iceberg and floe; the decks were covered with skins of seals and jawbones of whales, and in a huge cask amidship a young polar bear showed its ugly teeth, and growled savagely at the boys, who had already begun to torment him. To me there has always been the attraction of a romance in the return of one of these Arctic adventurers—it is the sort of fascination one feels when stalking a hooper or a loon. They come to us from the bleak and sombre north, and bleakly behind them rises the northern winter. And then the wild strangeness and remoteness of the wilderness into which they have penetrated—mountains of ice that reel together in perilous madness—iron-bound seas which the tempest cannot ripple—the angry flush of the aurora upon the night!

Meanwhile the horse and his rider stood immovable upon the pier-head. Hacket had scanned attentively the faces of the crew as the ship was moored, though he had shown no sign of recognition even when stout Captain Manson waved his hand to him on landing. But at length a young, strongly built sailor, who had been taken possession of by a pretty girl the moment he put his foot on shore, freed himself from her embrace, and approached the horseman. He had one of the typical faces of a district where the Scandinavian blood is mixed with the Celt's—the fair skin, the soft blue eyes, the curly yellow hair, the frank tone and fearless carriage of the North Sea rover. He nodded coolly to Hacket (who returned his careless greeting), and then coming close up to the horse, and laying his hand upon the straggling mane, said in a low significant whisper—so that the horseman alone could hear—

"We hailed the Crookit Meg, sir, last night, aff Rattray Briggs."

* * *

Tam or Tammas Corbie, the lawyer, was perhaps the sharpest man in Balmawhapple. At the burgh school, and at the Marischal College, he had as a lad carried everything before him. He was possessed by the passionate liking for out-of-the-way learning which seems to come naturally to some men. With a little patrimony of his own to start with, he elected to try the bar, and for some years he appeared to be on the fair way to the bench. But suddenly and unaccountably he broke down—utterly and irretrievably. There had always, along with the real love of letters, been a scampish element in the man, which had led him to prefer the shady side of literature and law. As he grew older the taint infected his whole nature; and by-and-by the intellectual thirst was succeeded by a thirst of a more dangerous kind. So when he had lost his last client he left the Parliament House, and returning to his native town became its legal adviser. Even at home, however, his reputation was dubious. He was, as I have indicated, a clever, shrewd, learned lawyer, who might have made his mark anywhere; but as he seldom went to bed sober (being invariably, indeed, as his cronies said, "blin' fou" early in the evening), and as he was, even at his soberest, more remarkable for keenness of scent and sharpness of tongue (and his nose was keen and his tooth sharp as a weasel's) than for honesty, veracity, or general trustworthiness, his business gradually diminished, and he had latterly become the adviser mainly of that section of the community which is more or less beyond the pale of the law. Yet, socially, he still kept his head above water; for he was a magnificent whist-player, and among a small community such a gift is invaluable. He played by a sort of instinct; the tipsier he got the more masterly was his management of his cards; even when "blin' fou" he seldom lost a trick.

On the evening of the day on which the Jan Mayen arrived, Corbie was seated in his office, as it was called by courtesy— a wooden shed which overlooked the harbour, and which smelt suggestively of stale fish, tar, and whisky. He had had interviews during the afternoon with a smuggler, who had left a small keg of brandy behind him; a poacher, who had neglected to remove a hare and a brace of wild-fowl; a farm wench, who had instructed him to raise an action of aliment against a gay Lothario of the farmyard; a farmer, out of elbows, who wanted the lawyer to back a little bill on the bank; and now he was closeted with the last client of the day—an elderly woman, neatly dressed in the style then common among the class to which she belonged—a short gown over a thick woollen petticoat, a coarse wincey apron, and a close white mutch, with a black hood over it, now thrown back upon her neck, and exposing her fresh comely face.

A huge spirit-bottle—belonging to the "tappit-hen" variety —half-full of whisky, a jug of water, and a tumbler, were on the table beside him.

"Tak' a seat, Lucky," he was saying, "tak' a seat, and I'll be wi' you *quam primum!*" He had been rummaging through his drawers for some old papers; and musty letters and mildewed processes were scattered in wild disorder on the floor. "The Cairn-catta Mortification—faith it was a mortification to the laird—sax hunderd poonds or thereby oot o' that sour moss to ony hizzy in the parish, forbye the taxed expenses before the Lords. I needna keep the papers— there's nae mair to be made o' *that*, I'm thinkin'," he added pensively, throwing the bundle into the fire, "though it was

a guid-gangin' plea for mony a year. The laird's far doun the
hill, and young Harry's a dour whalp. It needs a lang spoon
to sup kail wi' Cloutie; but I ken a thing or twa may bring
the lad to reason. The Skilmawhilly Augmentation—a weel-
kent case, Lucky, reported at length, wi' mony *obiter dicta* o'
the bigwigs, in the first volume of the Decisions of the
Faculty. Auld Skilmawhilly never could thole the minister,
and they gaed at it like cat and dog. Sir Islay was coonsel
for Dr Drumly, and it was gran' to hear him proponin' his
pleas in law for the Kirk. Whilk, Lucky, were to this effec',"
he continued, putting on his horn spectacles, and partly
reading from the print—"that, though the infeudation of
teinds to laymen was forbidden by Innocent III. under the
heavy penalty of the want of Christian burial, and the yet
heavier one of eternal damnation, yet that by the Act 1567,
cap. 10, commonly known as the Assumption of Thirds, it
was enacket that the Commissioners of Plat—and sae on for
saxteen pages. Indeed, Lucky, he could speak like a buik,
and he drove Skilmawhilly clean dementit, though that daft
body Polkemmet ca'd him 'a Hielan' stot'—for, you see, he
cam' from the coonty o' Argyll."

At this juncture—Corbie turning round to replenish his
glass—the old woman made a nervous attempt to interpose.
"Jist for ae minute, Mr Corbie, for ae minute."

"Presently, presently, Mrs Cruickshank—what's to hinder
you and me having our cracks? Ye'll mind Polkemmet, a
daft auld body, as I was sayin', but he loved his joke, and he
had a pleasant wut. He sattled Skilmawhilly fairly when the
laird took Yonderton to coort for stealin' his bees. Ye see
Yonderton's orra man was fast asleep in the field, wi' his head
aneath his oxter, when the bees swarmed upon the back pairt
o' his person. They fand an auld skep, and were gettin' the
swarm fairly skepped when Skilmawhilly cam' on the ground.
'They're my bees,' quoth Skilmawhilly; but Yonderton wudna
alloo it; and sae they gaed to the shirra. Skilmawhilly man-
teent that he followed the bees from his ain door, and saw
them swarm where they did. But it was pleaded for Yonderton that, possession being nine-tenths o' the law, they were noo

his lawful property ; and that though, if they had swarmed on a tree, it might behove the owner to cut the branch, it cudna be expeckit that sic a liberty wud be taken wi' his man's legs. So the pleading stood, when Polkemmet, pittin' his wig back, and movin' his chair a bit,—whilk, Lucky, was his manner when he was ready wi' his joke,—said that he was prepared to advise the cause. 'I'm for Yonderton,' says Polkemmet, 'inasmickle as the bees libelled, from the place they settled, must hae been bumbees.' He! he! he! Ye may believe, Lucky, that they were braw times when Polkemmet was shirra; but it's fifteen year noo, since they made him a lord—a paper lord"—he continued thoughtfully, turning again to the tappit-hen—"a Senator of the College of Justice, whereof I am an unworthy member."

The old woman's impatience could be restrained no longer. "I canna bide, Liar Corbie," she exclaimed; "if ye wunna hear me, I maun e'en haud the gait."

This appeal was attended with success. Corbie lay back in his chair, and the old woman, drawing her seat close to him, began her narrative in a low confidential tone. For some time he found it hard to keep his mind from wandering (the whisky had begun to tell), and more than once he interrupted her when some familiar technical phrase gave him an opportunity of airing his erudition, and of becoming discursive and anecdotical.

"Ye dinna mean to tell me that you've intromittit wi' the effec's?" he exclaimed, when at length the old woman paused for a moment to recover her breath. "Then you're within the *ratio decidendi* o' the coort in the action at the instance o' Umquhile Dagers against Christian Penny—sister to Bessie wha lived in the Langate—ye'll mind Bessie?—in which summons o' poinding, Lucky, it was fand and declared by the Lords, that though the defender had only intromittit wi' a little timber bed and a pint-stoup which pertained to the defunct, yet was she liable as Universal Intromissatrix——"

"O man, what's Christian Penny to me, or Bessie, forby?" cried the old woman, driven fairly desperate. "I cam' to speak to you aboot auld Yokieshill — John Hacket — John

Hacket and my sister Elspit—we had news on Mononday that Elspit is dead—and ye wunna listen to a word I say."

"Joe Hacket!" the lawyer exclaimed with an oath, rising unsteadily to his feet, "what for did you not speak oot your errand at ance? Keep your seat, my guid freen', keep your seat; but we'll steek the door in the meantime, and syne we'll no be interrupit." He cautiously drew the bolt; and then sitting down close to the old woman, he listened in perfect silence and with the keenest attention to her narrative. The expression of his face changed as she proceeded; before her whispered communication was over he was another man. The story had quite sobered him; and when she had departed—leaving some soiled and barely legible papers with him—a certificate of marriage, a notice of death, an old number of a local journal—he continued to sit and ponder gravely over the dying embers of the peats.

"A Deil's bairn," he muttered to himself. "A Deil's bairn did I say? Na—na. The verra deevil incarnate—Hornie himsel'. But suppose that Joe Hacket was married on Elspit —Elspit Cheyne, she was—how would Harry stand then?"

At this moment steps were heard outside, the door was violently flung open, and Captain Knock of the coastguard— "the Commodore," as he was called—in his faded naval uniform, entered the office.

"Come awa', Corbie, come awa'—they're waitin' for us at the Provost's; the Doctor is mad for his rubber. What in the name o' the saints has keepit you sae lang?"

The Balmawhapple worthies of the year One played their nightly rubber at the Provost's lodgings—for the Provost was a bachelor, and except his housekeeper Mailie—the "Provost's ae lass"—had no inconvenient impedimenta. To-night —it was not yet seven o'clock, but in those days they dined in the forenoon—Dr Caldcail and the Provost were seated before the chess-board, with which they were whiling away the time until the other players arrived. The Provost was a poor hand at the game, whereas the Doctor was an adept at this as at other games requiring skill, coolness, and address. But, as we are waiting, my dear old friends may, meanwhile, have a paragraph to themselves.

Of Provost Roderick Black it is perhaps enough to say that he was a hero after Mr Carlyle's heart. He possessed indeed a fine capacity for silence. He had also a fine capacity for snuff. It was insinuated by superficial and discontented burgesses that these were his main characteristics. But that was a mistake,—a most sagacious soul looked out at you from under the shaggy eyebrows. The eye was cloudy, the brow heavy, the limbs loosely put together and ill-arranged; but any one with a knack for construing the hieroglyphics of character could see that behind this rather unpromising exterior there was much to admire and love,—the bland temper, the homely energy, the shrewd integrity of a very genuine and typical Scotsman.

Dr Caldcail had been coined in an altogether different mint. He was a clergyman belonging to a school of which the last survivor died out when I was a boy. Farmers and theologians; the keen-eyed controversialists of the Church court and the Academy, but dull as ditch-water in the pulpit; gay with French *esprit*, but without a spark of spiritual life; who, in a manner, sincerely accepted the statutory creed of the Church, and yet in their life and conversation quietly set aside the Christianity of which they were the official representatives,—it is a perished race. Dr Caldcail was in person dried and shrivelled—a piece of parchment or vellum, tough and yellow as leather,—his legs in his tight-fitting gaiters, when he mounted his grey mare, being the merest spindle-shanks. He was a famous chess-player, a famous whist-player, a fine scholar, a man who had spent many years on the Continent, and could speak French and Italian like a native, a *bon vivant*, a gallant among ladies, especially the great ladies at Pitfairlie and Slains (Jean, Duchess of Gordon, loved him dearly—he played a rubber with her every night when she was drinking the waters); but among his people he affected the bluff and homespun farmer, and was indeed a hard hand at a bargain. He would as soon have parted with a tooth without value as with a shilling, and he never sold the oats or "sma' corn" off the glebe, except during the famine years when wheat was at 100s. the quarter. He took his snuff with the grace of a courtier. He rapped out his clear sharp sententious retorts like pistol-shots. He handled his rapier with the dexterity of a practised dialectician,—as became the friend of David Hume and Voltaire. He was as wiry and vigorous at seventy as he had been at seven-and-twenty,—there was nothing about that spare body of which death or disease could lay hold. Bright, alert, and rapid in the intercourse of society, he was dull and tedious in the pulpit, and a deadly bore in the General Assembly—to which, however, he was sent regularly once a-year by his less active brethren.

This was the man who was now indulging in a sort of monologue while he moved his pieces or watched his adversary's moves. The Doctor's tongue was "aye waggin',"—even the solemnity of whist could not silence his vivacious commentary,—and of course chess with a much inferior foe was mere child's play.

"Ha! ha! Provost, what say you to that? Queen in check, and impossible to relieve her.—Mary Stuart or Marie Antoinette? What precious scamps these French fellows are, to be sure—as bad as Geordie Buchanan when he defamed his mistress, or Murray when he sold his sister. You pit the pawn forrit—what's the gude o' a pawn? My leddy's page wi' his bit pasteboard sword against Cœur de Lion.—But, Provost, I never could understand how Davie Hume cared to row in the same boat wi' Geordie Buchanan. I would as soon lie heads and thraws wi' that hairy John the Baptist, who is deevin' the Whinnyfold lads oot o' their sma' wits. O man, but he's a lousy Apostle.—Aff goes the queen, and I'll mak' you a present o' the castle.—But, as I was sayin', Davie whiles gaed wrang, aboot Mary Stuart, and miracles, and particular providences, and the standard o' taste. What could he ken aboot miracles mair than the rest o' us, and to say that nae weight o' evidence could persuade him that

Lazarus rose from the dead was maist unphilosophical.—
Deed, my lord, you're getting into deep water—that king o'
yours is close pressed as Saul at Mount Gilboa, or poor King
Jamie on the field o' Flodden.—Not that I wud say a word
against David Hume, with whom I had much pleasant converse at Paris when I took the grand tour wi' my Lord Tilly-
whilly in the saxty-five—before I was transported to this
blessed Bœotia.   To think o' that body Warburton settin'
himsel' up to refute *him* as he pretendit : he micht as well
hae refuted the Bass Rock.—Ye wudna daur say check to the
king?   Faith, Provost, I hae you noo.   What's your next
move?   As sure as gospel that's a groat into my pocket—we're
playing for groats, mind.   Fritz himsel' could not have pued
his men thegither after sic an unspeakable and unaccoontable
blunder.   There are mair things in heaven and earth in the
way o' perfec' unreasonableness than the unassisted intellect
is capable o' conceiving.   Never lose your temper, laird ; it's
neither dulce nor decorum to fa' into a fit.   Put on the pieces,
and I'll gie you a knight.   A knight, and we'll mak' it saxpence this time.   But you maun look sharper after your
queen—you had a keen eye ance for the queans, Provost, if
a' tales be true—*Gratiæ solutis zonis*, as the poet says.   O
the little rogues !—there were some remarkably fine women at
Paris in the saxty-five!   And to think how many o' my auld
acquaintance are dead !—Whist ! whist ! my lord.   We have
nae confession in the Kirk o' Knox, at least between auld
haverels like you and me, and a minister of the Gospel is
bound to walk warily.   Surely that's Corbie and the Captain
in the street.   Lord, how it blows !—there's mair than the
east wind lowse this nicht !   Bring up the haddies, Mailie,
and I'll look oot the Glendronoch—*dissipat Euius curas
edaces*—it's a fine speerit, Glendronoch (tho' it needs mixing),
and as the auld Abbé used to say to me when uphauding
Purgatory, 'Ye may gang farer and fair waur.'"

"And here's the buiks," says the Provost, bringing out a
well-thumbed pack of cards, as Corbie and the Captain enter
the room.

"I say with Jack Cade," the Doctor exclaims cheerily, as

IN THE YEAR ONE.

he clears the table. "The first thing we do let's kill all the lawyers."

"We'll finish the rubber first, if you please," says the Provost, with a chuckle, as they cut for partners.

So they sat down; and for two or three hours the game proceeded with varying luck amid comparative silence.

The wind had risen during the evening, and now it was blowing a gale. There was no sound in the streets, except the rattling of the windows and the distant roll of the surf— the townspeople, for the most part, were safe abed. Early to bed and early to rise made us healthy, wealthy, and wise in the year One. The second rubber had newly begun, when there was a modest rap at the street door, and Mailie entering, announced—

"It's Watty Troup"—Watty was the burgh idiot— "speerin' for sneeshin'."

But that was hours ago, and they were preparing to lay aside the cards and gather round the blazing peats for the final tumbler and the penultimate "eke," when a louder and more peremptory knock arrested the players.

"Here's Alister Ross," said Mailie, opening the door, "wants to see the Captain."

"Bring him ben," quoth the Provost. A remarkably handsome young fellow in the uniform of the coastguard, carrying a cutlass of the old-fashioned pattern, and with a pistol in his belt, entered the room.

"What's up, Alister?" said the Captain huskily to his subordinate. "What's up? What an infernal din the wind is making! Speak oot, man."

"I don't think it will last, sir; it is taking round to the land, and the fog is rising. But I've just heard that the Crookit Meg was seen aff Rattray Briggs this morning."

"D—n the Crookit Meg! She's the curse o' the coast," sputtered the Captain. "But they can't land a keg to-night, —Skipper Dick himself couldn't make the Bloody Hole in this fog, and the wind blowing dead in shore. There'll be a heavy sea aff Dunbuy: he'll not risk it."

"That's true, sir; but they might run round to the Ward,

and if I'm not wrong, it will be clear before daylight. I'd better warn our men at Whinnyfold."

"Ay, ay, my lad, aff wi' you—the Grookit Meg and them on boord o' her are kittle cattle. And—Alister—a word in your ear. I'm an auld man and ye're a young ane. Dinna lippen to that little quean, Eppie Holdfast—there's mair maidens than mawkins in this country, and mony a strappin' lass is thinkin' lang for a stoot lad. Hoot awa', man, dinna glower ; that hizzie is no to be trusted. She'll beguile you if she can. Her brither's on boord the lugger, and it's my opinion Harry Hacket kens mair o' baith the cutties than he wud care to tell at the town-cross."

So Alister went out into the darkness, and the Captain returned to his cronies, who were gathered cosily round the fire.

The Captain was a well-known figure in Balmawhapple—a short, stout man, with a face like a harvest moon—a face beaming with whisky and fun—but without any neck to speak of ; so that when he became hilarious towards the end of the evening he went off every now and again into a sort of apoplectic fit, from which he would emerge out of breath, and with the tears running out of his honest eyes—testifying to the violence of the process of recovery. His friends were used to these paroxysms of choking, and allowed him to take his own time in coming to. What between spitting, and sputtering, and stuttering, he was not what is called a ready speaker ; but, on the other hand, he had a vast command of "nautical" language, and a very vivid and prolific fancy—in short, he swore like a trooper and lied like Munchausen. But he was a general favourite, and he was specially popular with his men ; for he had a kind heart (that universal solvent), an open hand, and an unquenchable thirst for "news."

"Ha ! ha ! Captain, this breeze will bring the woodcock across the water ; we must have a day on the Ardlaw. That's the cover for a cock."

"The cover for a cock ! " sputtered the Captain, attempting to relight his pipe, which had a chronic habit of going out. "There's not a decent cover on this side o' Benachie. Give me the Loch o' Skene for cocks, ay ! and for jacks too. Why,

Doctor, when I used to shoot there wi' auld Pitfoddels, we could have walked across the loch on their backs!"

"Noo, Captain, that's a lee," said Corbie, who as the night advanced was apt to grow pugnacious and opinionative.

The Captain began to spit and stutter, but before he could bring his guns into position to open fire on the enemy, the agile Doctor interposed.

"Hoots, Captain, dinna mind him. We a' ken Corbie. His bark's waur than his bite. And Pitfoddels was that *rara avis*," he went on, trying to create a diversion—"that *rara avis*, an honest lawyer. Ha! ha! Corbie, what say you to that, my man?"

"There's mair honest lawyers than honest D.D.'s, Doctor. That's what I say. The çanon law compared with the ceevil is superficial, unphilosophical, and sophistical."

"The civil law!" the Doctor retorted. "Why, the men who made it—if my friend Gibbon is right—were some of the greatest scoundrels unhung."

The lawyer was fairly roused. "Ye ken little of the Roman law, my freen', of whilk in its main features the Scots is a verra reasonable imitation. The Romans were a great people, and their law is a maist remarkable system o' jurisprudence. They had a perfec' respect for fac's—ay, Captain, a perfec' respect for fac'. For what says the *Corpus Juris*? 'Nam plus valet quod in veritate est, quam quod in opinione.' That's the main distinction, Doctor, between the lawyer and the D.D.,—the lawyer seeks diligently for facts which he can verify, the D.D. blethers aboot a hash o' doctrines which are incapable of identification. Nor did Justinian—if ye like to ca' the haill body o' laws after the ruler in whose reign they were codified —haud wi' your Whig freen's on this side, or your French freen's on the tither side o' the water. Dootless we have made changes in oor laws, says he, but why?—'quod non innovationem induximus, sed quoniam æquius erat.'"

By this time Corbie had talked himself into high good-humour and comparative sobriety, and when shortly afterwards the party broke up, he took the Commodore under his wing, and saw him safely housed.

"The maut's aboon the meal wi' Corbie," the Doctor said to himself, as he strolled towards the manse; "but what a lawyer's lost, because he canna drink in moderation!"

* * *

The streets were wet with mist when the young coast-guardsman opened the Provost's door. An occasional oil-lamp shone with a sort of nebulous radiance into the thick fog; but a good deal of circumspection was needed to avoid the pitfalls on either side of the narrow footway. He met no one except one solitary woman with a child in her arms, who came towards him as he quitted the town. The wind had driven her long hair into her eyes, and she looked, as far as he could judge in the uncertain light, poverty-stricken and dishevelled. "It's no a nicht for the likes o' you to be oot, my lass," he said to her kindly, as a fierce blast nearly tore the rags from her back and the infant out of her arms. "The likes o' me!" she replied, with a hoarse hysterical sob, as she disappeared into the darkness.

Alister had now left all the streets behind him; but a single light still burned ahead. The house from which it proceeded stood on the very margin of the sea—between the sea and the roadway. The outer door was partially open, and pausing for a moment before he entered, Alister gazed into the room from which the light came. It was an ordinary cottage interior—a but and a ben: in what appeared to be the kitchen a bed was let into the wall, and at the bed-side there was a shelf for books, on which some half-dozen volumes were deposited. A very old man sat on a three-legged stool before the fire—an old, spare, and wizened man, in a homespun suit of corduroys, with a square leather apron fastened close up to his chin, and a pair of horn spectacles upon his nose. The spectacles appeared to be more for ornament than use,—the wearer looked over them, not through them. Shrewd sagacious eyes planted in a face which must always have been strongly marked, and which was now deeply lined by ruts which time and care had worn.

Shrewd grey eyes, yet with that dreamy light in them which denotes the passion of the student or the abstraction of the mystic. The lamp was hung on the wall, and the light fell full upon the volume which lay on his knee—a folio volume printed in picturesque old-fashioned type, and held together by quaintly worked clasps of brass or tarnished silver—the sort of book which used to lie about many an English farmhouse, and now at Christie's or Sotheby's is worth its weight in gold.

This was the cottage which Adam Meldrum had occupied for many years.

Alister paused a moment, and then pushing back the door entered the room. A pleasant cordial warmth came into the old man's face, as he laid aside his book.

"Dinna move, Uncle Ned, I canna bide. I'm awa' to the Ward, where it's like enough the Crookit Meg will be afore me. But it's a wild nicht,—I wonder you left the door aff the sneck."

"I forgot it," said the old man simply. There was a wonderful gentleness and sweetness in the voice.

"I see how it is—you have been at the buiks again. I wish I could bide, Uncle Ned, for a screed of an auld play; but I just lookit in to say that you might bar the door, for I canna be back before morning. Only I had best tak' the lantern wi' me—the mist's verra thick, and the road across the Saddle Hill is no fit for a Christian—even in daylicht."

Alister lighted his dark lantern, and the old man went with him to the door.

"The mist's rising," he said, looking round the sky; "and the moon will be up by one. I promised to get a tarrock's wing for Eppie. It's a sin to kill the puir birds, but she's a wilfu' lass, and wins her way wi' maist o' us. Look round by Pothead as you are passing the morn's morn, and you'll maybe find me at Charlie's Howff. Gude nicht, my lad—God bless you."

"Gude nicht, daddy, gude nicht."

There is something always strangely impressive in passing

out of the noise and bustle of a crowded city into the darkness—in exchanging the light and warmth of human life for the vast spaces of night, and the solemn company of the stars.   You become at once a citizen of an altogether different world, and invert at a step your relationships.   The interests of the streets out of which you have passed cease to be engrossing: these are the self-same stars under which the ships of Ulysses sailed; that is the Greater Bear, that the Lesser, and that the Belt of Orion.   And if, as on this evening, a thick wet mist hides the stars, and disturbs in a portentous way the proportions of the objects on the roadway or by the roadside, the effect is hardly less striking.   As Alister with the occasional aid of his dark lantern felt his way through the darkness, he could hear the roll of the surf at his feet muffled by the mist, and the occasional plaint of a plover as it rose from the beach and went past him on the wind to the inland mosses.   From Bowness, where the fisher-people stay—Bowness itself being blotted out by the mist—the old road leaves the shore and mounts the hillside, thus cutting off that extremest angle of the land from whence the lighthouse flashes its welcomes and its warnings across the deep.   At the summit of the Saddle Hill there is the Ale-house tavern—a hostelry well known in the old posting days when this was the sole road to the south.   Alister did not meet a living creature; only when near the summit, looking in a break of the fog across the peat-hags, he saw that lights were flitting about the mansion-house of Yokieshill—where "auld Laird Hacket" lived.

On reaching the hostelry he found the house still open, and men and women on the move.   A horse, steaming in the mist, stood saddled at the door.

"What's up, my man?" he said to the ostler; "you're late to-night."

"It's young Hacket," Jock the ostler replied, pointing with his thumb across his shoulder.   "He's speakin' a word wi' the mistress.   They say the auld laird's in the dead-thraws.   God save us—it's a wild nicht for flittin'.   Yokieshill is sair to pairt wi' his gear; he wunna dee, he swears, till he sees his liar, and

Harry's awa' to the Broch to fetch Corbie. There's been some queer splores up the glen, if a' the folk says is true——"

"Stand out of the way, you lout," said a deep voice at his elbow, and throwing himself on his horse, young Hacket galloped off into the mist.

Jock shook his fist at the vanishing figure. "If he disna keep a ceevil tongue in his ugly head, the unhangt thief," he muttered, as he retreated to his den in the loft among the straw.

Alister resumed his march. He had by this time passed the crest of the hill, and had begun the descent to the low-lying lands of the Ward. On this side the fog had lifted. The vast expanse of a boundless ocean was dimly visible in the starlight. He passed Fontainbleau lying high and cold among its rocks ; and his heart beat more rapidly as he noticed that a light was still burning in an upper room of the lofty farmhouse. "It's Eppie's room," he whispered softly to himself. The surf was thundering up the beach at Long-haven ; the spray that came from the Bloody Hole wetted his face. At this moment a shrill whistle roused him from his dreams. He paused abruptly, laying his hand on the pistol in his belt. The whistle was thrice repeated—a whistle that to a less attentive ear might have passed for the cry of a startled whaup. Then a dim figure cautiously approached, and a low voice said, "Is that you, Harry Hacket? They're waitin' for you at Hell's Lum." Then the speaker paused for a second, and then with a startled oath, "By the Lord, it's the gauger," disappeared as swiftly and noiselessly as he had come.

Alister hurried on. "It's impossible they can land to-night," he muttered, as he heard the surf boiling among the fissures along the coast. But he hurried on until he had reached the Hawklaw, a vast mound of sand that rises among the bents of the Ward. From thence he could see the whole Bay of Slains. The bay was white with foam. The waves were rolling up whitely upon the sand. Then he went on to the station, where he found one of the men standing at the door with his pipe in his mouth.

"Well, Colin, anything up?" he asked.

"Tim noticed a smart craft in the offing just before sun-down.   It had the raking masts of the Crookit Meg, but they must have changed the rig.   It bore away to the south.   Tim went down to Collieston to see the captain; it's no possible they can land this side o' Newburgh.   There was a bleeze on the Hill o' Gask after dark, but it might have been the lads at Achnagatt firin' the whins."

A bright peat-fire was blazing within.   Alister threw himself upon the unoccupied bed in the guard-room, telling Colin to waken him if the wind went down.

But there was no word of the Crookit Meg that night.

* * *

Dr Caldcail was an early riser, and when he looked out next morning from his bedroom window the wind had fallen, the sparrows were chirping cheerily among the boor - tree bushes, and the October sea was sparkling in the October sunshine.   The manse was built just outside the burgh—the Peel burn separating it from the Kirkton—on a pleasant emi-nence above the beach.   Adam Meldrum's cottage stood on the other side of the highroad, closer to the sea, and thus the minister and the old boat-builder and bird-stuffer were next-door neighbours.   The alliance between these curiously as-sorted friends was very close and cordial.   "Uncle Ned" never went to church; but the Doctor, with a twinkle in his eye, good-humouredly accepted the situation.   "I make no man's creed but my own," he said with Swift; and to him the Dean of St Patrick's, after David Hume, was the first of men. Neither Adam nor the Doctor was an unbeliever, but both were old men who had seen much of life; and while most of the Doctor's convictions had by wear and tear grown thin and tentative and provisional, Adam had drifted away into a theology of his own—a theology extracted mainly from the Old Testament, the plays of Shakespeare, the *Religio Medici*, and Edwards's *Ornithology*.   Uncle Ned had as much con-tempt for the Doctor's sermons as the Doctor himself could

possibly have had; preaching was the process by which his
friend "gat that trash aff his stamach," the absence of which
made him an honester and wholesomer companion.

They were close allies, and indeed the Doctor was probably
the only man in the community who did the crazy bird-stuffer
anything like justice. But then the community was never
quite certain when the Doctor was serious. His jests, like
his sermons, went over the heads of his hearers. When he
told the councillors of the burgh on an occasion of civic
festivity that a bailie is made once a-year, but a poet or a
naturalist only once in many years, he took the precaution to
veil the compliment in the obscurity of a learned language
("Consules fiunt quotannis, et novi proconsules, Solus aut rex
aut poeta non quotannis nascitur"). So no harm was done;
on the contrary, the Doctor's acquaintance with the tongues of
antiquity was looked upon as a credit to the town.

Adam was not a native of the burgh; he belonged to the
fertile lowlands of Moray, but he had been little more than a
lad when he migrated to Balmawhapple. The great sorrow of
his life had driven him away from his own people; but of it and
of them he never spoke; and he had long ago taken root upon
the bleak and stormy headland where "the broch" stands.
For many years he had lived a solitary life, until "little
Alister" had been thrown upon his hands by an unthrifty
nephew,—"little Alister," now two-and-twenty years old, six
feet one in his stockings, and (in spite of his six feet) in love
over head and ears with Eppie Holdfast of Fontainbleau.

Adam, as I have said, was partly boat-builder and partly
bird-stuffer; this morning, seated on a three-legged stool, he
was hammering away at an old boat. It was placed on a slip
which he had constructed close to his cottage, so that in either
capacity he had his tools at hand. The Doctor, strolling down
to the beach in his slippers after his early breakfast, greeted
his neighbour with a jest and a quotation — as was his
wont :—

"On such a stool immortal Alfred sat!"

"Ay, Doctor, but he lat the cakes singe."

"And you object to the comparison? Good; but tell me,

my learned Theban, why Shakespeare did not put Alfred into a play?"

"That's a question that neither you nor me can answer—nor yet the General Assembly. Nae livin' man can tell what Shakespeare would, or could, or should hae done in ony conceivable circumstances—he is just simply unaccountable."

"But where's the young fellow, Alister Ross? Is he on a journey, or making love, or making war, or baith? It's a presentable lad, let me tell you, and they think a deal of him up the way."

"Alister gaed to the Ward last night; he was to have been back early. I pairtly promised to meet him at—Fontainbleau."

The Doctor gave a whistle. "Sits the wind in that quarter, eh?

> ' Old as I am, for ladies' love unfit,
>   The power of beauty I remember yet.'

But don't let him burn his fingers with that little French witch; she's not a craft to ride the water wi'."

"Eppie is a gude lass in the main," said Adam, "though ill-guidit it may be."

"Tush! I forgot that she, too, is one of your scholars. But just give Alister a hint; I saw her at the Memsie ploy, and I didn't quite like the way she was carrying on with Harry Hacket. An honest lass should keep clear of that nice young man. By the way, what's become of Lizzie Cheves?"

"They tell me she's somewhere about the Kirktoun—wi' her bairn. Puir lass!"

"Ay, ay, Adam; there's a heavy account some folks will have to settle by-and-by. Baith you and me believe that, if we believe naething mair. And there's little to choose between us, if Brimstone disna lee."

"That's true, sir. Heaven is aboon a' yet; there sits a judge that nae king can corrupt. I howld wi' you and wi' Shakespeare, baith respectable authorities. I mind weel the day," he continued, "when Rob Cheves was married on

Esther Cheyne—they were a happy and a handsome pair.
He was keeper at Yokieshill; he had been twenty year with
the laird.   Mony a queer outlandish bird he has sent me, for
Rob was a dead shot.   It never was known how he cam' by
the mischance : some said that the gun burst, ithers that it
was the laird's doing in ane o' his mad fits.   Howsomever
he lost his place—they were ever hard folk the Hackets—and
syne he lost heart and was gude for naething.   I was coming
hame early ae summer morn from the Teal Moss, where I had
been seekin' a strange deuck's nest, when I saw a woman sittin'
by the dyke-side wi' her head in her apron.   It was Esther
Cheyne.   Puir Rob had tried a rash cure !   The doctor could
do naething for his crippled leg, and Rob kent that he was a
sair burden upon the wife, wha was workin' her fingers to the
bane to keep him, and so—and so—'Esther,' he had said to
her wi' his last breath, 'I could wark nane for mysel', and I
was just hinderin' you.'"

"A pitiful story, indeed !"

"Ay, but that's no the warst.   When they were turned
awa' by the auld laird, young Hacket kent brawly hoo it was
with the bonnie bit lass that had been the sunshine o' her
father's hoose.   She was little better than a bairn ; and he lat
her leave wi'oot a word.   He never lookit near them again.
And ye ken what Lizzie is noo!   'Vengeance is mine, saith
the Lord, I will repay ;' but, Doctor, if Rob had lived, the
loan would hae been repaid lang syne—wi' usury."

"All in good time, my friend.   The mills of the gods grind
slowly, but they grind exceeding sure.   'Dii laneos habent
pedes.'   And troth here comes Corbie himsel', on auld Jess,
hittin' her feet at ilka step ; a wisp o' straw round her hind-
legs, my man, and ye wudna mak sic a noise in the world.
Truly, the body's lookin' gash.   What ails you, Corbie ?
Have you no a word for a freen' ?   Though your glorification
o' the Ceevil Law was maist unceevil, and ye micht hae letten
the Captain draw his lang-bow at pleasure—it hurts naebody
—I bear no malice."

But Corbie, looking like a man who has got a mortal scare,
and turning neither to the right hand nor to the left, went

straight on to "The Royal," where he stabled his steed.
Then the news got abroad. The laird of Yokieshill—Joe
Hacket—was dead, and Corbie (a ghastly comforter) had
been with him till he died. But the dying man had been
unable to sign the will which the lawyer had prepared. It
was of no consequence, however, Corbie explained, with a
curiously absent and preoccupied air, as he quitted the grey-
gabled house among the moors—of no consequence; the
deed had only declared Harry to be—what in point of law
he was without any deed whatever—owner of Yokieshill, sole
heir to his father's goods and gear, heritable and movable.

The minister and Uncle Ned looked at each other.
"There's something in the wind yonder," said the former.
"Faugh!" he added, as a whiff of stale fish and blubber was
wafted across the bay, "I am of Sir Toby's opinion, 'A plague
o' these pickle herrings!'"

II.

POOR Queen Mary paid but a brief and troubled visit to the
country of her birth; but some of the domestics who came
with her from France remained in Scotland after their mistress had sailed across the Solway. Among these was Marie
Touchet, who had been body servant to the Queen, and who
was married in the spring of 1566, at the Palace of Holyrood,
to a trusty retainer of the Earl of Erroll—one of the loyal
noblemen who through good and evil report adhered to Mary.
Loyalty had been a passion with the courtly and comely Hays
ever since Robert the Bruce, after the disastrous eclipse of the
great house of Comyn, had conferred on his tried friend the
barony of Slains, which at that time included nearly the whole
district that lies between the Ugie and the Ythan. It was
only natural that the retainers of the great house of Erroll
should be in favour at Court, and thus it happened that
Anthony Holdfast had been permitted to take with him to
his distant home among the sea-swept moors of the north the
favourite servant of the Queen. Marie had been born among

the leafy woodlands of Fontainebleau; and Anthony, who was
desperately in love with his charming little wife, gallantly proposed that her new home should be christened or rechristened
after the place where she was bred. It was a pleasant fancy
enough; and Marie was duly grateful, and thanked her Scotch
husband in her pretty though rather incomprehensible French-
Scots very sweetly for his loving devotion to *la belle France*
and to herself. Yet there was a tear in her eye, and her gay
smile grew wistful and doubtful when she compared the Fontainebleau of her girlhood with the Fontainbleau to which she
was welcomed. The contrast between the sunny plains and
the leafy forests of the South and this gaunt farmhouse upon
the barren seaboard of the *Mare Tenebrosum* was certainly
very striking. As the melodious syllables of " Fontainbleau "
sound curiously out of place among "Gasks," and "Achna-
gatts," and "Yokieshills," so the blithe little Frenchwoman
must have felt ill at ease for a time among her novel surroundings.

The Holdfasts of Fontainbleau, though neither lords
nor lairds, clung like limpets to their rocks; and thus it
came about that in the year One a Mrs Holdfast was still
tenant of the farm. Her husband, Mark Holdfast, had died
a month or two before his youngest daughter was born;
so that for more than seventeen years Mrs Holdfast had
been a widow. She had had a numerous family; but the
eldest son Mark was at least twenty years older than his
sister Euphame. For after the birth of five sons in succession there had been a long break—an interval of ten years
and upwards; and then Dick had come, and then, a year
later, Euphame or Eppie. The elder sons had all swarmed
off from the family hive,—some were farmers, some were
sailors, some settlers in the backwoods. Mark, the eldest,
was tenant of Achnagatt, the farm which "marched" with
Fontainbleau; and Mark had married about the time that
Eppie was born. So that Eppie and her nephews and
nieces were nearly of an age, and might have been boon
companions and bosom friends if Eppie had chosen. But
in point of fact the relations between the two farmhouses

were not particularly cordial. Young Mark and his comely
wife and her comelier daughters were the simple, unpretending, honest sort of people that are to be met with in
any average farmhouse on the eastern seaboard; but in
Eppie there was a strain of unfamiliar blood. *They* were
soft and gentle, and perhaps rather inclined to flabbiness,
physical and intellectual; she was keen, piquant, exacting.
They were contented with their lot; a fitful fire burned
in her veins. The Achnagatt girls were shy, timid, and
undecided; the girl at Fontainbleau looked you straight
in the face as a skua looks at you without winking. Her
bright black eyes might have been thought somewhat over-
bold in a less perfectly moulded face; but such a face
disarms criticism. The Norsemen, who peopled these northern coasts, had no part in this girl. Eppie was half a
Frenchwoman and half a gipsy.

This was how the estrangement between the two houses
came about. Old Mrs Holdfast had been a masterful
woman. She was Euphame Keith in her maidenhood, and
the Keiths, from the great Marshal down to the farmer at
the Mains, were as obstinate as mules; but this latest wild-
flower softened her into graciousness. There was a charm
about her madcap Dick which a mother's heart could not
altogether resist; but Dick had taken to the water like a
duck; had years ago deserted the family nest; and was now
seldom within hail, except sometimes of a moonlight night,
when a skittish little cutter, of questionable pedigree, was in
the offing,—a skittish little cutter which, like the Flying
Dutchman, was often heard of, but seldom seen, so seldom
indeed that there were people who held that The Crookit
Meg was a myth. (Whether Dick Holdfast will find a place
in this chronicle is not yet certain; it will be a casual
glimpse at most.) So that all the jealous affection of a
severe, intense, and reticent nature had been concentrated
upon her youngest daughter. The girl was the spoilt pet
of her widowhood. Eppie was perfect, immaculate, without
flaw or blemish of any sort. To eyes not blinded by love,
this little gipsy-cat was by no means without flaw or blemish.

Flawless, indeed, she would have missed her main attraction, like that kind of china which is only perfect when cracked. It would have been better for herself and for them all had she been broken in — to decorum; but then, perhaps, the wild violet, or rather the sweet-briar, flavour of her life—it is the sweet briar and not the sweet violet which scents the garden at Fontainbleau—might have evaporated; and this history might not have been written.

Mark, as I have said, was a plain man,—plain in manner and plain in speech, if not in person. His affections were deep though by no means effusive; and he had a specially warm place in his heart for his mother, and for Eppie too. But he felt that a character with some very curious and unaccountable traits, which he did not pretend to fathom— they were not in his line—was being allowed to run to seed; and he spoke his mind frankly and bluntly. This was the beginning of the breach which gradually widened as Eppie's moods grew day after day more wilful and restive and incalculable. For Mrs Holdfast would believe no evil of Eppie; and shut her ears and hardened her heart against whoever ventured to hint that this undisciplined favourite would inevitably prove a heart-break to her mother. Thus a false element came into her life; while, on the other hand, Mark, after a single repulse, washed his hands of the consequences, and went his way. But he too felt sore, angry, vexed: it troubled him that any one should come between him and his mother; and he silently resented the injustice, as he considered it, of her choice. Thus division was established, with the usual consequences.

> " When love begins to sicken and decay,
>   It useth an enforcèd ceremony,"—

a ceremony which is never more irksome than when it grows up between those who are near of kin or near in love; and Mark adored his mother. But Eppie was not troubled; so long as she was permitted to go her own way unchallenged, she was supremely tolerant because perfectly indifferent.

Yet there had been a time—now some seasons past—when Eppie's fate hung in the balance.

* *
*

Fontainbleau is built on a heathery plateau upon the summit of the Heughs. Any one acquainted with the coast knows Longhaven,—a ravine or chasm which penetrates for wellnigh a quarter of a mile into the solid land; and at the upper end of this ravine the old farmhouse stands—or stood within the memory of living men. There is another chasm a hundred yards farther south called Pothead; another beyond it called Hell's Lum. Opposite Hell's Lum, and nearly blocking up the passage from the open sea, is the island of Dunbuy. This is the last of the great granite headlands; thereafter the cliffs break away, and the coast sinks down to the sandy bents which enclose the Bay of Slains.

The farm of Achnagatt lies behind the sandhills which shelter it from the sea, and is separated from Fontainbleau by the great south road that now is, and by an affluent of the Whapple. Fontainbleau has no shelter of any kind,—it stands, as I have said, upon the summit of the cliff, and the fierce winter winds beat upon its windows day and night. Sometimes, when the winds have churned the waves into yeast, the windows that look to the east are white with the driving foam. No tree can take root upon that inclement seaboard; the alder-bushes whenever they rise above the garden wall are cut across as by a knife. What may be called the arable district of this country is singularly unpicturesque; but when, leaving the plateau, we descend into the chasms along the coast, we enter another world,—a world of romance and mystery, of light and shade, of stern strength and tender beauty, where the measured beat of the wave and the sorrowful complaint of the sea-mew only add to the impressive solitariness of the scene. The path which leads from Fontainbleau to the shore, zigzagging among bracken, winding round boulders, resting beside bubbling spring or mossy bank of ferns and primroses, the blue sea and the white sea-birds

framed in every variety of green, is one of the most delightful that can be imagined.   The promontory between Long-
haven and Pothead consists of a succession of heathery knolls,
sparsely planted with scraggy spruce and juniper - bushes,
where the earliest woodcock is sure to alight, it being the first
bit of cover this side Norway.   At the extreme point even
the heather wears off, and the bare rocks rise naked and
jagged from the water, yellow with lichen and brown with
tangle.

They used to call a particular ledge or niche on this headland "Charlie's Howff."   This was the natural observatory
from which Uncle Ned took his bird's-eye views of nature.
And the cool sparkling water of the Rood well, bubbling
up from some unfathomable depth below the sea, was the
only stimulant which the old naturalist on his rambles could
be persuaded to touch.   It was older, he asserted, than
the oldest vintage in the Provost's cellar: of an age indeed
to be computed, not by years of annual magistrates, but by
great conjunctions and the fatal periods of kingdoms.   So it
went well with the bread and cheese which he carried with
him when on the tramp.

"What brings you here, Uncle Ned?" little Eppie would
inquire—little Eppie, then about ten years old.

"If you lived in the High Street of Edinbro', Eppie, you
would sit at the window to see the folk gae by.   So I sit here
to see my freen's pass—the sea-birds, and the porpoises, and
the whales.   It's the calendar that shows me the time o' year.
When I notice the lang wedges o' wild swans and bean-geese
and loons and lang-tailed harelds and eider deucks flyin' past
to the south, I ken that autumn is over and the winter
comin'.   Then when they begin to return it is a sign and
a testimony that the spring-time is at hand.   Sae when the
whales are blowin' like waterspoots, and the grampuses rollin'
about like barrels, and the solans fa'in' like bullets into the
water, the fisher-bodies are advised that the great herrin' shoals,
that bide in the deep sea till the heat o' summer, are nearin'
the shore.   Truly there's nae month in the year like June, wi'
the bays a' swarmin' wi' fish; tho' indeed the haill year is a

perfec' perpetual feast to them that remember Him who designed the birds and the beasts, and young and auld bairns—
like you and me, Eppie."

At other times he would be accompanied by Alister, the
sturdy schoolboy, who lived under his kinsman's roof, and
then the children would have famous days of scrambling
among the rocks.   Eppie could climb like a squirrel or a
cat; her eye was perfect; even when on a narrow, slippery
ledge, with the surf boiling below, her head never failed her.
It seemed that a spice of danger added to the zest of her
enjoyment, putting her upon her mettle and bracing her
nerves.   If she could induce Alister to venture along a ledge
from which he could not return without a helping hand, she
would skim round about him like a sea-mew, and laugh un-
sympathetically at his terror.   But in truth the boy was a
daring cragsman, quite as venturesome in reality as Eppie
herself; and he had taken the eggs of the shag and the
peregrine from crags which had never been scaled before
by anything heavier than a conie or a fox.

Then they would return to Uncle Ned's seat, and at the
old man's feet share his frugal meal, listening lazily in the
sunshine to his discursive talk.

"There's a leam-fishing in St Catherine's Dub," he would
say, pointing to a deep gash in the rocks.   "Lang syne,
Eppie, a great Spanish barque—the St Catherine by name—
struck upon that reef.   It was a ship of the great Armada,
and it carried the Admiral's flag.   It went to the bottom wi'
every sowl on board.   They say that a great store o' gowd
lies at the bottom o' the Dub,—that was the clash of the
country-side when I was a wean.   But lang or ever the
Armada sailed the Danes kent ilka landin'-place alang the
Heughs.   They were wild folk, fearin' neither God nor man.
Mony a farmhouse they harried, and they burned the kirks,
and spared neither mither nor maiden.   But in the end a
great battle was fought at the Ward—it began in the dawnin'
and lasted far on thro' the nicht—and the saut-water thieves
were forced back to their ships.   It was a grand deliverance,
and the Yerl built a kirk on the battle-field, for it was said

that mair than mortal men took part in the fecht. That's
an auld wife's story, it may be; but that the battle was won
wi' God's help we may richtly believe. The kirk stood for
a thousand years, and may be standin' yet: for ae wild winter
nicht a mighty wind arose, and blew for a week, so that no
man could stand against it. When it ceased the kirk was
gone—it had been owercassen by the sand; and indeed the
sandbank itsel' may be seen to this day at the Water o'
Slains."

Then as the boy and girl grew older he would take them
with him into that imaginative domain where he spent so many
of his days.

"When you are a bigger lass, Eppie, you shall read the
plays of Shakespeare,—and you too, Alister. There has been
nae man like Shakespeare born into this world. He was
acquent wi' a' the devices o' man's heart; and yet had he
spent his time like mysel' in inquirin' into the ways o' birds
and beasts, he could not hae been mair familiar wi' their
ongoings. There's the teuchit—wha ever was mair pleased
wi' its divertin' wiles, which indeed have always seemed to
me mair like understandin' than instinct; for afore it could
steal awa frae its nest and rise anon on broken wing, it must
hae considered sariously hoo it could best beguile us :—

> ' I would not, tho' 'tis my familiar sin
> With maids to seem the lapwing, and to jest
> Tongue far from heart, play with all virgins so.'

How tenderly he peeps into the nest of the cushey doo—
there's never mair than ae pair of young cushies in a nest
—whar her golden couplets are lying saft and snug. And
Juliet desires a falconer's voice to lure her tassel-gentle back
again—just as Alister whistles a plover oot o' the lift; and
Coriolanus will be to Rome as the osprey to the fish who
takes it by sovereignty of nature; and Antony, leaving the
fight in height, claps on his sea-wing and like a doting mallard
flies after the Egyptian witch; and the shy Adonis is the dive-
dapper peerin' thro' a wave; and Duncan has nae thocht or
suspicion o' that bloody midnight business, because the castle

o' Macbeth is haunted by the swallows, who have built their
pendent nests at ilka window; which pruves that the air is
sweet and delicate, and better than doctors' drugs for an auld
king.   Puir auld Duncan!—as he sits there wi' the sunset
touching his grey hairs, list'nin' to the twitterin' o' the swallows, he looks a sweet and gentle and contentit auld man:
and a contentit auld man, my dears, is the happiest o' men.
But, O my bairns, the death-warrant had been signed, and
the bluidy designs o' twa black hearts—a man's, ay, and a
woman's—had been registered in hell.

> ' Within the hollow crown
> That rounds the mortal temples of a king
> Keeps Death his court, and there the antic sits.'

You've heard of Leddy Macbeth, Eppie, from your spellin'-
buik; some ither day I'll tell you about Juliet and Coriolanus
and Antony and Cymbeline, and the thrang o' kings and
clowns and fair women wha have been embalmed for ever in
the imperishable pages o' the chief o' poets."

This sort of talk went over their heads often, no doubt;
yet children are far wiser than the people who make stories
for them suppose.

"Did he belang to the Broch?" Eppie asks.   The Broch
rounded her horizon.

"Na, he was never sae far north.   Yet he kent the sea
weel,—though whar he saw it, oot o' his dreams, I canna tell.
The sea," he went on, "that responds like the weather-glass
to every impulse of the breeze—the always-wind-obeying
deep—until as the gale rises it loses its equilibrium a'thegither,
like a man oot o' his wits—as mad as the vexed sea—must
hae been regarded by Shakespeare in a' its moods.   Timon,
weary o' the warld and its fickle praise and blame, would
mak' his grave beside the sea, upon the very hem o' the sea,
whar its licht foam might beat his gravestone daily.   And for
my ain part, bairns, I would love to lie within hearin' o' the
swell—for the sea never sleeps, and it may weel be that even
amang the mools we micht hear its voice—when ither voices
are heard nae mair.   Moreover, the sea itsel' is full of life,—

being the image or visible manifestation of Him who is the centre and the source of life.   The vital force o' oor Maker is nowhere else sae veevidly personified.   Therefore, my bairns, the sea to an auld man like me has a hopefu' soun'—it speaks o' vitality and immortality,—like him who said ' Thou shalt not leave my soul in hell, neither shalt Thou suffer Thy Holy One to see corruption.'   The auld prophet indeed believed that the sea was unquiet because it was sorrowful,—there is sorrow on the sea, it cannot be quiet, says he ; but Jeremiah's knowledge of the sea was leemited, and he lived before the art o' boat-buildin' had been brought to oor present perfection, so that there was a prejudice against the saut water amang his countrymen.   But Shakespeare kent weel that the habitual motion o' the sea was pleasant and blythesome ; for when Perdita dances Florizel wishes her a wave o' the sea that she might do nothing but that ; and in verra truth, the fa' o' a wave and the footfa' o' a blythe lass are twa o' the sweetest soun's in this astonishin' warld."

It cannot be doubted, I think, that the ideal domain into which his companionship with Uncle Ned brought Alister Ross tended to enrich a character that would otherwise have been mainly noticeable for simplicity, shrewdness, and natural candour—a clear and limpid soul such as the gods love ; but somehow or other the influence was, or seemed to be, wasted on Eppie : the ideal ran off her, as water off a duck's back. Uncle Ned loved her as if she had been his daughter, and perhaps he loved her none the less because he felt, as the old Puritans would have said, that he was fighting for her soul— that the struggle between him and the Devil for this "precious piece of childhood" was still a drawn battle.   Her wilfulness, her insensibility, the spirit of mockery by which she was possessed, were purely impish ; yet her dauntless courage, her directness, her brightness, fascinated and dazzled him.   Her heart was still torpid, he would own ; but love might thaw the ice, and breathe a woman's soul, a woman's sense of duty and devotedness, into the cold bosom of this wilful kelpie.

But, as I have said, the ideal solution which was to thaw her selfishness into sacrifice, her impishness into womanliness, had not yet begun to work. She was seventeen years of age; a choice piece of workmanship; in splendid health, and without a touch of fear. On her eighteenth birthday (her birthday fell in the winter-time—she was born in the terrible winter of '82) she had sat with Uncle Ned at "Charlie's Howff," while the great white gulls sailed majestically along the cliffs, and the raven and the peregrine screamed at the intruders out of the sky. There had been a sprinkling of snow during the night; the frost was keen, and the limpid stream that trickled from the Rood well was being gradually translated by incrustation into a pendent crystal,—an enormous icicle.

"See, Eppie," said Uncle Ned, pointing to certain sharp and delicate imprints upon the snow, "mony hae been here this mornin' besides you and me. That's a rabbit's foot, and that's a roe's. What has brocht the buck doun to the sea? He'll be oot o' sorts, likely, and wantin' a taste o' the saut water. A haill thicket o' patricks hae been scrapin' on the lee side o' this drift. And here's the lang taes o' the woodcock, and—Gude guide us, Eppie—the webbed fute o' a wild-goose! There hae been some fine ploys here in the starlicht! That's a hare's seat beside the hedge : pussie has washed her face, and curled her whiskers, and noo she's aff to the neeps. There's many a simple history, my dear, to be read by the hedgerows and the burn-side in the winter time : and I never weary o' spellin' oot the letters. I'm an auld man noo ; but they're a' as wonnerfu' to me as when I was a wean. For it's true what the Apostle says, tho' aiblins no in the sense he intendit : Ever learnin', and yet never able to come to the knowledge o' the truth. For the truth is unfathomable and unsearchable."

"I don't see what good it has done you, Uncle Ned," says the young realist in her blunt fashion. "What's the good of a thing that's good for nothing?" she adds, in the very words of the philosophy of David Hume.

* * *

Alister loved Eppie, but Eppie did not love Alister. In this, however, there was no disparagement of Alister: for Eppie loved no one except herself. In point of fact, Eppie liked Alister as much perhaps as she was capable of liking. There was a subtle vein of sensuousness in this chilly nature; but Love?—of that as yet she knew nothing. Alister was strong and active, a fine specimen of the Scandinavian type of manliness; and Eppie saw that he was true and simple and warm-hearted—and yet she did not love him. She admired his rustic bravery, his open-mindedness, his faith in herself, as well as the frank blue eyes and the stalwart limbs of his outer man,—somewhat in the way that a man admires a handsome woman, with whom he is minded to flirt, but whom he does not mean to marry. That was all.

Once indeed she had nearly thawed. They had been out in the Fontainbleau skiff, fishing and fowling, and they were floating homewards in the autumn moonlight—a fathom or two from the cliffs. The glamour of the moonlight was around them. Birds of calm sat brooding on the charmed wave. An occasional auk floated past with the tide, its head under its wing. Then they came to a huge stack of snow-white rocks on which the moonlight rested broad and full. Half-way up the cliff a blue heron—a bird seen once in fifty years or so, and associated with quaint and fantastic superstitions—was perched on one leg in a cleft of the precipice. It was blue in every feather as a summer sky at morning. The ledge where it had posted itself was exactly like a niche carved on purpose to hold a relic or a little statue or a picture of a saint. The moon was full, and the bird looked as if the cliff had been made for it. Something in the solitariness and the strangeness of the surroundings touched Eppie. She was sitting on the same seat with Alister, and a sort of pathetic gleam came into her eyes. He stole his arm round her waist without speaking. She did not resist; her head lay upon his shoulder; she nestled closer and closer. This unaccountable tenderness—what did it mean? It was beneath these cliffs that other earlier lovers—as we partly know—had pledged their troth; and why not Eppie?

But when the boat touched the shore she sprang from his arms, and thereafter she did not speak to him for a month. They had been brother and sister ; now they were lovers ; and the whole soul of the wilful girl rebelled against the claim which in a moment of incalculable weakness she had seemed to allow.

Then Alister was despatched to a station in the south, and they did not meet again for a year or two. When he came back, in the summer of the year One—promoted to a fair place in the service—he heard that old Hacket was on his deathbed, and that Harry Hacket would be the new laird of Yokieshill.

This, I think, was the turning-point of Eppie's life. Had she yielded at that time to the soft persuasions of her better nature, she might have been saved.

III.

It was during the year of Alister's absence in the south that Eppie's acquaintance with young Hacket began—at some harvest-home or other rustic merry-making. The Hackets belonged to the gentry ; but the old laird of Yokieshill was a complete recluse, having withdrawn himself before his boy grew up from the society of the county. He was in bad odour both as master and neighbour. Insolent and overbearing by nature, he became morose and savage as the darkness deepened round him. It was a gloomy house, haunted by memories of evil-doing, standing gauntly among the melancholy moors. Mrs Hacket (she was one of the Logies,—Jean Kilgour of Logie) had died when her boy was born ; and thereafter no woman of the better sort had entered its doors. There was a tacit antipathy between father and son ; a dreary childhood—how unutterably dreary is the shy isolation of a child !—had matured into a sullen manhood ; and altogether the outlook for Harry Hacket when he came of age was one which the most poverty-stricken hind on the estate need not have envied. He was grossly ignorant; he had no companions except his gun and his dogs; his conscience was obtuse; paroxysms of passion had acquired for him the reputation of a bully, while, in truth, the habitual ill-usage to which he had been exposed, by crushing the animal spirits and the native elasticity of childhood, had made him a coward.

"The stars in their courses fight against Sisera," the Doctor said, discussing with Uncle Ned the character of the young squire.

"Ay, Doctor, but what business had the stars to tak' ony part in the strife? Hoo are we to guide oor battles if the stars come doun and fight like the auld gods on this side and on that? But there's some men who never get a chance: they are reprobates from the beginning. Heaven and earth have conspired against them. It's ane o' the mysteries o' this warld which metapheesics and theology have clean failed to expiscate. But between oorsels, Doctor, I've aye had great sympathy with Sisera. The stars werena verra particular in their choice o' tools. A nail in a sleepin' man's lug—it's no fair."

Yet this swaggering young fellow was presentable enough. Although he knew nothing of the dainties that are bred in a book, he had a certain measure of natural shrewdness which served to keep him out of any quite fatal scrapes. He was strongly built; his features were massive; his crisp black hair had a natural curl; the large black eyes were sombre but penetrating. Their stealthiness was not visible to the casual observer,—the stealthiness of a wild animal which has been hunted from its cradle, whose ancestors have been hunted from immemorial time. There was an underbred look about him, it is true, which would have made him, in spite of his broad chest and masterful air, distasteful to a woman of true cultivation; but then the girls about Yokieshill were not gifted with the keen and educated perceptions of the gentlewoman. The lasses who worked on the neighbouring farms were, many of them, sufficiently comely; and as their moral standard was not high, the fact that Merran Shivas or Kirsty Murrison had been seen with the young laird in the gloaming was rather a

feather in her cap than otherwise. Harry had no scruples on
this or on any other subject ; desire and its gratification went
hand in hand ; and by the time he was five-and-twenty he had
contrived to win for himself an unsavoury repute among honest
women.

It was not to be wondered at in the circumstances that Harry
Hacket should have sought the society of his inferiors. He
could not, in fact, help himself. He was shut out, by his
father's habits and by his own, from the great houses of the
neighbourhood. Man is a gregarious animal, and Harry
Hacket was driven by the social instinct, by the craving for
companionship, to the public-house and the bothie. Then he
was the young laird. A great part of the land round about
had been inherited or acquired by his father. The fortunes
of many of these simple people would by-and-by come to
depend on his goodwill. He was not loved ; but he was
tolerated, invited, encouraged. He and his father were barely
on speaking terms. The old man had grown very miserly ;
it was his last enjoyment in a world which he did not love
and more or less despised. Harry might commit as many
follies as he pleased, but he must not expect his father to pay
for them. At that time smuggling by land and by sea was in
full swing ; foreign wines and silks as well as home-made
spirits were at famine prices ; the illicit traffic was a lucrative
one. Harry was driven by his necessities to consort with men
who habitually and successfully evaded the law. Even by
these men he was not trusted : a true instinct warned them
against one who was destitute of the rudimentary principles
of honour which are current among thieves, who was at heart
a coward ; but then he was useful to them. Had he been
openly hostile, the son of the resident proprietor, who was
constantly wandering about the moors with his gun and his
dogs, might have come inconveniently in their way. He
would certainly have learnt that the Black Moss was frequented
not by wild ducks only. Harry was proud in his coarse ignorant fashion ; he would not have married a cottar's daughter
even to spite his father ; for in his own conceit he belonged
to the upper class which could do what it liked with the

lower; and he internally resented the familiarities which he was forced to accept from his associates.

This is not a nice character, but it was one very common in Scotland in the year One,—the home-bred son of the miserly or impecunious laird, whose education had been neglected, and whose morals had been worse than neglected. Uncle Ned was very tolerant: he believed that, rough-hew them how we may, a divinity shapes our ends; that the world would go topsy-turvy were there no hand behind the scenes to keep the puppets on their feet; and that without some such unseen direction education becomes an utterly hopeless enterprise. But even Uncle Ned admitted that Harry Hacket was a difficulty; and when, in spite of such warnings as he could give her, Eppie Holdfast's name began to be associated with the young laird's, he turned away with a dull but poignant feeling of pain and displeasure in his heart to which his simple nature had been hitherto unused.

But Eppie was not blinded.

* * *

I don't want to do Eppie any injustice. She was a remarkably fine animal—her physique was splendid—she had magnificent vitality. Her skin was pure and her eye bright with perfect health. But she had never been broken into harness, and at length she became unmanageable. What strict control and discipline might have effected I cannot pretend to say— something, not everything, for the vice was in the blood. It requires something more than the wise direction of man—it needs the fire of Almighty God—to warm the cold and calculating instincts of a worldly nature into the glow of sacrifice and the ideality of love. There were all sorts of superficial contrarieties in Eppie's nature; she was hard yet cunning, icy yet sensitive, frank yet reticent. On one side she seemed rude, blunt, imperious; yet she had that native capacity for treachery which is bred in the bone of the wild-cat and the hawk. The girl was utterly fearless; yet nature had armed her with the stealthy arts with which she arms the weaker

animals. You say that this is an unnatural combination?
But there are no vital inconsistencies in such a character as I
am sketching. Given an original basis of urgent and clamant
selfishness, and to compass its end any disguise can be assumed, or rather it can shape itself into any mould. Poor
Eppie must have committed some dreadful crime in a prior
state of existence, for even in her bluntest moments she was
watchful—ever on the alert to guard against surprise.

Eppie was not blinded. But Harry was the young laird;
and his wife might be—should be—would be—a great lady.
Why not? said Eppie to herself. But to become a great lady
it was necessary to marry this man; and then she had to ask
herself if she loved him as she would love her husband. Well
—she was not quite sure of her feelings—he repelled and attracted her as the loadstone attracts and repels. She knew by
repute that he was sulky and passionate; she had a sort of
moral conviction that he was a coward. He might have be-
haved badly to girls—to do Eppie justice, the worst of his
iniquities were not known to her; well, girls must look after
themselves as she meant to look after herself; but cowardice
—that was a crime in a man which it was difficult to forgive.
And then there was Alister. Poor Alister! Lord of his presence and no land beside, as Uncle Ned would say.

"Harry," said Eppie, as they stood on the Saplin Brae, "I
don't know that mither would like me to ride so far."

"Oh, never heed, Eppie; we'll be hame before dark."

Eppie was a bold rider, and she looked splendid in the
rustic habit which her own deft fingers had woven. Her
steed was only a "shalt" or "shaltie," a half-bred, half-broken
native of the farm, yet a wiry and indefatigable little beast.
The breed of Highland ponies has died out now, more's the
pity.

It is the spring-time, a soft wind is blowing from the south,
and the braes of Fontainbleau are white with cowslips. Eppie
looks splendid: her face is flushed with the excitement of the
gallop up the Saplin Brae to the ridge above Yokieshill; the
young laird has dismounted to tighten a girth and adjust a
stirrup; he gazes up into her face with eyes that are brimful

of passion. He has never had a toy like this before; his longing to clasp it, to seize it, to make it his own, takes away his breath at times; he is mad with desire. They have raced up the steep ascent; the horses took the bits between their teeth and flew like the wind; and now they are resting on the summit. And at their feet is the old house of Yokieshill, and the mosses round about that the wild duck love, and the blue sea edged with a white line of breakers, and circled by the Sandhills of Slains. And all the land between is owned by the laird of Yokieshill, who is dying at home in his bed.

The tempter selected an exceedingly high mountain from which to show the tempted all the kingdoms of the world and the glory of them.

Harry Hacket was but a coarse and rustic edition of Mephistopheles; yet he judged rightly when he brought Eppie in their rides to the Saplin Brae. For from thence she could behold all the goodly heritage which she coveted; and distance gave the gaunt old Scotch house a charm which would not have stood the test of a closer acquaintance.

"Let me call you Eppie," he had asked on one occasion as they stood on this spot.

"My name's Euphame," she had answered calmly "There's aye been a Euphame Holdfast in Fontainbleau or ever there was a Hacket in Yokieshill; but you may call me Eppie if it pleases you, I am sure."

"And you will call me Harry?"

"Surely," she answered, returning his ardent glance with a shrug of her pretty shoulders. "Harry's a prettier name than Hacket."

"What ails you at Hacket?" he said, gloomily, for he secretly hated the name which belonged to his father as well as to himself.

"Oh, the name's guid enough for them that owns it, she replied, with airy indifference. "Naebody of course would tak' it for choice."

After this fashion it had been settled that "Eppie" and "Harry" were to be substituted for "Miss Holdfast" and "Mr Hacket." Bitin' and scartin' are Scots folks' wooin';

and the more he was hurt by the sharp tongue and the dangerous teeth of this chilly and unapproachable damsel, the more furiously did his passion blaze.

And now the gay knight and his fair damozel are pricking on the plain. In that barren treeless country, and to these hard weather-beaten men and women of the coast, the shadowy coverts and the wide park-like spaces of Pitfairlie —for which they are bound—form an enchanted domain. The sea is a sharp taskmaster: never at rest itself, its unrest creeps into the blood of those who live on its shores; its companionship implies a constant strain. To cross from Balmawhapple into the Pitfairlie woods was to reach a haven of repose after painful wrestling with the east wind; the wavy outlines, the deep shadows, the soft greenery of the park rested eye and brain wearied by the poignant light. And then, to add to its attractions, there was "the auld admiral," who brightened it by his wit and enriched it by his goodness —my dear old friend, who wore his seventy years lightly like a flower, and whose keen tongue and mother wit were crisp and bracing as a winter morning.

Pitfairlie was delightfully situated. In front of the castle a noble chace dotted with forest trees—magnificent limes and chestnuts—retreated slowly till it lost itself in a thicket of spruce and brushwood. The approach swept in a succession of fine curves along the brink of the river. There were no gates to shut in the face of the people; nothing to indicate exactly where the lawn terminated or the outer world began. Cottages were scattered here and there among the cover; blue smoke curled in lazy wreaths over the tree-tops.

They rode through the castle grounds, till they came to the barren upland, where the plover and the moorfowl breed. It was a glorious ride; the road continually ascending from the rich banks of the river to the region of the heather and the pine, and disclosing a new coign of vantage at every turn. The picturesque antiquity of the historic abbey, the lordly breadth of the modern mansion, the rose flush of my lady's flower-garden, the blue curves of the river gleaming through the spring greenery of the woodland, the low backs of the bushless downs crowned with shining crests of purple heather, the white swans upon the lake ruffling their snowy plumage, or dipping their long necks into the clammy weeds, I do not wonder that the Balmawhapple poets of the year One should have waxed eloquent in praise of the fair Pitfairlie domain.

They drew up their panting horses in the middle of the encrimsoned downs, and turned their faces homeward. A gorcock crowed lustily, startling the gathering shadows of the night. There was no sound or trace of man; the wild Highland cattle that fed upon the scrubby herbage were the only denizens of these dreary flats. Obstinate, mouse-coloured, picturesque little brutes, with shaggy manes and shaggy heads crowned with long branching horns, who looked at the riders with brown, tranquil, meditative eyes as they went past. The ox-eyed Juno!

"O dear me, how delightful it is!" sighed Eppie to herself. And then as they rode home in the dark—if it is ever dark in these high northern latitudes — Harry made her understand at last that he loved her as such men love. Eppie was in a dream: dreaming was a new sensation to her; for Eppie, as a rule, slept the sleep of the just, or at least of a perfectly healthy young animal. Two voices sounded in her ears—the voice of the man beside her, and the voice of another who had been her playfellow in the old days; and while she listened in an unfamiliar reverie to Harry's story, she thought of Alister. But all the time she knew, or fancied she knew, that she had made her choice; for her own self-love was deeper and more vital than any other. Ambition had the whole, or wellnigh the whole, of her heart; Love only an obscure corner. And for his part, Harry, even in that gust of passion, felt that he was a fool; was even then mentally calculating how he could win her on the easiest available terms.

But the upshot was that in the meantime Eppie had two lovers in hand, to neither of whom, however, had it been finally and irretrievably pledged.

So the months passed, Eppie still on her guard, and
hedging as they say on the turf: grave and silent with
Uncle Ned, mocking and masterful with Harry Hacket,
but watchful always; until on an August evening of the
year One, Alister Ross, looking remarkably handsome in
his new uniform, returned to Balmawhapple.

"What is to come of it all?" Eppie asked herself nerv-
ously when, on the day following his return, the blue-eyed
sailor, browned with sun and salt-water, and grown from a
boy into a man (though there was still a boyish sparkle
in the honest untroubled eyes), presented himself at Fontainbleau.   Eppie in her grave matter-of-fact way was not much
of a humourist; yet she smiled to herself — rather uneasily
to be sure — when somehow or other the vision of a cat
playing dexterously with *two* mice (until she had decided
which to eat first) inopportunely occurred to her.   "What
brings him here when he is not wanted?" she said, pettishly;
and indeed she was angry with him and with herself, and
would have rated him soundly had she dared.   But Alister
looked so big and strong and gentle and comely that the
angry words died upon her lips.   "Is it possible that I
am afraid of him? Is it possible that I——" and then
Eppie, who had been watching him as he made his way
through the moor, ran up to her room without completing
the sentence.

The Jan Mayen entered the harbour at Port Henry on
the first day of October 1800, the day before Laird Hacket
died; and the reader will be kind enough to understand
that while I have been chatting with him about old times
and old stories three weeks have passed.   The stooks at
Fontainbleau have been gathered into the farmyard, and
the Achnagatt "clyack" is to take place to-morrow.

IV.

It was the forenoon of the day on which the Achnagatt harvest-home was to be held; and Mrs Mark and her daughters were busy in the kitchen preparing "sowens" and other delicacies for the entertainment. I have not got a copy of Mrs Dods in the house, and cannot therefore give you any authoritative recipes for the dishes that were being made ready. There were bannocks, and oat-cakes, and piles of fresh butter, and basins of yellow cream, and an ample supply of Glendronoch. The girls were pictures of health; their short petticoats disclosed serviceable, though by no means clumsy, feet and ankles; their arms were bare and bespattered with the flour and oatmeal which they were baking into the delicious home-made bread of the farmhouse, —not the arms more white than milk of which the poet sings, but good, honest, sturdy arms, tanned a little by the sun while milking, and reddened a little by the fire when cooking. The girdle was suspended over the peats, and there was a constant running to and fro between it and the baking-board. Cousin Kate was considered the prettiest of these unsophisticated Graces; but Kate was the housewife too; and indeed a sort of commander-in-chief, who looked after her father's accounts and took charge of the dairy. Mrs Mark's exertions in bringing these nice girls, and one or two rather violently disposed schoolboys, into the world, associated as they had been with a growing tendency to plumpness, had induced her to hand over the active duties of preparing for the feast to her slimmer daughters; while she and Miss Sherry—who had been brought out from Balmawhapple by Mark on the previous evening—sat in the ingleneuk with their spinning-wheels,—the constant companion of gentle and simple at the time of which I am writing. Altogether the kitchen was highly picturesque. The girls flitting to and fro, with their sparse petticoats and upturned sleeves, in the frisky mettlesomeness of earliest maidenhood; Miss Sherry, with her old-fashioned spinning-wheel (which is being again

introduced into our drawing-rooms in an inane and irrelevant
way); the long array of shining pots and pans and willow-
pattern plates suspended in a haik above the dresser; the
gipsy-looking girdle; the wide, homely, hospitable fireplace;
the ruddy glow of the peats; the gathering shadows of the
October night;—it is one of those "symphonies" in light
and shade which are not easily forgotten, especially by
children, artists, and lovers.

Miss Sherry was an institution of Balmawhapple, where
she and her sister Grace lived in one of the nicest houses of
the town.   Each of those old patrician mansions had its
motto (*had*—for they are all gone) carved in good broad
Scots over the doorway.   "Feir the Lord."   "Flie from
syn."   "Mak for lyf everlastin."   "No this lyf is bot vanity."
"Svear note."   The house occupied by Miss Sherry and her
sister had belonged to the Earls Marischal, and their defiant
distich—"They haif sayd: Qhat sayd they?   Lat them say"
—was nearly as characteristic of its present occupants as of
the old fighting Keiths.   These elderly Scotch ladies of the
year One had indeed small regard for what would now be
termed public opinion and the proprieties.   Miss Sherry was
one of this race of old Scottish gentlewomen; for though by
no means rich, and mixing rather with the middle than with
the upper classes, she had a strain of gentle blood in her
veins which made her fifteenth or sixteenth cousin to all the
great people in the county.   The old Admiral loved Miss
Sherry and her caustic speech; he called her "cousin," and
always sent the sisters a fat goose on New Year's Day.   He
made a point of calling upon them whenever he visited the
burgh (which he represented in Parliament—the Provost and
two other freeholders forming the constituency; and a very
good constituency it was — holding remarkably sound and
constitutional opinions), and drank a glass of their elderberry
wine without wincing, and indeed in the cheeriest possible
spirit.   Her niece, Mrs Mark, was naturally proud of the
connection; and Miss Sherry was always a welcome visitor at
the farm.   She was a neat, natty, daintily dressed old lady;
and her sharp face and keen eyes (which had seen seventy

summers) were nearly as fresh as her grandnieces', and disclosed a fund of shrewd intelligence and sarcastic life. She
had witnessed in her time a good deal of hard living, and
hard drinking, and hard swearing, without being prudishly
scandalised. Yet her directness of speech and somewhat
easy morals belonged to the outside, and there was a sound
heart and high principle behind.

"And the Doctor bid me tell you," Miss Sherry was saying,
as she sat burrin' at her wheel, "that he'd be here before
dark and bring John Skinner wi' him—(that harn's not what
it used to be). The auld man's beginnin' to fail—he's no
sae soople as he was when I mind him first; but he has a
gran' voice for a man o' his years—he's auchty if he's a day—
and he sings his ain sangs verra sweetly. We maun hae the
Ewie wi' the Crookit Horn, or *Tullochgorum*. It's fearsome,
Marion, to think how auld we are gettin'; it's saxty years last
June since he was clapt into the Tolbooth by the sodgers, and
his wife—puir thing—at the doun-lying. Weel-a-wat, the
Doctor may flyte as he likes at the like o' us"—all these old
Balmawhapple ladies were stout for Episcopacy—"but he'd
best let *that* flee stick to the wa'. He's a snell body the
Doctor; he wunna argue wi' an auld wife like me, and if
I drive him into a corner he jist taks his pinch o' snuff, and
tells me that I maun hae heard that the deil and the dean
begin wi' ae letter; when the deil gets the dean the kirk 'll be
the better; and then he mak's me the yeligant bow which he
learnt at the Court o' Louise Quinze—so he says—and
marches aff wi'oot waitin' for an answer. But he's a steady
hand at a rubber—that I maun alloo—and after a', the body's
kind in his way—though pecooliar."

"What's become o' your feyther, lasses?" Mrs Mark observes to her daughters. "The barn must be ready by this time;
and the folk 'll be arrivin' shortly. Sae run and dress yoursel's,
my dears, and auntie and I 'll see that the cakes dinna singe."

So the three Graces rush up the wooden stairs to don their
finery; and Miss Sherry resumes.

"I maun speak to the Doctor about oor Kirsty,—she'll hae
to stan' the session. Kirsty considers a lad jist perfec' salva-

tion ; and I've aften tellt her how it wud end. Yet when she cam' to me wi' her head in her apron, I cudna believe my ears, for she's a dounricht fright. 'Kirsty Meerison,' says I, 'it's not possible—an ill-fa'ured limmer like you! Wha in the name o' mercy 's the feyther o' the wean?' 'Indeed, Miss Sherry,' says the impudent hizzy in a bleeze at the notion, 'I could hae got plenty o' feythers.'"

"Dear me," says Mrs Mark, "I'm sorry for Kirsty."

"But it's the same wi' them a'—a lad's jist perfect salvation. And there's Mark's sister, Eppie Holdfast—she'll be comin' to the ploy, nae doobt?"

"She wudna say when Kate gaed up to see. The auld mither has been but poorly this month back——"

"It's little Eppie cares for her mither," Miss Sherry retorted, "and she'll come if she chooses, you may depend on that. I dinna like the clash I hear aboot Eppie in the Broch. There's that nice lad frae Moray—at least they say that baith he and Uncle Ned belang to Fochabers—Alister Ross is clean daft aboot her ; but Eppie, they tell me, hauds up her nose at him. And they do say—but ye'll ken best, Marion, though there's aye water whar the stirkie drowns—that she's ower thick wi' young Hacket——"

"Harry is laird noo," Mrs Mark interposed.

"To be sure, we a' ken that the laird's dead," says Miss Sherry. "He was an acquaintance o' mine in auld days, afore he gaed gyte—never a freen'. There were some bad stories aboot him lang syne, and if puir Rob Cheves hadna been a fule, we micht hae gotten some verra enterteenin' information noo that Joe Hacket's safe awa'. And young Hairy's a bad boy, or I'm mistaen. Bourd not wi' bawtie ; and if Eppie comes, I maun gie her a word o' advice. Mark should look after her a bit."

"Eppie 'll gang her ain gait, auntie—we maunna mell. But I shouldna wonner if baith Alister and Harry Hacket were at the ploy to-night——"

"Harry Hacket !" exclaimed Miss Sherry. "It's no a week sin' the auld man was buried. It wudna be decent, but it's little for decency he cares."

"Weel, auntie, I dinna ken; but Mark met him on the road yestreen, and he thocht it was neeborlike to ask him to come across. Mark's very simple—honest man!—but Hairy was as ceevil as could be, and Mark thinks he'll come."

Then the guests began to arrive.

* *
*

The farm lads and lasses were sent to eat their cakes and sup their "sowens" in the barn; whereas Dr Caldcail, Mr Skinner, Captain Knock, and one or two more of the better sort, were ushered into the parlour. Mark gave his friends a cordial greeting and a tremendous "grip"; and they forthwith gathered round the hospitable board, where the savoury messes prepared by the Graces were steaming invitingly. A cold turkey, a red-hot haggis, crappit-heads, mealy puddings, a roly-poly—these old Scotch dishes were worthy of the worthy people who were bred upon them. So long as the *Noctes Ambrosianæ* survive—and the *Noctes* will live when the Radicals and Republicans who sneer at the ambrosial nights and their ideal gluttony are eaten of worms (the poor worms!)— the memory at least of this national and historical fare will be kept fresh and savoury,—embalmed in immortal prose.

"Mr Skinner will ask a blessing on these mercies," says Mark; and then they set to, and ate as they could eat in the year One.

A sweet and venerable old man was John Skinner, genial and easy-tempered as a singer of songs should be, yet with a quiet tenacity of character and conviction that could have nerved him to die had it been required of him for what he deemed to be the truth of God. The evil persecuting days, when he had been dragged from his bed to jail for venturing to minister to the scattered remnant, had passed away like a bad dream; and now, loved and honoured by gentle and simple, he saw his children's children at his knee, and peace in Israel. He had been a poet of the people before Robert Burns was born; and now "puir Robbie" was dead, and the old man mourned for him as for a brother.

Captain Knock, who was seated beside the comely hostess, was in great force.

"A remarkable turkey, Mrs Holdfast, a verra fine turkey indeed, and you maun favor me wi' the receipt for the stuffin', which is maist excellent. But if you had seen the breed we had at Tillymaud! they were simply stu-pen-dious! I mind the Admiral dining wi' me ae day. 'Captain,' says he, 'that turkey weighs fifteen punds good.' 'Fifteen punds!' says I. 'I'll wager a dozen of Bordeaux that it's thirty if it's an ounce.' 'Done!' says he—and we had it oot o' the dish and weighed upon the spot. It was five-and-thirty punds, as I'm a leein' sinner! The Admiral wudna believe his eyes; but he sent the hogshead a' the same, and gude claret it was, and weel liket for mony a day. We ca'ed it the thirty-five."

Miss Sherry for her share had a minister on either hand,— the kindly representatives of the rival creeds.

"The Doctor tells me, John Skinner, that ye are leavin' us for gude and a'. That maunna be: the bishop's a worthy man and a gude son; but it wud be a sin to tak' you from your auld freen's."

"Indeed, Miss Sherry, I'm beginnin' to break, and the lasses are a' forisfamiliate, and in spite of the Gude Book and a bit sang at times the house feels lonely, tho' Kirsty is a canty and couthie lass."

"And the Pharos o' Linshart," said the Doctor, "will be darkened! Have you considered how the Longside lads will wun thro' the Longate bogs on the mirk nights?"

"We are unaccoontable beings," replied the old man, softly. "Will you believe me, Miss Sherry, that I canna thole the notion o' extinguishin' that poor little Pharos, as oor reverend freen' ca's it? It has burned there for fifty years as steady as the Polar star. I was tellin' the laird that he maun execute a mortification on its behalf; but he says that in that case the auld man maun bide to see that it burns fairly. Indeed, Pitfour has a kind heart, and I sent him a bit rhyming letter o' thanks for a' the gude he has done to me and mine."

"You maun gie me a copy, John Skinner," says Miss Sherry. "I dearly love your verses—yours and Robbie's;

tho' the Doctor here is a' for Pop, and Swift, and Addison—
feckless bodies wi' their fushionless English trashtrie. But
you see he has nae ear for music, puir man!"

"Come, come, Miss Sherry, that's not fair. I could ance
dance *Tullochgorum* with the best of you; and I agree with
Rob that there's a wild happiness o' thocht and expression
—that's what he wrote you, Skinner, if I remember richtly—
about the *Ewie wi' the Crookit Horn*, which makes it one
o' the best o' Scotch sangs. But, my dear freen', do let us
hear a verse or two o' the epistle to Pitfour."

"My memory is no what it used to be, tho' indeed to this
day I can repeat the maist part o' *Chryste-Kirk-o'-the-Green*.
But there's twa-three lines that—wud you believe it!—brocht
the tears into my auld een as I penned them;" and the old
man repeated in a low voice the simple lines which some of
us have not forgotten :—

> "Now in my eightieth year, my thread near spun,
> My race through poverty and labour run;
> Wishing to be by all my flock beloved,
> And for long service by my Judge approved;
> Death at my door, and heaven in my eye—
> From rich or great what comfort now need I?"

There was a shadow of a tear in Miss Sherry's keen eyes as
he concluded, and the Doctor exclaimed somewhat testily,
"Hoots, hoots, my freen', this will never do. You'll set us
greetin', and what wud Mrs Mark say to weet eyes at her
ploy?"

"To be sure, to be sure; yet, as we a' ken, Doctor, joy wi'
jist a touch o' regret is ever the sweetest. And tears and
smiles are aye meetin' in this changefu' warld. 'Seria non
semper delectant, non joca semper. Semper delectant seria
mixta jocis.' Beggin' Miss Sherry's pardon."

"That's true, my freen', and we'll talk nae mair Latin, tho'
indeed no man can write better Latin than John Skinner.
And that reminds me that I've never got the copy o' the
Batrachomyomachia Homeri latinis vestita cum additamentis
(your pardon again, Miss Sherry) that you promised to send
me."

"It will be ready by the New Year. It's still in Charles Chalmers's printin' office."

"Mark is lookin' at you, Doctor," says Miss Sherry.

"Mr Skinner," Mark shouts from the bottom of the table, "I hear Sandy Scott tunin' his fiddle. They'll be waitin' for us in the barn. But we maunna part till you sing us the *Ewie*."

"Mark," said the old man, "I've never sung the *Ewie* since my dear Grisel left me. But there's a wheen verses to the tune o' 'Auld Lang Syne' that might not come amiss at this time."

And then he sang, in a remarkably pure and clear voice for a man of eighty, to the air that goes direct to every Scotsman's heart, a verse or two from the *Auld Minister's Sang*.

> "Though ye live on the banks o' Doun,
>   And me besooth the Tay,
> Ye well might ride to Faukland town
>   Some bonny simmer's day.
> And at that place where Scotland's King
>   Aft birled the beer and wine,
> Let's drink, an' dance, an' laugh, an' sing,
>   An' crack o' auld lang syne."

"Noo, Doctor," said Miss Sherry, "mind, ye are promised to dance a strathspey wi' me."

"Indeed, Miss Sherry, my dancin' days are past, forbye it was the minuet we mainly practised at the French Court in the year saxty-five. But," continued the Doctor, gallantly, "I never could resist the solicitations of the gentle sex. Ye will have your fling at Pop, Miss Sherry; but wha could compliment the leddies like Pop?—

> 'Fair tresses man's imperial race ensnare,
> And beauty draws us with a single hair.'

So I maun do my best wi' my auld legs," he added, looking down complacently at the knee-breeches and black silk stockings then commonly worn as evening dress by the order to which he belonged.

* * *

The fun had become fast and furious before Eppie arrived. She was dressed with excessive simplicity,—she always dressed simply. She had discovered that the simplest dress set off to best advantage her shapely figure and finely poised head.

The Doctor, rather out of breath with the strathspey, was seated beside Miss Sherry when she arrived. "What a grand creature it is!" he said. "But she's oot o' her place in a farmhouse. She should hae been bred in a palace. She's fine as Desdemona. She might lie by an emperor's side and command him tasks."

"Gude be here, Doctor," said Miss Sherry. "I howp she disna think o' lyin' by onybody's side yet. Eppie's jimp eighteen; and I never did quite like the expression o' her face. Gie me a sweet honest face like Kate's; that's the face that wears best."

"Nothing venture nothing have," quoth the Doctor. "If I were a young man I wud risk a fa' for Eppie."

It was clear that more than one at least of the young fellows present were of the Doctor's opinion. Eppie had known, as if by instinct, the moment she entered, that both Alister and Hacket were present; and she had barely greeted her aunt before they were by her side.

"No," she said, merely bending her head to the young men, "I canna dance; mother's poorly. I've promised Cousin Mark to be his partner for a Hoolachan." Cousin Mark, commonly known as Mopsy, was a chubby-cheeked curly-headed little fellow of eight, who doted on his youthful aunt. "But I maun be hame in an hour."

She had made up her mind that the situation was too dangerous. So she would dance with neither.

Alister retreated; Harry looked black as thunder. Then the fiddle struck up; the floor was quickly covered by the dancers; the girls were swiftly swung round by their partners in the frantic passion of *Tullochgorum*; the pace grew faster and faster; there were wild shouts and shrieks and laughter. Little Mark clung to Eppie, and was whirled off his feet in the delirium of the dance. It was a grand romp to an air that puts mettle into the clumsiest feet—the sort of Bacchanalian riot in which these grave people give vent to the suppressed excitement of their lives. Out of such moments they snatch a fearful joy, unfamiliar to the grey sky of a land that seldom brightens into imperfect sunshine.

Eppie and little Mark threw themselves on a bench in a dim corner. Even in the noisy rapture of the dance, Eppie, whose head was always cool, had had time to whisper to Harry (who was leaning against the wall, watching her moodily), "Harry, I maun speak to you. There's word from Dick."

So when the dance was finished, Harry sauntered up sulkily to the place where she sat with the boy in the partial darkness. He was in one of his black moods.

"Rin awa', Mopsy," she whispered to the boy; and then turning to Harry, and looking him straight in the face with her careless unshrinking eyes, "Dinna glower, Harry," she said. "You might have the sense to see that I couldna dance wi' you the night. But, sulky or no, it's the same to me—only I maun gie you the message I gat frae Cummin Summers. He was waitin' ootside to see you, but he couldna bide langer. They were fishin' on the Gutter Bank last night. The Crookit Meg is cruising aboot the bank, waitin' for the neap-tide. He spoke to Dick and the skipper. They will run for Pot-Head on Monday night whenever it's dark, and they'll ken from the licht at Port Erroll whar they can land freely. Now, go; see, they are lookin' at us."

"But, Eppie, why are you so unkind? It's weeks since I saw you, and now you haven't a civil word for a poor devil. Let me take you home."

"No—no—no," she exclaimed, hastily. "Watty is here wi' his lantern; it's only a minute's run. Bide whar you are, Harry; there would be a clash if you gaed wi' me."

"Stay, Eppie, one minute. What are we to do with the gauger?" looking askant at Alister, who was now seated at the other end of the room with one of the Graces. "I hear he's at your place every Sabbath afternoon, he and that crazy fule Uncle Ned." (Eppie frowned.) "It'll be clean impossible to land a keg if he's in the way; oor men winna face him.

Well, this is the last job of the kind for me; I'm sick of the risk. And, Eppie, anither word. You said that you would like a cross like Lady Yerroll's. Now, the skipper is to get one at Antwerp—a gold cross set wi' pearls from the Braes o' Gicht. I gaed him a dozen wi' him that I got whan divin' as a boy——"

Eppie was touched. "Harry, that was kind of you. A gowd cross——"

At this moment they were interrupted by the Doctor and Miss Sherry.

"What do I hear about a gold cross?" said the Doctor, who saw, with his quick tact, that the situation was difficult, and who was ready to shield, as far as he could, a pretty girl like Eppie. "We'll have no papistrie in Buchan, Mr Hacket —not even to oblige Miss Sherry, who is hand and glove wi' the Pop. No, no, Miss Eppie, if we are to introduce the cross into a land which has profited by the Reformation, it maun be a less debatable article, and mair becomin' a sweet lass like yoursel'. There is another Pop for whom my freen' Miss Sherry has nae particular regard—in fact, no regard at all—and he wrote some most delectable verses,—in English, I grant you: he didna understan' the Scots, mair's the pity— aboot his Belinda's cross—

> ' On her white breast a sparkling cross she wore,
>   Which Jews might kiss and infidels adore.' "

The Doctor rattled off his nonsense gallantly, resolved to see Eppie out of the scrape if possible. Hacket, with a sullen salutation to Miss Sherry, had turned away; Eppie had drawn herself up to her full height, and stood at bay with a curl on her lips, and the unpleasant look in her eyes. Miss Sherry was ready for battle.

"Eppie Holdfast," she said, "it becomes a maid to walk warily. The Doctor kens that I'm nae a preceesian"—here she turned round; but the Doctor, seeing the conflict inevitable, had fled—"and I've nae patience wi' the Pharisee who because he has a sore nose threeps that a' the warld should wear plasters. But there's a line across which an honest lass

canna venture; and Harry Hacket is no an improvin' freen'
for an honest lass. It's no that he's wild, Eppie—maist young
lads will get into a scrape at times; but he's hard and cruel.
He wull seek a' that you can gie him, and then leave you
without a thocht. Tak' my word—I kent his feyther, and
I ken himsel'. They're like ane anither as twa peas—baith
in body and soul. Listen to me, Eppie. There are things
which I canna speak o' to a young lass like you; but had you
seen Merran Cheves last week fished oot o' Port Henry——"

Eppie could listen no longer. Her heart had beat louder
than it had done even during the reel,—though her lips did
not cease to smile, and her eye did not quail.

"Harry—Mr Hacket—is naething to me—less than naething," she said, with a cold *hauteur* that would have become
a queen.

And then she turned away, and went home without another
word. The warning could not have come at a less fortunate
time; for to-night, for the first time, her heart had softened to
Harry—a little bit—a very little bit.

Do not misunderstand me. It was pity that softened her—
not love. Ever since Alister's return it had become daily
clearer to herself that some unknown spiritual force had taken
possession of her soul. She resented the unfamiliar durance,
strove against it as a captive against his chain. She had been
mistress of herself till now, except for one brief intoxicating
moment months ago upon the moonlight sea; and it humbled
her to feel that her heart was growing stronger than her will.
She was angry with both her lovers. She spoke coldly to
Harry; to his rival she was brusque and repellent. But if
Alister had been able to lift the veil, he would have known
that she was already won.

The moonlight was still brilliant upon the moors, though
Eppie had been hours in bed. She woke suddenly from a
vaguely troubled dream to acute and vivid consciousness. She
had owned to herself as she lay down that Love was winning
the day, and yet she made the admission with reluctant bitterness,—O, the pity of it, the pity of it! Here was the young
laird at her feet, with all the broad acres of Yokieshill in his

hand as a bridal gift, and yet she could not take it. Why not? Was it possible that life without Alister could be such a forlorn business as she now pictured to herself it must be? The potent attraction which draws a girl to the one man in the world *for her* is not much believed in nowadays; but in the year One the Divine Right of Kings and Lovers was still acknowledged—at least by the vulgar in remote parts of the country. But when she woke of a sudden from her troubled dreams, all this reluctance had unaccountably vanished. The knot somehow had untied itself while she slept. She rose from her bed; for she felt instinctively that at such a moment the man she loved must be near at hand. We look on the faces of the sleeping and they awake; is there the same magnetic force in Love? Anyhow she saw, as she drew aside the curtain, a dark figure standing below her window,—his long shadow projected across the moor. She knew it was Alister, and, unseen, she stretched out her arms towards him. "Dearest, dearest," she murmured, with a passion of yearning that surprised herself; and then, blushing, ashamed, hardly believing as yet in the new bliss which had made her for the moment feeble and "foolish" as a love-sick girl, she let the curtain drop. But Alister had not witnessed the transfiguration of love; and as he turned away his heart was sore.

* * *

Uncle Ned was working next morning in the small and secluded apartment where he kept his birds,—now whistling softly, anon talking discursively to himself, a habit which he had acquired in his long solitary rambles.

"I dinna believe that ony boonds can be set to the sagacity o' beasts and birds,—especially birds. They have undoubtedly a quicker and finer sensebeelity than fowr-legged beasts,—which is not to be wondered at considerin' their daintier and mair delicate upbringin'. That storks will live only in republics is a proposition that is unsupported by credible testimony, and would not indeed increase ane's opinion o' the poleetical intelligence and discrimination of the bird. Yet I can well believe that resting on ae leg while haudin' up the ither, she keeps a chucky-stane in her claw, which droppin' when she is like to sleep, the noise waukens her. Nor is that auld story incredible which affirms that when the geese pass Mount Taurus they stap their pipes fu' o' gravel to avoid gaggling, and so by silence escape the eagles,—for it is jist clean impossible to circumvent a wild-guse."

Then, as the work proceeds rapidly under the deft fingers, his thoughts wander away to the great master of his imaginative life.

"The Doctor maintains whiles in his humorsome way that Shakespeare is but a *nominis umbra*, and that Nature hersel' fashioned the plays as she fashions the crystals and the shells. And indeed it is true in a sense. But there is mair than the inevitable instinct o' the silkworm in Lear and Hamlet and Macbeth. It seems to me whiles that ilk ane o' the great plays incarnates a master passion o' the sowl: love wi' its bitter sweetness in Juliet; and jealousy, which is cruel as the grave, in Othello; and anger and desire and madness and patriotism and ambition. But as I grow auld I have a queer fondness for *Measure for Measure*, which they say he wrote when a lad—tho' I canna believe it; for it traverses a' the problems o' life and death, justice and injustice, order and anarchy, the strict operation o' law and the finer compensations o' equity; and contains the latest judgments of that maister mind on ilka chance o' the game in this vast tennis-court, where men and women are the ba's."

"So Uncle Ned is at his auld tricks again?" quoth the cheery voice of the Doctor at the door. "Shakespeare and the musical glasses, as the Vicar says?"

"Sit down, Doctor, sit down. I'm in that humour that if I canna speak to you or Alister, I maun speak to mysel'. And sae our musical freen' Mr Skinner means to leave Linshart, —troth, I'm grieved to hear it. Mony a nicht, wadin' after wild deucks across the Rora mosses, the licht o' that kindly beacon has warmed my heart. There is naething mair lonesome than these lang watches beneath the stars,—when we feel that we are being carried swiftly thro' boundless space,

when oor bit warld seems but an insecure and narrow perch.
If we lose oor hold, Doctor, hoo far do we fa'? But that's
mair than a' the doctors can tell. We see aboot us for a bit,
and then, as Hamlet says, the rest is silence. If you'll move
the Tammy Nory to ae side you'll find that a safter seat,
Doctor."

"And that's a Tammy Nory," the Doctor replied, lifting the
bird and seating himself in its place; "and perhaps you could
tell me, Uncle Ned, what's the difference between a Tammy
Nory and a John Dory."

"Noo, Doctor, I'm no prepared at present to enter on a
metapheesical discussion. But I wanted to speak a word to
you about Alister. The Commodore says that he does his
wark verra weel; but it's clear to me that the lad has tined
heart a'thegither."

"Alister is bewitched, Uncle Ned, clean bewitched; and
the little French monkey at Fontainbleau has done the mischief. What sweet oblivious antidote can physic love?—give
him a dose of it and the boy will mend. I saw the witch at
Achnagatt last night: she has got a great big blustering horse-
fly in her web, and she means to—to—eat him. What fools
the women are, to be sure—and the men too! Yet it seems
to pay: *Fortuna favit fatuis.*"

"Ay, Doctor, the Deil's aye guid to his ain. But I can
mak' naething o' Eppie noo. Speak to her and she jist sits
and looks at you wi' her black gipsy eyes, wi'oot answerin' a
word. A maiden has nae tongue but thought. True; yet
there's something uncanny and bye-ordinar' in Eppie's silence."

"Hang it, man, dinna fash her. It's you and Miss Sherry
will drive her across the dyke. She's no the first witch I've
kent,—they were in covies at Paris in the year saxty-five. Wha
can tell what thochts pass thro' these inscrutable creatures,—
specially at eighteen or thereby? The Dean declares that
women's prayers are things perfectly by rote, as they pit on
one stocking after anither! Nae doobt they sattle doon after
a bit; but they need a light hand at startin'. But here's
Willie Macdonald wi' the papers,—let's hear what the *Journal*
says."

A battle might be lost, or a crown cast away like a bauble, without Uncle Ned being a bit the wiser. He took little or no interest in the politics of the grosser world : whereas the fact that the puffins arrived each year at the Scrath Rock on the thirtieth of April was really momentous. But the Doctor was a keen politician.

Any reader who cares to consult a file of the *Journal* for the year One may do so at his leisure. He may possibly light upon the very number which Dr Caldcail unfolded in Adam Meldrum's inner chamber on that October morning. The career of Galloping Dick the highwayman, he will observe, has been brought to a close on the Aylesbury scaffold. Marengo has been fought, and Seringapatam taken, and Tippoo Saib killed. Possibly the most vivid reminiscence that these names will conjure up to him is old Mrs Baird's pious ejaculation when she heard that Tippoo had chained her son to a brother officer,—" Lord pity the chiel that's chained to oor Davie ! " But from the columns devoted to the latest London news (ten days old) he will learn that smuggling is alarmingly on the increase, and that the laws for its suppression are to be vigorously enforced.

* *
*

The Achnagatt "clyack" was held on the Wednesday ; the Crookit Meg was timed to reach Hell's Lum on the Monday night. So much for the days of the week : I must refer you to the columns of the *Journal* if you are anxious to identify the days of the month.

Eppie was curiously restless during these intervening days. She sat talking dreamily to her mother, who was ill in bed, or wandered aimlessly about the farm and among the rocks. But no one came near her. There was the occasional white sail of a passing ship at sea. A flock of golden plover wheeled over the house : the melancholy wail of the curlew was heard from the distant mosses. The men were at work in some outlying fields. Mennie, her mother's old servant, flitted uneasily about her pale mistress, who seemed to her experienced

eye to be growing thinner and frailer each successive day,—
wasting away with the wasting year. And the weather was as
still as the house; the noisy equinoctial gales had exhausted
their passion, and the days were soft and moist and warm,
though the sun was invisible through the dull steamy haze
that rested on land and sea. It was that ghost of the Indian
summer which visits Scotland in October.

At last Eppie could bear it no longer. She got Watty to
saddle Bess, and she started by herself for a canter across the
moors. The swift motion brought the blood into her cheeks.
The little mare galloped gamely, and for an hour her mistress
did not tighten the reins. Then of a sudden the pony came
to a dead stop,—she had cast a shoe. It was well on in the
Thursday afternoon.

Fortunately the mischance had occurred on the Saddle-hill
within a few hundred yards of the Alehouse Tavern. There
is, or was, a smithy on the other side of the road. Eppie
dismounted and led the mare to the smithy, which was growing effulgent as the darkness gathered. Rob Ranter, the
smith, was absent; but a little imp, who had been blowing
the bellows to keep his hand in, undertook to fasten the shoe
which Eppie had picked up when she dismounted. The
people of that district have a curious liking for diminutives,
and this little imp of the forge was familiarly and affectionately
known as "the Deevilikie." Meantime Eppie, gathering up
her skirt, sauntered across the road.

On the bench in front of the hostelry a familiar figure was
seated. It was our old acquaintance Corbie, — the honest
"liar." A pewter measure of spirits stood on the table before
him: it was obvious that he had been drinking hard. Eppie
eyed him curiously and coldly as he greeted her with drunken
gravity.

"Ay, ay, my bonnie young leddie,—a sicht o' a sonsy lass
like you is guid for sair een. What wud you be pleased to
tak'? Lucky will be here presently. Come awa', Lucky, and
attend to the young leddie. And so as I was sayin' when
interrupit by your lordship," he continued, and a wicked
gleam came into the drunken eyes—"I gaed doun to Yokies-

hill to see Joe Hacket—na, na; I'm wrang—Joe was the
auld laird, and the auld laird's dead and damned.   Preserve
us a', that's actionable, and *veritas convicii non excusat* as they
say in the Coorts.   Or as the Doctor pits it verra pleasantly,
letters of cursing, says he, being the exclusive privelege o' the
Kirk.   Weel, you maun understan', as the morning was fine
for the time o' year, I had the mear oot early and rode aff to
veesit a client or twa.   And first I gaed to Mains o' Rora, for
the new millart has a gude-gangin' plea regardin' the sma'
sequels o' the outsucken multures,—bannock, knaveship, lock-
and-gowpen, and siclike.   And Rora himsel'—the doited body
—winna lat the tacksmen at Clola cut their peats in his moss,
for he manteens, you see, that the clause *cum petariis et tur-
bariis* is no in the charter.—Anither gill, Lucky, anither gill.
—But that, my dear, is a contestation that is not regarded wi'
favour by the Coort, for the servitude o' feal and divot may be
constituted by custom, in like manner as the clause *cum fab-
rilibus* (whereof our gude freen' Rob Ranter is an ensample)
has fa'en into disuse.   But these are kittle questions o' heritable richt, which maun be decided by the Lords o' Coonsel
and Session,—the market-cross o' Edinbro' and the pier and
shore o' Leith being *communis patria*.   And sae, my Lord,"
—as he became tipsier he turned more frequently to the
Court, which he fancied he was addressing—"being arrived
at Yokieshill, as aforesaid, I tauld Mr Hairy Hacket that it
wud be convenient if he wud sattle the sma' accoont for business undertaken by me on the instructions o' his late feyther.
You maun understan', my Lord, that the accoont was maist
rediculously sma'—nae aboon twa hundred poonds or thereby.
Weel, he glowered at me like a hell-cat, and swore that not
one doyt or bodle or plack o' his should gae into the pocket
o' a drucken scoon'rel;—drucken scoon'rel, my Lord, these
were the verra words, for I made a note o' them at the time,
and I wull tak' the oath *de calumnia* if your Lordship pleases.
'Mr Hairy Hacket,' says I, 'ye'll pay my taxed bill o' expenses
by Mononday mornin', or by the Lord! I'll see you oot o'
Yokieshill.'   At this he jist gaed fairly gyte.   Says he, comin'
up to me pale as death, and catchin' me by the back o' the

neck, 'Oot you go in the first place, you leein' scamp,'—
'leein' scamp,' my Lord; and whan he gat me ootside the
door, he whistled to an ugly savage tyke that was lyin' in the
sun. 'Nell,' says he to the bitch quite coolly, takin' oot his
watch, 'if this infernal swindlin' scoon'rel is not ootside the
yard afore I count ten, gie him a taste o' your teeth.' Mercy
on us, the beast looked up in his face wi' a low snarl.—What's
come o' the mutchkin, Lucky?—Ay, ay, Mr Hairy Hacket,—
infernal swindler—leein' scamp—drucken scoon'rel,—verra
gude,—a conjoined action for defamation and assault,—
damages laid at twa thoosan' poonds,—not a penny less.—
Is't you indeed, Miss Eppie? Dear me, so you've come a'
this gait to see the Lords o' Session and Justiciar'.—Come
awa' ben, my dear, come awa' ben,—auld Joe Hacket is in
the dock for bigamy, and I'm ceeted to speak—ceeted as a
wutness,—if I'm no ower fou," he added with a dazed look.
"Yes, my Lord, I was present,—John Hacket, bachelor, and
Elspet Cheyne, spinster—for life and for death, for better and
for waur. But whar's the lines?" Here he pulled some
papers out of his pocket and flung them loose upon the table.
"They were ill-matcht, my Lord, ill-matcht. She couldna
thole his black looks—I dinna wonner—and she ran aff wi' a
sodger within the year. It was noised at the time that the
ship gaed doon in mid-sea. But auld Mrs Cruickshanks tells
me—what did Lucky say?—it was the day the Jan Mayen
cam' hame—troth, my Lord, I feel that a taste o' speerits, if
the Coort wudna objec'——"

Here his head fell forward on the table, and in another
minute he was fast asleep.

Eppie had heard the first sentences of the lawyer's harangue
without the least show of interest. She saw that the man was
tipsy, and she stared him straight in the face with her native
chilly indifference. She did not pity him, nor was she afraid
of him: let any man, tipsy or sober, dare to lay a hand upon
her! So she sat down at the other end of the bench without
uttering a word, and began switching the dust out of her habit
with her whip. But when "Yokieshill" caught her ear, she
turned and listened with closer attention. The legal and Latin

phrases were, of course, quite unintelligible to her; but she contrived to follow the main current of the rambling narrative. This drunken, disreputable lawyer had become master of a secret which made Harry Hacket—what? Her heart stood still with sudden fright. Who and what was the man with whom she had established such perilously close relations? Was he the laird of Yokieshill, or was he not? And the whole story was to be found in these papers that lay scattered about the table. She saw the imp bringing her pony out of the smithy, and she rose to go. Then, with a sudden impulse, turning her back upon the boy, she swept the scattered papers together and thrust them into her pocket. Corbie stirred and muttered in his sleep, but he did not waken. Then she mounted her steed and rode away.

Watty was waiting for her at the farm-door, and took the pony. Eppie ran up-stairs to her room. It was dark,—the half-veiled moon was rising from the sea like a nymph half-submerged, shaking the water from her dripping locks. She got a light, and then she pulled out the papers which she had —well—appropriated. Even to Eppie the significance of the story they told was clear as day. The first paper was a certificate showing that an irregular marriage had been celebrated at Inverurie on the 14th of May 1768 between John Hacket of Yokieshill and Elspeth Cheyne, spinster, lately residing with Joshua Cheyne in Clola. (Eppie knew that the late Mrs Hacket—Harry's mother—had been a Kilgour—Jean Kilgour of Logie.) Then there was a letter of somewhat later date with the Maryland post-mark, enclosing a draft in favour of Betsy Cheyne or Cruickshank. The last letter was written from some place in Maryland, and stated briefly that Elspeth Cheyne was dead. She had died about a week before the letter was written. The date and the signature were illegible; but Eppie found from the post-mark that it must have been posted during the year then current—the year One. That was all, but it was enough: it was clear that at the date of the Laird's second marriage his first wife was alive; Corbie had not exaggerated when he swore that he could turn Harry Hacket adrift. His father had left no disposition of his estate; and Yokieshill belonged not to Harry the bastard, but to the legal heir—whoever he might be.

* * *

The Provost and Bailies of Balmawhapple were met in solemn conclave. A special messenger from the south had arrived on horseback that morning—Friday morning—bringing an official letter addressed to the Provost. On the cover, in a bold masterful hand, the words "William Pitt" could be plainly read.

A crowd of excited sailors and fisher-folk were gathered round the door of the Council Chamber, for rumour as usual had been busy. The Jacobins were in possession of the Metropolis—the French fleet was in the offing—the Provost was to be knighted—a new battery was to be built on the Ronheads. It seemed, however, to be generally understood that Corbie was in possession of authentic intelligence; and his diplomatic disclaimers were treated with ill-concealed incredulity.

"Sir Roderick, indeed! A compliment to the burgh! Na, na, they're ower busy to send compliments sae far north. And the Provost's a decent and deservin' body, wha winna mak' a fule o' himsel' at his time o' life, tho' it's true, as they say, that there's nae fule like an auld fule. A new battery? It's not to be denied, Mrs Lyell, that the rickle o' auld stanes at the Ronhead is fa'in' to pieces; but whar's the siller to be fand? The Jacobites were bad eneuch, and the Jacobins are nae better, I grant you; but if we're to be eaten oot o' hoose and lan' wi' these murderin' taxes, there'll soon be little love for King George left in the country-side. Pawt-triotism, my freen's?—it's not possible to be a pawtriot wi' Glendronoch at twenty shillings a gallon. And as to the French man-o'-war aff Collieston——"

Here the Provost appeared on the steps of the Town Hall, and beckoned to the lawyer. Corbie obeyed the summons with alacrity.

"Look here, Corbie," said the Provost, when they were

out of earshot of the crowd, "this is no a matter for argument, nor yet for a joke. I have never mysel' had dealings with the free-traders; and tho' it is said that there are folk in the toun wha dinna objec' to traffic wi' them—our freen's in the Council bein' agreeable to wink when needfu'—I'm willing that byganes should be byganes. But, Corbie, my man, there maun be an end o' the trade noo. They have heard in Lunnon that a' that trash o' French treason comes across the water on boord the luggers; and the Commodore has been warned that he'll lose his place if anither cargo is landed this side o' Newburgh. A troop o' sodgers will be here next week, and ilka yard o' the coast will be watched day and nicht. Noo, Corbie, ye ken verra weel what you're aboot, and if you should hear by chance that ony o' your acquaintance hae a taste for Hollands and French brandy, you might advise them privately to stick to the native speerit, as being, in the meantime at least, *safer* for the stamack. Dinna say a word, my man—least said, soonest mended—I'm awa' to get the Doctor to compose a bit note to Mr Pitt, for neither Bailie nor Provost, I reckon, has the pen of a ready writer."

Corbie was sharp enough when sober (he had slept off yesterday's debauch), and he saw the drift of the Provost's speech quite plainly. The Provost, he knew, was, till roused, the soul of good nature and good fellowship; and the mere fact of his delivering this elaborate address proved that he was roused now. It was clear that the authorities had re-solved, willingly or unwillingly, to set their faces against the trade; and that any one who was interested in it—and who was not?—had better look to himself with all convenient speed.

But Corbie was puzzled how to act. After his experience of yesterday he would have no more dealings with Mr Harry Hacket except in a court of law—Harry might go hang for him; and besides, it was awkward that the documents on which he mainly relied should have unaccountably gone astray. He knew for certain that the Crookit Meg was daily expected: he knew that the cargo was of altogether excep-

tional value. What was to be done? The increase in the
strength of the coastguard was not to take place for some
days: could the landing be effected before the new-comers
arrived? It had been whispered about that the cargo was to
be run on the Monday night; but if the Crookit Meg was
communicated with in time, it might be possible to get everything made snug before the close of the week then current
—which would be a deal better. And if it came to the worst,
there were the twelve hours after sunset on Sunday; and in
the year One—in a district, moreover, where an easy-going
Episcopacy had survived—Sabbatarianism was not rampant,
least of all among the free-traders and the fisher-folk.

During the course of the afternoon Corbie had a word or
two in his office with Peter Buchan—"Young Peter" as he
was called, to distinguish him from his father "Auld Peter."
Peter had returned from the Greenland seas on board the
Jan Mayen a week or two before (being, indeed, the smart
young fellow who had greeted Harry Hacket on the pier at
Port Henry); and he was now engaged in his usual winter
pursuit—cod-fishing off the Gutter Bank.

It was not quite dusk when one of the large yawls used in
the deep-sea fishing left the south harbour for the Gutter
Bank. Peter Buchan was at the helm. "It's a mighty fine
night for the big cod," he remarked casually, as they stole
past the pier-head, where a private of the coastguard was
seated, whistling drowsily as he polished his pistols.

* *
*

The fishing hamlet of Port Erroll is built along the ledges
of the North Haven cliffs; while the fishing-boats are drawn
up out of reach of the breakers on the bleached sands of the
cove. Seen from a distance—from a distance, remember—
these whitewashed, red-tiled cottages present an appearance of
most picturesque confusion. A quaint gable end with a most
preposterous little window peeps round the corner: one old-
fashioned mansion has mounted bodily on the back of its
neighbour: were a single wall in the lower tier to give way,

the whole community would incontinently topple into the sea.
Slippery steps compounded of mud and water and the remains
of slaughtered fish connect the various storeys of this perpendicular hamlet, and lead ultimately, after a series of successful
manœuvres, to the beach on the one hand and the upper
world on the other. Nets and great black pots and dried
fish and the wings of sea-fowl are suspended along the walls;
and ducks, and gulls who have been made captive in their
youth, and a large scrath with a look of insatiate gluttony
stamped on its ugly face, explore the recesses of an ample
ash-pit, which has not been emptied within the memory of the
oldest inhabitant. An ill-favoured and ill-conditioned sow
waddles greedily from one tempting abomination to another,
and disputes with lean and weather-beaten curs the savoury
nuisances of the dung-heap. Amid the dirt, innumerable little
bundles of rags and tatters—the progeny of the fertile sea—
wallow with unspeakable zest, and as we discover in these
parcels of filth the bright eye and the roguish smile, we are
more than ever impressed by the unquenchable *élan* of boyhood. Nowadays such a community would be held to offend
grievously against all the conditions on which health depends;
but in the year One sanitary science was in its infancy, and
these worthy people—those of them, at least, who escaped
the perils of the sea—never thought of dying, except of old
age.

The sun has set: lights begin to twinkle among the cottages. It is the Sabbath night, and the inmates are sitting
lazily at the doors of their dwellings. Then a bell is rung,
and the women rise and walk leisurely towards the chapel on
the rock—a building as grey and weather-stained as the rock
itself. Some of the men follow. The evening service has
begun, and forthwith the music of the great sea-psalm echoes
across the bay :—

" The floods, O Lord, have lifted up,
    They lifted up their voice ;
    The floods have lifted up their waves,
    And made a mighty noise.

But yet the Lord that is on high
  Is more of might by far,
Than noise of many waters is
  Or great sea billows are."

Presently the rough voice of the Missionary in urgent intercession with a jealous God is heard through the open door,—
though the words of the prayer cannot be distinguished.   But
were we to enter we could guess that the congregation are
preoccupied and inattentive,— even the preacher becoming
ultimately aware that the thoughts of his hearers are wool-
gathering.   So the service is brought to an abrupt conclusion,
and the congregation stream out into the twilight.   All eyes
are turned at once and instinctively towards the sea.   Yes—
a blue light is burning on the water, a couple of miles from the
land.   One or two of the men disappear from the crowd, and
scramble away to a ledge where a heap of brushwood has been
collected; a piece of tinder is ignited with the old-fashioned
"flint and fleerish," and presently the brushwood is in a
blaze.   These are signals—signals between the sea and the
shore.   If you were versed in the language of the craft, you
would understand that the blue light from the Crookit Meg
was a note of interrogation—"Is the coast clear?" and that
the red blaze from North Haven was the answer—"It is all
safe at Hell's Lum."
    Then the women and children go indoors, and in parties of
twos and threes the men ascend the steep footpath leading to
the mainland, and turn their faces to the south.

V.

I CANNOT tell exactly what passed through Eppie's soul
during the two days that followed her interview with Corbie
on the Saddle Hill.   Her mind was in a whirl.   The unfamiliar restlessness which had taken possession of her increased more and more.   She was as unquiet as the flock
of plover which continued to wheel round the farmhouse—

haunting and hurting her with the burden of their plaintive lament. Her chilly serenity had deserted her,—she was anxious, nervous, excited. A medical man who had felt her pulse then for the first time would have fancied that there was fever in her blood. Ambition had twisted its fibres round her heart; and she had seen her way at last to the high place which she coveted. She had, in a fashion, persuaded herself that she was in love with the Prince,—this bluff Prince Hal, who had ascended the vacant throne, and who kept a seat for her by his side. And it was true that she had thawed to him; he had been considerate in his rough way: the world, she began to feel, had treated him hardly— had, it might be, even harder treatment in store for him. And, had her heart only been free to consent, there was a certain innate largeness in Eppie's nature, almost or indeed more than masculine in its supercilious magnanimity and indifference to public opinion, which would have kept her obstinately loyal to one born under an adverse and evil star. Yet it was, in truth, a very different force—a far more potent attraction—that had shattered at last the crust of her self-regard. The beginnings of life are full of mystery : so are the beginnings of love. Why Eppie's heart should have selected this precise moment to assert its rights will probably never be known : Eppie herself did not, I believe, know any more about it than the rest of us. But the fact remains : it was the secret sweetness of the hopes and memories with which the thought of Alister suddenly and unaccountably suffused her soul that had softened her,— softened the keen hard eyes, and made the world which she saw through the mist of unfamiliar tears a world of unfamiliar tenderness. Ah! my poor Eppie, why did you not waken a little earlier ? Is it possible that you can yet free yourself from the net which your own selfish pride has woven ? can yet escape from the entanglements, the mean and base entanglements, in which you are caged? Or is it too late for redress ?

Alas! the punishment of sin by some mysterious law is often delayed until the sin has been put away from us, and traitors to love are tried and convicted when their treason is dead and buried.

There is a piercing wail of delicious pain which we sometimes hear in music, as when the Mermaid's Song in *Oberon* is sung low and softly at twilight. Such a passion of longing and sadness and exquisite abandonment took possession of Eppie's soul. It startled her, but it soothed her. She was mesmerised by the sweet subtle persuasive desire that had nestled itself like a bird-Cupid in her heart.

She scarcely slept during these nights. She heard the murmur of the sea,—not the loud beat of noisy waves on pebbly beaches (for the high cliffs divide us from the strife at their feet), but the still small voice of the mighty tides which circle majestically round the world. Her window was open,— she was as hardy as the plovers whose shrill challenge when a whitret or a fox came prowling past disturbed the mystery of the silence and the darkness. At times she heard Mennie stirring about her mother, and she rose in her bed and listened softly. A thrill of tenderness for the pale, silent, suffering woman in the room below touched her as it had not touched her before. The pitifulness of the doom which had thrust this strong masterful will aside made her heart ache. Could it be that Fate was to bear her, was even now bearing her, yet farther away from the little kingdom whose policy for many a year she had guided and inspired? Death is sad enough; but the few dreary days during which the sceptre of high command is falling from the listless emaciated fingers are even sadder.

So that when the Sunday evening came and Alister arrived, Eppie's whole soul was swelling on the unfamiliar tide of tenderness. Tears came into her eyes on the slightest provocation. She had begun to understand that divine necessity of life which joins its joy and its sorrow together in mystic inseparable union. We must needs reach the heights of joy before we perceive that they dip for ever into an abyss of sadness. Eppie had reached this height. If Alister speaks out to-night, her casual glimpse into the deep places of the soul may become an habitual mood. And Alister means to speak out.

But the stars in their courses fought against Sisera.

* * *

I do not believe that in all their after-lives that soft October evening, when the mellow autumn twilight melted into moonlight, was forgotten by Alister and Eppie. Eppie had at length abandoned herself to the stream which was bearing her gently to the Happy Islands; Alister was infected by her dreamy bliss. They wandered among the rocks where they had wandered as children; they crossed in mere wantonness the *mauvais pas* at the Bloody Hole; they laughed gleefully when their old friend the peregrine rose screaming and scolding from his rock. The Scrath Pillar was black with cormorants, who were balancing themselves in all sorts of grotesque attitudes on impossible pinnacles; they laughed again at the uncouth gambols of the solemn and funereal birds. Then they went into the house, where supper had been prepared for them by Mennie. Eppie ran up to her mother's room, and returned radiant. Mrs Holdfast was a shade better, and would see Alister. So Alister was taken into the sick-room, and the sick woman smiled into his face, and pressed his hand with an air of soft entreaty. Was she resigning to the lover the mother's jealous rights in her wilful pet? In these last hours the soul, "beginning to be freed from the ligaments of the body," rises into a finer air, and sees right and wrong, the true and the false, the noble and the ignoble, as they are seen by the eyes of immortality. But neither Eppie nor Alister knew that when the wan woman laid her trembling hands upon his hand it was a farewell blessing she meant to convey to him. Then they returned into the little parlour which opened into Eppie's sitting-room, where they found the simple fare of the farmhouse—oat-cakes, fresh butter, fragrant honey, creamy milk (do not scorn it,—on such fare the Ossianic heroes were bred)—arranged for them on a heavy oaken buffet, elaborately carved in fruit and flowers, which Marie Touchet may have brought with her from Fontainebleau.

Alister had been commissioned by Uncle Ned (who was confined to the house by a feverish attack) to implement a promise which he had long ago made to Eppie. The *Saints' Rest*, the family Bible (in which Eppie's was the latest entry among the births), and one or two manuals of Calvinistic divinity lay on the window-sole of the parlour; but there was no *Shakespeare* in the limited library of the farmhouse. The whole of that wonderful fable-land (except for Uncle Ned's reminiscences) was a *terra incognita* to Eppie, who indeed, from her childhood, like the old lords of the district, had loved better to hear the lark sing than the mouse squeak. This day Alister had brought one of the prized volumes in his pocket, and when the meal was finished Eppie insisted that he should read her "a bit of a play." Their conversation had begun to flag; the girl had grown shy and conscious— adorably shy and conscious; the open book was a barrier behind which she instinctively retreated. She pushed the volume across the table, and sat looking at him as he turned the leaves, with her hands in her lap. The volume had opened at *Romeo and Juliet*. Juliet?—ay, here was a braver Juliet, and as he ran rapidly over the earlier incidents of the tragic story, which is bitter with the bitterness of things too sweet, his thoughts wandered away from fair Verona to return to the Fontainbleau farmhouse. Romeo's boyish rapture, indeed, could poorly compare with his steadier and manlier love; but Juliet's novel abandonment of passion suited Eppie's mood. Here at last, set in articulate speech, was that ideal world of which she had been dreaming—dreaming since she awoke. She sat looking at him, her lips apart, her hands pressed together, as if fascinated. Had he spoken at that moment, all might have been well. But when he came to

> "It was the lark, the herald of the morn,
>   No nightingale——"

Eppie started up: "Stay, Alister, stay, I hear mither movin'," she exclaimed in a voice that sounded tense and excited, as she darted out of the room.

Alister's heart was full. Love had told him that Eppie was altered. Her voice was softer—her mood more playful and yet more tender. There was an unfamiliar moisture of happiness in her eyes. Alister was a simple lad ; but love quickens the apprehension. He felt that the spring-time had come at last.

He waited for her to return. He would take her in his arms, and whisper the story of a devotion of which after all Romeo's wayward vehemence was but a dim reflection.

> " See, how she leans her head upon her hand !
> O that I were a glove upon that hand,
> That I might touch that cheek ! "

No—no,—the direct energy of his passion would employ no such tortuous diplomacy. And Eppie,—this new Eppie, so changed from the Eppie who had listened with chilly acquiescence——

At this moment he heard a low whistle outside—(the window was open)—" Hist—Hist—Miss Eppie—Miss Eppie ! "—and then a scrap of paper wrapped round a pebble fell upon the floor at his feet. He sprang to the window through which it had been flung ; but though the moonlight was clear as day on the moors, this side of the house was in deep shade, and he saw no one.

Then he picked up the scrap of paper which had become detached by the fall. He looked at it involuntarily ; involuntarily his eyes followed the words. There were only a couple of hastily scrawled lines ; but he staggered as if struck by a blow. " Darling Eppie," it said, " Eppie darling, dinna let the gauger leave—by hook or by crook keep him from Hell's Lum." And it was initialed " H. H."

I need make no mystery about this fateful scroll. Harry Hacket on his way to the Cove had learned at the Alehouse Tavern that Alister (whose movements had been anxiously watched) was still at Fontainbleau ; and he had immediately despatched " the Deevilikie " with the lines which he had hurriedly scrawled at the bar. " The Deevilikie," with the perverse ingenuity of his connection, had cleverly conveyed it to the wrong hand.

* * *

"I swear by the God who made me that it is false!"
Eppie exclaimed passionately, as with a bitterness of pain
past all words she clung to her lover,—seeking with one last
frantic despairing effort to detain him.   Treachery was ab-
horrent to every instinct of the better nature which love was
fashioning, and this was treachery of which she was accused,
—mean and base and senseless treachery to the man she
loved.

But Alister would not relent—would not indeed listen;
the simple honest heart had grown implacable in a moment.
Had he known women better he would have known that this
mad passion of despair was genuine,—that no actress could
have thrown all that heartbreak into spoken words,—that
only an agony of love and longing could have forced this icy
maiden to cling to him as she did.

But he did not believe her—her treason was too patent,—
even thus with her arms about him she was only obeying the
mandate of his rival.

Then the clock struck ten : the rosy hours as they read
together had slipped away unnoted.

"Ten o'clock, by God, and the men at Collieston."

It was the first time that any one had heard Alister take
that high name in vain : but he was not himself.

Then without another word he tore himself from the
clinging arms, and went out swiftly into the moonlight.

There might yet be time.

The image of Love had been irreparably fractured; but
the failure of duty might be repaired.

Eppie stood where he had left her,—dreary, hopeless,
heartbroken.   Then she cast herself in hard tearless silence
upon her bed, where she lay for hours without moving,—her
face turned to the wall.   When, in the first light of the chilly
dawn, she rose up pale and silent, with black circles round
the coal-black eyes, the bloom of young desire, the purple
light of love, had passed out of her face.

* * *

Uncle Ned had that evening been as restless as Eppie. He was feverish and unsettled. His books, even his birds, had failed to interest him. He was continually going to the open door,—voices were sounding in his ears that seemed to come from the sea. When it was close upon midnight he looked out again. The moon was high in heaven,—night was as clear as day. For many years he had tramped about the country by moonlight. To most of us Nature is only known in her waking moods;—we are asleep during those ineffable moments when she is dreaming, when the shy birds are fishing in the river mouth, when the owl and the fox and the dormice are alert, with listening ears. But the night side of her life was as well known to Uncle Ned as the other. The short summer nights were over for the year, and the old man had felt with a pang that, in the meantime at least, he would go no more a-gipsying. But the splendour of the moonlight tempted him until he could resist no longer. There was a bank of whins above the Water of Slains from whence he had often watched the water-birds all night. Yes, the air was soft and warm, he could take no harm. And if he should? How could a lover die better than in the lap of his mistress? "Diana's foresters, gentlemen of the shade, minions of the moon," he said, with a soft laugh. Then he went into the inner sanctum, to take a farewell look at the birds. There was a small family of kittiwakes—downy little morsels—which he had still in hand. The group was not quite to his mind, so he sat down and deftly touched them here and there. Then he rose, and locking the outer door, took the road to the Ward, walking rather unsteadily at times. His feet did not seem to move as freely as they once did, he confessed, rather sadly.

I know that whin-bank myself—once, long ago (when on a summer fishing ramble), I slept among the furze. Then I saw something by snatches of the life that Uncle Ned knew by heart. It is a memorable experience in its way. The unquiet and unrest of the daytime are gradually subdued as the evening descends. Anon the hoarse cry of the heron, the shrill plaint of the plover, or the wild cry of some belated sea-bird, break at long intervals the quiet murmur that comes seaward across the sandhills.   Then there is an hour or so of perfect stillness in the deep of the dead night, which lasts until the grey light begins slowly to gather along the sullen sky.   When we are able to look abroad the world is motionless and inanimate, and a heavy cloud of mildew hangs over the river.   The blackfaced sheep had begun to bleat when it was still dark, and now the voices of countless water-birds, who have been waiting for the retreat of the tide, answer each other mournfully through the damp air of the early morning.

"The air bites shrewdly," said Uncle Ned, by this time settled comfortably in a furze-bush.   "It maun be nigh the dawnin'.   What a congregation o' lang-necked herons—a perfect Presbytery!   I wonner to what religious persuasion they belang?   Maybe they howld wi' John Calvin—I suldna be surprised.   This brae is fairly alive wi' bunnies.   Dinna mind me, my furry friend; nibble awa' wi'oot stanin' on ceremony. The verra witchin' time o' night!   Surely Shakespeare is wrang when he mak's it of evil repute—there's far less evil afoot by night than by day.   But he pits the words nae doobt into the mouth of some sinful man, devoured by greed and ambition.   The noon of night—the innocent, angel-haunted hour—when even the inaudible and noiseless foot o' time may be heard by the listening ear.   See what a fair procession o' spiritual forces are on the move, passing across the face of heaven, like the Northern Dancers.   And there's the first streak o' licht in the east—the grey-eyed morn will be moving presently.   A heavenly birth!   Dayrise—that is the hour before the sun himsel' is up—to my thinking, is just perfectly divine.   The dew of thy birth is of the womb of the morning.   Truly thae auld Hebrew poets had a wonnerfu' knack of saying preceesly the richt thing at the richt time."

But it was soon clear to Uncle Ned that more than the birds were stirring.   In fact their clamour—quacking of wild ducks, shrill piping of sandpipers, screaming of sea-mews— proved that they had been disturbed by man.   And in the bright moonlight he discovered across the river a column of men moving down to the ford. The moonlight gleamed upon steel—the men had cutlasses in their hands. It was the coast-guard.

The incoming tide fills all the low ground which lies between the sandhills. When Uncle Ned arrived, the wide level space was flooded. A bright unquiet plain of waters quivered beneath his feet. But the tide even then was ebbing —running back like a mill-race; and now only a shallow streamlet flowed lazily through the centre of a wide sandy plain.

There was a little delay at the ford; but the men were quickly across. The path from the ford, passing below "Charlie's Pot" (a noted pool for sea-trout), leads almost directly to the bank where Uncle Ned was established. Here it joins the road which runs up-stream to Ardallie; down-stream across the sandhills to the fishing hamlets at Hell's Lum.

The night was so still that the hoarse cheery voice of Captain Knock was recognisable by Uncle Ned. "Well, you see, Alister, when I had skewered the first Johnny Craw-paw, I turned upon the ither twa. The ane was a complete Goliath o' Gath in the uniform o' the auld Guard. He cam' at me like a mad bull o' Bashan; but I caught him aneath his oxter, and he gaed down like a shot—dead as Julius Cæsar. The last o' the three—a little black pock-marked chiel, wi' a lang mustache—turned to rin, but I had him on the grun' before he could say Jock Wabster. I was a first-rate rinner, Alister, in those days—I had ta'en a' the prizes that simmer at the Strathbogie meetin'; so when the general —Marlboro', ye ken—comes up, 'Captain Knock,' says he——"

"I think, sir," said Alister, "that this is the place we spoke of; it commands baith the road and the foord."

"The verra spot—so get the men under cover, and a mouthfu' o' speerits," added the gallant Captain, diving into his pocket for his flask, "will keep the mildew oot o' the stamack." The men were lying down among the whins and heather, when Uncle Ned, looking towards the sea, saw the advance-guard of the free-traders appear over the sandhills. The richest cargo that the Crookit Meg had yet run was at hand. Slung in panniers on the backs of some thirty or forty hill-ponies, and guarded by the crew, accompanied by fisher-men and farm-labourers, silks from Lyons, gin from Holland, lace from Brussels (and one golden cross set in pearls from Antwerp), were being conveyed to the interior. At the head of the band came the "Skipper"—a noted smuggler of the day. Harry Hacket rode beside the leader; on his other hand a youngster, with a look of premature daredevilry in his face, but bearing a striking resemblance to Eppie, was laughing merrily—like a boy; and indeed Dick Holdfast (the spoilt urchin had been the merest youngster when he ran away to sea, leaving Eppie to monopolise all the tenderness of the mother's heart in that late autumn of her love) was even yet barely more than a boy.

The moonlight was still brilliant, though morning was at hand. The free-traders moved quickly; but at the ford there was a moment's pause. It had been arranged that one half of the party should keep to the river-road leading to the bog of Ardallie, whence the merchandise could be distributed at leisure; the other half crossing at the ford and making for the old tower of Udny—near which the great south road passed. Of this pause the coastguard took advantage. The men sprang to their feet, barred the way, and Captain Knock, who in spite of his brag was as brave as a lion, advanced upon the leaders. Alister was by his side.

"Hulloo, my freen's, have the goodness to stop for one minute. Now, Mr Skipper, what may be the meaning of this moonlicht flittin'?"

"Come, come, Captain," said a deep rough voice in reply. "Don't try any of your tricks upon us. We are good sub-jects of King George, and have no will to meddle with you. So please stand out of the way." The speaker was an Englishman.

The free-traders were taken by surprise. They had heard that the coastguard were at Collieston, and they fancied that the road was clear to the hills. But the cargo was worth fighting for ; and, if it came to the worst, they meant to fight. The crew of the lugger were heavily armed.

"Hang it, Skipper," said young Dick, throwing his plaid aside and drawing a pistol from his belt, as he pushed forward, "the sooner we get this business through the better." He was followed by the crew.

There was a confused tumult in the moonlight. Uncle Ned from his perch saw the flash of steel, saw more than one man fall, heard a pistol-shot or two, heard Dick's cheery voice and the Commodore's deep growl. It was clear from the first, indeed, that the fight was one-sided. The crew were outnumbered ; the fishermen and the farm-labourers had disappeared before a shot was fired, taking the ponies with them ; but the sailors' blood was up, and they knew besides that the venture in which each had an interest would be a dead loss unless they stood their ground. So many oaths were uttered, and some deep gashes given, before they yielded. Yet it was all over in a quarter of an hour or less, and Dick, with an ugly cut in his face, when he saw that there was no more fight in the men, managed to reach the close cover of the furze, and crawl cat-like along the bank. The rest surrendered.

Harry Hacket would have gladly escaped at the outset had it been possible. But he could not help himself; the crew were behind him, the revenue officers in front. He inwardly cursed his luck : this was the worst scrape of his life ; and in truth the whizz of bullets and the flash of steel made his blood run cold. He was a coward at heart ; the mere presence of danger—of death—unnerved and unmanned him. But the rage of despair sometimes takes the semblance of manhood. One of the coastguard had singled out the horseman (his features obscured by his broad felt hat), and rushed at him with cutlass drawn. Harry's heart beat as if it would burst ; but forced to face the instant peril, he drove his spurs deep into the mare's sides, and sent her at his assailant. He had only a heavy hunting-whip in his hand ; but he flung it in the man's face as he raised the cutlass, and it blinded him for the moment. Before he could recover himself, Hacket had seized the weapon. There was now only a single man

between him and the open. It was Alister. By this time
the taste of blood was in his mouth; the wild beast was
roused; he could have charged a battery without winking.
Alister was his rival; Alister was his foe. With a bitter
imprecation, raising the cutlass above his head, and digging
the spurs once more into the terrified animal—mad with
fright—he rushed at Alister. Down came the heavy clumsy
weapon; but Alister was unhurt. For just as the mare was
plunging forward, an old man had risen up out of the thick
whins, close in front of the young coastguardsman——

"Oh, bairns, bairns!" said Uncle Ned, lifting his hands.

To save his own life Hacket could not have diverted the
blow. The heavy weapon came down upon the old man's
head with murderous force. Hacket reeled in his saddle, the
horror of the deed had sobered him. He gave a wild startled
glance at Alister, into whose arms Uncle Ned had fallen, and
then, seeing that the coast was clear, set the mare at the low
fence, and disappeared among the sandhills.

"'The laird himsel'," muttered Alister, as he laid the old
man on the grass and knelt tenderly beside him. "God be
thanked," he continued, as he bound his handkerchief across
the wound, "it's just gashed his cheek. So, Mr Harry
Hacket, this is your doing—a braw nicht's wark, a braw
nicht's wark."

* * *

But Dick Holdfast's troubles that morning were not yet
over.

When he had crawled for half an hour through the furze,
he descended into the deep cleft cut by the burn of Forvie,
before it joins the greater stream. Then for the first time he
ventured to rise to his feet. Thereafter his path lay up the
course of the burn, until at a sharp angle, about a mile farther
on, he was able to plunge at one step into the shelter of the
sandhills. These sandhills are the dominant feature of this
arid land. The vegetation is salt and bitter; the prickly bent
wounds the hand; there are no living creatures to be seen
except the conies, or to be heard except the curlew; even

the hardy blackfaced sheep, when it loses itself in this Dead
Sea valley, simply starves.   And it is easy to lose your way—
these monotonous undulations are as bewildering as the monotonous levels of the desert.   But Dick knew his way well;
and before the morning was far advanced he had reached
the long tongue of rock which runs into the sea between Port
Erroll and Hell's Lum.   A sward of short sweet velvety turf
carpets the plateau; while on either side the black rock dips
sheer into the sea—five hundred feet below.

The morning was simply faultless; and—save for one
obvious blemish—the picture was as perfect as it could be.
The sea—or what of it was visible—was blue as the sky; but
the broad luminous plain did not carry the eye with it as it
sometimes does to the outermost horizon; on the contrary,
less than a mile from the land an impenetrable bank of fog
lay upon the water, a damp and humid veil.   To enter into
that bank was to leave the sheen of the sunlight, and all the
pleasant sparkle of the morning, behind you.

Dick, lying at full length along the sward, peered cautiously
over the edge of the precipice.   It was one of those places
where the brain is apt to lose control over the body; where
men born on the flats become sick and giddy; where the
perilous fascination of "knowing the worst of it" becomes at
times imperious and overmastering.   But Dick was visited by
no imaginative tremors.

"The verra place," he remarked, as he looked coolly about
him.   "The hoody's nest is not fifty feet awa', and it maun
still be possible to swing roun' beneath the bank.   I learnt
the trick from Cummin Summers; it's a trick worth learnin'.
Then down the laigh end o' that lang smooth shelf—I can see
a fute-print here and there—and then there's the deep gully
that takes you stracht to the water-side.   The bit o' rotten
rock at the corner is not canny—the maist part cam' awa' in
my hand the last time I passt—but it's only a bit loup after
a'.   And there's the graceless cutty hersel', I declare, safe and
snug in the Cut.   It needs a keen eye to be sure to discover
the Crookit Meg in Hell's Lum, she's as black as the verra
rock.   Dander has a' ready to rin—that's clear—but how the

three o' us are to handle her across the water is mair than I can tell. And not a breath o' wind in the sky. O for a bit breeze, and we might won thro' yet!"

Dick appeared to be satisfied with his survey, for he drew back from the brink and threw himself into a clump of heather.

"I wonner," he continued, "if I micht venture to. steal across to Fontainbleau; the sight o' Eppie is gude for sair een. And the auld mither! But the haill country will be up, and we maun manage to creep awa' or ever the boats won roun' frae Collieston. But what bit lass is this?" he continued, as the figure of a young girl appeared at the summit of the rocky footpath leading from Port Erroll. "If we're not to start till dark she might warn Eppie. A sweet slip of a lass—it canna surely be little Nan?"

But little Nan it was—the slim little maiden who had been a comrade of Dick's in the old days when he had run wild about the country-side. Not out of her teens yet, it would seem; little more than a "bairn" indeed; innocent as a lamb; adorably unconscious as bird or flower. Yet Nan had been early initiated in a sense into the mysteries of love, Dick having been her "sweetheart" when she was barely five. And even to-day—though she looks on herself as a great girl now: she is fifteen come March—she keeps a very soft place in her heart for Dick, for Dick the truant, who had found his land loves too tame, and who was now a rover upon the sea.

She gave a great start when she saw him. And then a glad cry of childish delight.

"O Dick—Dick!" she said, throwing her arms innocently round his neck. "But they have hurt you," she continued, with a half sob, as she noticed the cut on his face, and the blood plastered over his cheek.

The boy laughed gleefully as he stooped and kissed her—shaking the clotted curls off his forehead.

"And it's you, little Nan! And you've grown quite a big lass, Nan! And it's only a scart on my cheek, my dear! And how's auld Lucky? And is Wasp still to the fore?

And now sit you down, my bonny Nan, and tell me what brought you here in the nick o' time?"

She had come to spend the Sabbath with her grandfather at Port Erroll,—"for he's auld and doited, and Peter is aff to the sea," sobbed Nan, in an April storm of tears and laughter. "But, O Dick, whar, whar have you been sae lang?"

There was much to tell: but at last the boy roused himself from a pleasant dream. "Would it be possible, I wonner, to let Eppie ken that I am here?" he asked, somewhat anxiously.

"I'll tell her," Nan replied eagerly. "I ken the short cut thro' the moss——"

Nan was still speaking when a low cautious whistle sounded a note of warning—as it seemed to them. It came from among the rocks about the point.

They started to their feet. A flock of grey plover were wheeling overhead.

"Look, Dick, look!" she exclaimed breathlessly. Her quick eye had caught the gleam of steel in the low morning sunlight. "It's the coastguard," she said, pointing towards the land. "Oh, Dick, they will kill you."

"Stand whar you are, Nan; dinna muve. Gie Eppie a kiss frae me, an' the dear auld mither: and here's anither for yoursel', my bonny bairn. They wonna touch you, be sure; but dinna muve, dinna muve."

They were standing on the very edge of the cliff.

Sure enough it was the coastguard: the enemy had run him down at last. The tongue of rock was long and narrow, and the men were well between him and the land. Dick was in a trap: the door of escape was barred.

As the men advanced towards the spot where the figure of the girl stood erect and motionless against the sky, one of them raised his gun. But the other interposed. "Dinna, Colin, dinna—ye may hurt the lass. It's not possible that he can jink us now; he's fairly trapped."

The men came closer and closer to where she stood.

There were two of them—Colin and Jim—handsome dashing young fellows as one could wish to see among the rigging of a man-of-war.

Little Nan for the moment was in the heroic mood, or very near it. She stood there breathless—white-lipped— with round wide-open blue eyes—her hands pressed tightly together. But the heroic mood was not suited for Nan. As one of the men caught her roughly by the shoulder and pushed her aside with an angry oath—"D—n it, man, he's awa',"—she broke down of a sudden, and sobbed bitterly— bitterly as if her heart would break.

"Puir Dick!—puir Dick!"

The men crawled cautiously towards the brink; but they quickly drew back. The bank of turf on which they rested was a mere cornice projecting over a giddy void; it had been undermined by wind and rain; it shook, or seemed to shake, with their weight. The wall itself of which it formed the coping leant towards the sea; so that unless you chose to bend your neck, as Dick had done, clean over the abyss, it was impossible to scan the face of the precipice, or to see what was going on at its base.

And yet they did see something—something that arrested their practised eyes in a moment.

"The Crookit Meg, by God! the Crookit Meg hersel'!"

She was lying in a deep gash or cut in the rock, a splendid natural basin in which a three-decker might have rode. There was not a soul to be seen on board; yet the slim little craft looked instinct with eager life, like the captive animal through whose veins the yearning to be free pulses with a fierce thrill. Her half-furled sails flapped idly, as if wooing the reluctant breeze; a line that ran across her bow was fastened to the buoy outside the reef, where through the long summer days the Port Erroll boats are moored; yes, she is ready to slip away at any moment, like a bird in the hand or a greyhound on the leash.

"Not a soul stirring," says Colin, "and the sea like glass. There maun be boats at Port Erroll handy, we'll stop her yet. But, O Jim, my man, she's a rare beauty!"

But as it turned out, the boats at Port Erroll were not
"handy"; were, indeed, for some reason or other, quite the
reverse of "handy." They had been dragged far up the beach
past the big boulders, and the oars had been carefully stowed
away. It takes half-a-dozen men to move these unwieldy
craft, and there was not a man about the place that morning
who was not bedridden. The women stood at the doors, and
looked moodily at the "gauger bodies."

At last they succeeded in launching a boat; but in the
interval a good half-hour had passed.

The stout young fellows settle to their oars, however, and
pull like grim death.

But ere they round the headland, which rises sheer out of
the deep water, they feel a breath of air upon their faces; and
even as they round it they see, not the bare masts and the
black hull of the becalmed lugger among the rocks, but—the
Crookit Meg! the Crookit Meg in her finest dress and queenliest mood, a shining mass of snow-white canvas, stealing away
like a cloud.

And yet the breeze had barely touched her as yet.

"She's a precious beauty," said Colin again, unable, in spite
of his mortification, to repress a deep-drawn sigh—rapturous
as a lover's. They laid down their oars, and rising to their
feet, watched her as she stood straight out to sea.

But even while they looked, the freshening breeze filled her
sails, and she passed from their eyes as a dream passes. A
close, warm, steamy mist—thick and impenetrable as night—
rested on the water not five hundred yards from the shore.
Into this she entered,—cutting the solid fog cleanly—like a
knife. It was the last they saw of the Crookit Meg.

* * *

Eppie went down next morning to her mother's room in a
sort of stupor. Utter weariness and hopelessness had taken
possession of her. Her heart had opened out to the sun, and
a frost had come and nipped it to the core. To her the
blossoming spring-time had been the time of death—not of

physical death, but of spiritual—the death of hope, of joy, and of love.

Had Mrs Holdfast been herself, she must have noticed her daughter's apathy. But her hold on life had got weaker and weaker, the silver cord that moors us to time had been slackened, and she was drifting away to that still, strange land— the shadowy home of the shadows. The things of this world were falling from her. Even her engrossing love for her cherished pet had begun to grow feeble,—she was making new friends, seeking out fresh interests elsewhere. Where? Still there was a soft gleam of satisfaction in her eye when Eppie pressed her hand and kissed her cheek.

Eppie went mechanically about the duties of the house. She made no mistakes, but she was quite unconscious of what she said and of what was said to her. It was a close sultry day for October, but she had not the least notion whether it was fair or foul. Exciting scraps of news were brought into the kitchen, and stolidly discussed by the farm-labourers when they returned to their early dinners; but she did not notice that anything was amiss.

About mid-day she took her hat in her hand and went out of doors. She went as far as the garden. Some late yellow roses still hung on the bushes; she gathered a handful mechanically and stuck them into the breast of her dress. It had been her habit since she was a child; but if any one had asked her that day where she had plucked them, she could not have told.

There was a rustling among the elder - bushes, and the elfish face of the "Deevilikie" peered through the branches. Eppie's ear was sharper than a blackcock's, but to-day it appeared that her senses had grown torpid as her soul. The "Deevilikie" had to touch her dress before she noticed him. "Miss Eppie, Miss Eppie," said the imp, "I was bidden to tell you that for God's sake you're to meet him at Cairn-bannow. He'll be waitin' for you at fowr." Then he went on, leering at her maliciously, "There's been a gran' splore at Hell's Lum. So they say. The tae half hae been sticket and the tither drooned; the rest 'ill be hangit." And an expres-

sion of impish delight pervaded the impish face, which had
been turned prematurely into a leathery brown by the fire
of the forge.

Eppie never thought of resisting — resistance would not
avail her. She must dree her weird. She must meet her
doom. The stars had been too strong for her.

"I'll be there," she said, in a voice which sounded dry and
out of tune. "I'll be there in time."

Without even looking at the boy she returned to the house.
She told Watty to have the pony caught and saddled. It
could wait in the stable till she was ready, and he might go
with the men to their work. Then she mounted the stairs
to her bedroom, and changed her dress. Putting her hand
into the pocket of her riding habit, she found some papers.
She looked at them with a puzzled air; she could not at all
remember how they had come there. Then the scene with
Corbie flashed across her mind. Yes: they were Harry
Hacket's; she would take them to him. It was now three
o'clock; Cairnbannow was an hour's ride. So she went into
her mother's room, stooped down, and kissed her, and said,
"How are you, mither?" There was no reply—only a wan
smile on the worn face. Eppie kissed her again, falling on
her knees beside the bed. Then she rose up and went out—
the anxious questioning eyes following her to the door.

How long they followed her was never known. It was an
hour or two before Mennie could go back to her mistress,
and during that hour they must sometimes have sought the
door through which Eppie had passed, and by which she
would return. But she did not return in time; nor did
any one. The appealing eyes grew dim; the heart beat
fainter and fainter; and Mrs Holdfast died as she had lived
—a strong, solitary, self-reliant soul, a true daughter of the
masterful Keiths: recalling to me, indeed, when I think of
her, the bronze statue in the Wilhelm Platz at Berlin, under
which they have written (or is it only in the old church at
Hochkirch?) an inscription not easily surpassable in the lapi-
dary way—"words which go through you like the clang of
steel."

There was no sound in the sick-chamber that night : it had
ceased to be the chamber of sickness and had become the
chamber of death.   There had been no sound in it, at least,
since Mark, hastily summoned, threw himself on his knees
beside the bed, which, with its still occupant, had been made
smooth, and decent, and comely for the grave.   "O mither,
mither, but I did love you," cried poor Mark, who in the grim
reticence of his love had never said so much before.   But a
Scotsman is a grim animal.

Do not blame Eppie overmuch.   To do her justice (and as
the old proverb says, "It's a sin to lee on the Deil"), she had
no notion whatever that the end was near.

* * *

"And you will go with me, Eppie?" Harry asked ardently,
yet with the watchfulness of the hunted animal in his eyes.

"Ay, Harry, I will go with you," Eppie answered listlessly.

Hacket had ventured to return home after his escape.   He
put the mare into the stable himself, fed and groomed her,
then led her to an outlying byre at some distance from the
house, where he left her saddled.   Then he went up to his
own sitting-room, the room that had been his father's, and
opening an old-fashioned writing-table, began to examine the
letters and papers which it contained, throwing them, after a
brief glance at each, into the fire which still smouldered on
the hearth.   He was thus occupied the whole morning.   At
intervals he rose and scanned uneasily the distant highroad
leading to Balmawhapple.   Later he had something to eat ;
a little later he stole cautiously by an unfrequented footpath
to the smithy on the Saddle Hill, and despatched the imp
with the message to Eppie.   Then he returned to his room
and resumed his work.   If he was preparing for flight, it was
clear that he had resolved to leave no written evidence behind him.   One bundle of papers obviously startled him ; he
read them again and again ; then he tied them up carefully as
if he meant to keep them ; then, with a sudden impulse, he
threw the packet into the fire with the others.

Cairnbannow is a heap of whinstone high up among the moors. Some remote Hacket, riding blindly among the peat-hags, had broken his neck at this spot, and they had buried him where he fell and put the stones over him. The common people said that he had broken his neck on purpose; but that is a feat difficult to accomplish: accident is more potent than design in such cases. This, however, was the spot which Harry had selected for his meeting with Eppie. It was a mile or two beyond Yokieshill on the road to Ardallie—not the highroad, but a rough track through the moors used by the farm-carts that went in autumn to bring down the peats from the moss, and as a short cut by packmen and tinkers. The grouse sunned themselves upon the cairn in September; a little later on in the year a watchful blackcock looked round him from the summit. Eppie had once or twice ridden here lately; the coveted domain of the Hackets lay stretched below; so she knew the place.

The "lovers" met: Eppie listless and jaded; Harry restless, watchful, eager. They did not dismount; the horses moved on as they talked. Harry told her only that something had occurred which required him to leave the country without delay for a time: would she, oh! would she go with him? He pleaded for himself with a vehemence that almost woke her out of her lethargy. She looked at him with wondering inquiry in her eyes. Was he really going to leave? She had broken one lover's heart: was she to break another? Any love that had ever found a place in her own heart had been frozen in the bud; and even the old ambition appeared to be dead. She was utterly passive: either way it was the same to her.

Then she had said mechanically—for in truth she did not attach any definite meaning to the words, did not in the least realise that the moment for instant action had come—"Yes, Harry, I will go with you."

Her companion could not but notice her unnatural listlessness and abstraction. The sun was already setting, and yet she rode on without making any movement or showing any desire to return. The shadows of night came down upon the moors; but this pale impassive bride rode on silently beside him.

Neither of them had observed that the unseasonably oppressive weather of the past few days was about to culminate in a thunderstorm. The crisis was upon them. The huge white clouds which had been mounting out of the west all day had latterly grown ominously blue and slate-coloured, casting a lurid reflection of the stormy sunset upon the moor. The whaups passed by overhead with wailing cries. A gorcock which they started on the track flew a few yards, and then went down plump into the heather. A great convulsion of nature was at hand.

Between Yokieshill and Ardallie there was not in the year One a single dwelling-house; the barren moorland was unbroken by spade or plough; but at Pitlurg the high-lying table-land dips into the valley of the Whapple, and at the junction of the highroad with the hill-road — where the tollbar now stands—the Cottage Inn (what in Switzerland they would call the Chalet Inn) of Ardallie was placed. It was then kept by Jean Catto, and was mainly used by pedlars and smugglers. Many an illicit bargain — *pactum illicitum*, as Corbie said with a wink—was concluded in the widow's snug little parlour. It was a sort of half-way house between Balmawhapple and Aberhaddy.

The first heavy drops fell as they arrived at the door, and the "fire-flacht" was blazing across the dark before they had dismounted. Peal after peal rattled out of the heaven. And then the rain came down in perfect sheets of water. Yet in spite of the flood, the lightning continued to flash, and the thunder to growl and mutter like a caged beast, who ever and again breaks into a roar in the impotent violence of passion. No human creature could have stirred out of doors that night without danger of being washed bodily away.

The storm which cleared the air cleared Eppie's soul. She awoke and found herself seated in the cosy parlour of the inn. Jean Catto was bustling about her in a helpful way. "I maun sort the blue bedroom for you and your man," said Jean,

assuming that they were married folks ; and then she left her
to get supper ready.

Eppie's eyes opened wide ; her lips parted ; but she did not
speak a word. She stared after her hostess in dumb dismay.

At this moment Hacket, who had been seeing to the
horses, entered the room. Eppie rushed up to him with a
great cry.

"What does it mean, Harry? Where have you brought
me? I am ready to go. Please saddle Bess."

"It's not possible, Eppie, to move to-night," Hacket replied, the uneasy furtive look coming into his eyes. Nature
had treated Harry badly. Had it not been for those uneasy
furtive eyes, he would have been, though in a coarse, half-bred
style, really handsome. "You must let Jean Catto—they call
her Jean, I think—make you as comfortable as she can. We
will get away to-morrow by daylight."

A great dread took possession of Eppie's soul. What did he
mean? Now that he had got her into his power would he deal
fairly by her? Now that her good name was in peril, could
she trust him as she could have trusted the other? She could
have gone with Alister over the world secure in the innate
integrity of the man's nature : but Harry Hacket? That was
the wretchedness of it. She did not believe in the loyalty of
her lover.

What, indeed, did Harry intend by this girl—after all, only
a farmer's daughter—whom he had, wittingly or unwittingly,
induced to accompany him thus far? She had certainly com-
promised herself, whispered the mocking Mephistopheles who
is always at our elbow ready to take advantage of any slip we
may make. Why not win her now more cheaply—far more
cheaply—than he had fancied possible when they started that
afternoon?

I cannot for my own part be certain that the temptation was
seriously entertained by him. It was undoubtedly a temptation
that would appeal very directly to the sensual instincts of an
evil and cowardly nature. But I do not love Harry Hacket,
and I may be doing him injustice.

But as she looked at him, Eppie recovered herself. Her

immense superiority of mind made itself felt. Whenever they
had hitherto come into the direct stress of conflict, her moral
and physical courage had made her his master. She was to
win again to-night, always assuming, that is, that he had not
meant fairly by her.

"Harry," she said in a clear voice, coming up to where he
stood shivering before the fire. "Harry, look here. I winna
say which of us is to blame—it may be me, it may be you—
but you hae brocht me whar I sudna hae come. A lass
maunna lippen to a man if she wud keep her gude name.
Mine is gone. I canna gang back to Fontainbleau, except
you mak' me your wife. O Harry, it wud hae been better for
us baith if we had never met; but what maun be maun be.
Harry, you must marry me to-night."

She spoke with perfect distinctness in extremest simplicity.
Her good name had been inestimably dear to Eppie: it was
the one possession, besides her beauty, which ministered to
her pride; and Eppie, as we know, was proud as Lucifer.
Other girls might give themselves away if they chose; other
girls had soft hearts and weak heads. But she! And yet this
sulky booby of a lad had somehow contrived to compromise
her—as she fancied. There might be something of exaggera-
tion in the fancy; she was for the moment weak, morbid, and
unhinged. The excitement of the fever, which replaces the
lethargy of despair, burnt in her blood. But at all hazards,
this miserable sickness of shame which overcame her when
she realised her position must be put an end to—put an end
to by some instant decisive antidote. A terrible fatality had
driven her back upon her own self—hard, unloving, and un-
lovable; but that was no good reason why she should drift
helplessly to utter shipwreck. The words "utter shipwreck,"
if applied to other girls of that place and time, would have
been, I admit, a mere rhetorical expression, but to Eppie they
meant *that*, and nothing less. There was no ideal element, as
I have often said, in this girl; she had little or none of the shy
reverence for the right, for what is pure and modest and of
good report, which is the crown of womanhood. And yet her
vestal hardness and coldness had truly expressed a natural

attitude of her mind; she shrank from what was morally uncomely with critical annoyance and disapproval.   And now
there seemed to her only one method by which she could save
herself from the ugly gulf that opened before her feet—Harry
must marry her to-night.   It must be done now, at once, without an hour's delay; thereafter, though her heart broke (if
further breakage were possible), she could hold her head up
again, and look the world straight in the face—with her clear
unshrinking eyes, and in the arrogant simplicity of her rustic
pride, as she had done before.   Yes, she must be married to-
night.

He stood before the fire—silent, looking down.   He had
never seen her so moved before; there was a thrill in her
voice he had never heard before.   But he did not reply—
Mephistopheles was still at his elbow.   It was a pity that he
did not reply; it forced her to shoot her last shaft.

"Look at me, Harry Hacket," she exclaimed, after a long
pause, her face lighting up brilliantly with anger—or was it
scorn?   "I saw Liar Corbie after he had been wi' you at
Yokieshill, and he tell't me something aboot your feyther."
Hacket started, and moved uneasily.   "You can tell me
whether it be true——"

"It's a lie," he said, in a hoarse broken voice.

"And he gied me some papers."   Here he started again.
"Leastwise I've got them—by fair means or by foul I've got
them.   I felt that you were ill-used amang them, and my heart
was softened to you.   I thocht to do you a gude turn.   Noo,
Harry, I may be forced to bide here this nicht"—the rain was
lashing against the panes—"but Mrs Catto will lat me sit in
her room, I dinna doobt; and though I may be missed at
hame"—(Alas! Eppie, there is no one to miss you now)—
"yet when I get to Corbie's to-morrow—wi' the papers——"

Reader, you must remember that this girl's moral nature had
been utterly undeveloped, and that she was now at bay—a wild
creature at bay.   It seems to be assumed by many wise men
among us that the conscience in each soul, like the Greek
daughter of Zeus, is armed at every point from birth—"a
crownèd truth."   It is not so: it needs to blossom, to expand,

to mature : the sunshine and storm, the tears and laughter, the sorrow and sacrifice, of many a spring and summer, of many an autumn and winter, are needed to ripen it to perfect life.   Eppie's moral education had only begun the other day; she had grown into a woman ; but her conscience was still in its childhood, and love had been nipped in the bud.   Do not let us hate her because in her mortal terror she seized the nearest available weapon.   She knew not what she did.

It is possible indeed that she was unnecessarily terrified, and that her lover had not designed to harm her.   So at least he declared, and I am willing to believe him—for once.

"You need not fear me, Eppie," he said, raising his eyes at last.   "I always meant you to be my wife."

Marriage in Scotland is not attended with any unnecessary preliminaries.   Go into the next room, and declare before your landlady and her guests that you are man and wife, and the thing is done.   You are married past redemption ; the Archbishop of Canterbury with all his deans and archdeacons could not tie the knot tighter.   In some such primitive fashion, Harry Hacket and Euphame Holdfast were made man and wife.

A suspicion of the validity of the ceremony was sometimes expressed : but Corbie knew better.   "Consensus non concubitus facit matrimonium," said Corbie, when he went to the High Court; "and though it's undeniable, Mr Drumly, that only the ostler and the kitchen-wench, forbye Mrs Catto, were ben, yet nae plea against the credibility o' the witnesses has been proponed.   And as has been judiciously observed by Mr Erskine in his *Institute* o' oor law, whilk like that o' a' civileesed nations is imported from the Roman (tho' the English, to be sure, hae some cankered notions o' their ain), Mr Erskine, I say, has weel remarked that it is not essential to marriage that it be celebrated by a D.D., or even by the shirra —the consent o' parties being plainly expressed before credible witnesses ; for it is the consent o' the parties which alone constitutes marriage."

It was a wild and stormy night for a wedding ; but it would have been even darker to Eppie had she known all.   But it was not until the ceremony, such as it was, had been completed that an officer of the law, buffeted by the storm, but bringing a warrant for the apprehension of Harry Hacket of Yokieshill, on the charge of wounding Adam Meldrum to the danger of life, entered the inn.

Poor Eppie !

* *
 *

It was too true—dear old Uncle Ned had been wounded to the death. He was stupefied by the blow, and quite unconscious while they bore him to Achnagatt, the nearest farmhouse. He was carried into the best bedroom, where, in addition to prints of the storming of Seringapatam and of the Lord Lieutenant of the county, Mrs Mark's Pre-Raphaelite sampler, a *chef-d'œuvre* of the MacWhistler school of the period, was suspended over the fireplace. They put the old man to bed, and before the surgeon arrived consciousness had returned. His wound was bound up ; but the surgeon shook his head. Adam had lost a deal of blood ; the shock to the system had been tremendous ; he was over seventy. No : he might linger for a week ; he would suffer no pain ; but his days were numbered.

His friends gathered about him as he lay there serene and composed. Kate was a deft nurse, Alister got leave of absence from the Commodore, Dr Caldcail was a constant visitor. The old boatbuilder was wonderfully happy with his friends, young and old. His bed was placed beside the window, whence he could see down to the river, where the sandsnipe were piping to each other as they swept swiftly, like the shadow of a cloud, across the sand. One wild windy day a broken rainbow touched the clouds all morning, now melting into mist, anon growing vivid and consistent again. To the dying man it seemed in its perfect comeliness of colour, in its perfect shapeliness of outline, an earnest, a foretaste of the good things that were in store. "It compasseth the heaven about with a glorious circle, and the hands of the Most High have bended it." He never wearied of repeating these words ; which are indeed very great words—simply realistic, yet vitally ideal— as some great painter who puts a band of light round the head of the Redeemer. *The hands of the Most High have bended it.*

"Indeed, my bairns," he said (it was Alister and Kate now, not Alister and—another), "if Shakespeare hadna been born, I could have been weel content with the natural history o' the Auld Testament. But then, you see, the poets and prophets of the Hebrew people lived in a different warld; whereas Shakespeare is, as it were, ane o' oorsels. But they had undoobtedly a great enjoyment of nature. Beautiful upon the mountains are the feet of him that bringeth good tidings. Is there no balm in Gilead? is there no physician there? He kept him as the apple of his eye. But unto you that fear my name, shall the Sun of righteousness arise with healing in his wings. Ay, bairns, the men who wrote thae words were wayfarers who had abided wi' Nature in her secret places, until the sleepy magic of her music suffused their souls. With healin' in his wings! Dear me—it minds me somehow of the saft fa' o' the cushey's wings as she settles on her nest."

At another time he would discuss with the Doctor the conditions of that mysterious existence on which he was about to enter.

"Here we have no continuing city, but we seek one to come, said the Apostle. And anither saw the holy city, New Jerusalem, coming down from God oot o' heaven. Weel, Doctor, you and me may not have any sic veevid eemage of the New Jerusalem; for the warld is greatly changed since John lived in Patmos. Poor John! he must have got verra weary o' his bit rock, with the constant thud-thud o' the sea in his ears, and I canna wonner that he couldna thole it in the New Jerusalem. And there was no more sea! Indeed, Doctor, I canna say that I fear death; it is rayther that I am ashamed o' it, it being, as our freen' o' Norwich observes, the verra disgrace and ignominy of our nature. Yet death, as he says in anither place, is the cure o' all diseases—nectar and a pleasant potion of immortality. But the lang habit of livin' indisposeth us for dying. That's it, Doctor; we are the verra creatures of habit. I wonner what Elisha thocht when he saw Elijah fleein' into heaven like a laverock? He must have

been simply dumfoonded. But if the haill business was a
cunnin' deceit, as your freen' Mr Hume conten's, it was
maist extra-ordinar' clever o' the auld writer to mak' him
louse his mantle. And Elisha took up also the mantle of
Elijah which fell from him. For wha can help believin' it
after that?"

So he rambled on gently and sweetly to his friends beside
him; until, as his strength failed, delirium came and took him
back into the past.

"Sit doun beside me, Rachel, and sing me a bit sang. I'm
uncommon weary this nicht.——It's a rale bonny bird, the
grey plover. What—Rachel—gone? Ay, the bells are ring-
ing—the folk are at the kirk door—she's in the Laird's seat.
See how the sunshine o' heaven touches her brown hair. She
sits abune the lave like a saint in glory! But sic a woman-
like smile, sic a bird-like twitter o' a laugh, when she meets
me in the yard. 'Surely, Adam, surely,' she says softly.
How caller the air, how the birds sing, this Sabbath mornin'!
'And, Adam, mind ye bring me a sprig o' heather from
Benachie!' I was on my way to the Hielan's for a week—
for a week only. Ay, darlin', a hatfu' o' heather, and a heartfu'
o' love! And so we parted—for ever."

He paused and looked about him, and then the old story
was resumed.

"A week thereafter I stood again in the doorway. I had
tellt the corries o' the joy that was in store for me—the
heather had taen a rarer bloom, sic gowd in the sunset, sic
purple glooms in the gloamin', I had never beheld before. I
waited a moment in the trance, for an unaccountable dread
cam' suddenly upon me. Even as I waited a woman clad in
black passed oot—her eyes red wi' weepin', her cheeks soiled
wi' tears. I kent my doom before a word was spoken. She
looked at me—I had the bit sprig o' white heather in my han'
—wi' sad, pitiful eyes. 'It is all over,' she said, 'Rachel is
in heaven.'"

He fell back upon the pillow, the eyes bright with fever
gazing blankly into the sky, until, after a strained pause of
inquiry, they cleared, and he added softly, "A great crood

that nae man can number—an endless thrang o' warlds—but Love will bring the beloved."

So it went on, in broken snatches, until the end came— the gentle and peaceful end of a gentle and peaceful life. The delirium had left him, and he had bidden farewell to the Doctor—not without a touch of the old humorous twinkle in his eyes. "Gude-bye, my auld freen', gude-bye—

> ' If we do meet again, why we shall smile ;
> If not, why then this parting was well made.'

And, Alister—my dear, dear boy—you will keep the birds, but gie Eppie the buiks. Puir Eppie!" Then the voice sank to a whisper, "Rachel!—Rachel!—nineteen and seventy-three—dootless, a lang reckonin'—but—this mak's— these odds—a' even."

So with the unforgotten name, and a scrap from the beloved book on his lips, Uncle Ned passed away.

* *_{*}

The High Court of Justiciary was crowded by ten o'clock on the morning of the last day of the year One. Harry Hacket was to be tried on that day for the killing of Adam Meldrum, and the prospect of the trial had excited considerable interest in the northern metropolis. The social position of the accused, the audacity of the outrage, the growing feeling against the severity of the Excise laws, rumours about the romantic circumstances in which the irregular marriage with Eppie Holdfast had been contracted, had contributed to draw a crowd of idlers to the dingy courtroom. Corbie, propitiated by payment of his account (with legal interest), had insisted on coming all the way from Balmawhapple to instruct counsel, and was now seated within the bar in consultation with one of the clerks of Messrs Tod & Trotter, Writers to the Signet—the agents employed for Hacket. In a dim corner of the court, with a thick veil drawn across her face, sat the criminal's young wife—

Euphame Holdfast or Hacket, as she was called in the indictment.

Corbie employed the interval before the judges entered in obtaining opinions on certain questions of legal procedure in which his clients were interested from the clerk at his side. It was a tempting opportunity, moreover, to air his own erudition, which had been growing somewhat musty of late.

"Noo, you maun understan', Mr Drumly, that by the sett o' the burgh, the sea-greens belang to the feuars. But the deeficulty arises—What's a sea-green? 'A variety o' sea-kail,' says the Doctor jocosely; but he's a daft body. Indeed, Mr Drumly, I've heard him declare that the *Decretum et Decretalia* o' the Canonists are superior in maist respec's to the *Corpus Juris Civilis!* But the truth is that the study o' deeveenity obscures and stultifies the faculties o' the understandin', whilk on the contrar are recreated, refreshed, and whetted by the law. Noo, the sea and the sea-shore are onquestionably *inter regalia*—that I wunna dispute—but it disna appear to me, and it certainly to the best o' my judgment has not been sattled by the Coort—at laste at the Hoose o' Lords—that the sea-shore, being *inter regalia*, extends beyond the ordinary leemits o' the tide. Whereas it is the land covered by the spring-tides whereof a sea-green consists, accordin' to oor institutional writers, and mair particularly Lords Stair and Bankton. Says I to the Provost—'Dootless, Provost, the value o' the property is sma''—for you see the Broch is entirely bigget on rocks which rise perpendicular from the deep sea—' but the question o' law being of general importance, a declaratory action at the instance o' the Provost and Bailies o' the burgh against his Majesty's Advocate as representing the Crown———'"

At this moment a macer entering announced "The Court."

The audience rose.

Their lordships sat down, and the audience resumed their seats.

"It's Pitblethers, Kilreekie, and Fozie," said Mr Drumly.

"The Lord hae mercy on Harry Hacket," Corbie rejoined piously. "If it's within the leemits o' possibeelity, Fozie 'll hang him." Lord Fozie had an evil name among the criminal classes.

"Any objections to the relevancy, Mr Pittendreich?" asked the Justice-Clerk, when he had arranged his petticoats, and opened the scroll - book in which he made his notes, and taken a look at the prisoner, who had been brought up from below.

"Certainly, my Lord." And then Mr Pittendreich rose, and, taking up the indictment, tore it (figuratively speaking) to tatters. Thereafter my Lord Advocate in reply proved that no prisoner had ever had the satisfaction of being hanged on a more logical, coherent, and strictly relevant document. I don't mean to go into the legal argument; you will find it reported at length by Mr Cowpen (afterwards Lord Drumsaddle) in the first volume of his Justiciary Reports. It was exactly one of those nice points which the Court may settle by a toss - up with perfect safety. I had forgotten, to be sure, that a man's life in this case depended upon the solution, but so had the lawyers on either side; for indeed they hanged right and left in the year One, and thought no more of a man's life than of a rat's.

Then my Lords, modestly arranging their petticoats, retired to the robing-room to consider their judgment.

The Lord Justice-Clerk, Pitblethers, was one of Pitt's politicians,—a pleasant speaker, a strong partisan, an agreeable and well - informed man of the world, but not much of a lawyer.

"Well, Kilreekie, what do you say?" asked the Justice-Clerk.

"Faith, Pitblethers, ye may mak' a kirk or a mill o't. There is gude reason and nae reason on baith sides o' the Bar. I'm rather for lettin' the youngster aff; if we pit him to the jury, they're like to hang him. And did you notice the lass in the black veil under the gallery?—that's Mistress Euphame Holdfast or Hacket, I'll be bound; and an uncommon handsome lass she is. We'll susteen the objections, Pitblethers, if you please," said Kilreekie, who was a judicious admirer of the fair sex, though a cynical critic of his own.

"Well, my Lords," said the Justice-Clerk, "I recollect his father, old Hacket, on the Inverness circuit after Culloden, and he married a very nice girl—Jane Kilgour of Logie—by the way, a sort of cousin of my own. What say you, Fozie? My impression is that the major won't hold water. And as you say, Kilreekie, the jury are safe to hang him."

"And it wudna be the first o' the clan, Pitblethers, that has undergone a process o' suspension, if the auld Border thieves havena been misca'ed." The Justice-Clerk, who belonged to an old Border family, rather prided himself on his descent.

"I presume you agree, Fozie," the Justice-Clerk continued, disregarding the interruption, "that we can't sustain the relevancy? The definition of the *locus delicti* is quite too defective."

"We'll ca' it the *locus pœnitentiæ*, if you like, Fozie," Lord Kilreekie interposed again.

Fozie shut his eyes, wagged his head, and addressed a few inaudible observations to his cravat, in which the word "hangin'," however, occurred.

Lord Fozie, however, was in the minority; and it was agreed that the Justice-Clerk should deliver the unanimous judgment of the Court.

There was an eager intensity of interest in the prisoner's gaze when the judges returned. Hacket had divined truly enough that his fate depended on the decision of the preliminary pleas.

Lord Pitblethers made his points neatly, and sustained the interest to the end. More than once the prisoner felt that it was all over with him; but Pittendreich rubbed his hands and chuckled. He knew what was coming. "But," continued his Lordship, "we are unanimously of opinion that the words in the major to which objection has been taken is a fatal misdescription. It appears to us——"

"'Deed, my Lord, that's soun' sense if not gude law," exclaimed Corbie, unable any longer to restrain himself. He had that morning, as well as the night before, been revisiting with some old cronies a certain well-known tavern in the Advocates' Close.

The interruption caused a general burst of laughter, and the noise made by the macers in their efforts to restore silence prevented the audience from becoming acquainted with what remained of his Lordship's opinion—which came indeed to a speedy conclusion. The jury were discharged; the witnesses were liberated; and Harry Hacket had saved his neck.

* * *

So Uncle Ned died: and sooner or later—it is but a question of sooner or later with us all—the other members of the secluded society on that weather-beaten coast, who were so bright and cheery in the year One, were laid out of the way of the east wind. Captain Knock, "Liar" Corbie, Doctor Caldcail, Miss Sherry, my friend Alister and his pretty wife Mistress Kate (for men have died from time to time, and worms have eaten them, but not for—love; and the blow to Alister, though stunning at the moment, was not fatal) have finished each of them his or her bit of work in a world where there are always plenty of fresh hands. Pitblethers, and Kilreekie, and Fozie, have ceased to be a terror to evil-doers, and a praise and protection to those that do well; and their places are occupied by the men of a new world, who have forgotten the tongue of their grandfathers, and speak that astonishing English of the Scotch bar which has so often perplexed an amazed Legislature.

Eppie came of a long-lived house; and I can still recall the bright-eyed old lady, in her black silk gown and wonderful white hair, who occupied the many-gabled house among the moors when I was a boy. In my time she was Lady of Yokieshill; and only a confused tradition of Harry Hacket's misdoings survived. For the popular feeling against the man who had dealt that savage blow at Uncle Ned was too bitter to permit him to return, and he went abroad. Eppie did not accompany him. She had fought his battle obstinately so long as his life was in peril; but after the trial she came back to Balmawhapple, and lived in close retirement under Miss Sherry's hospitable roof.   She sent Cousin Kate on her marriage morning a lovely little gold knick-knack, which had been an heirloom in the Holdfast family since Marie Touchet's time (the initials M. S. and the Scottish lion being faintly engraved on the inner shield), but she was not at the wedding. She and Alister never met.   Then some arrangements had to be made about the property, which continued to be managed, or mismanaged, by our friend Corbie; and then Harry died, and it was found that Eppie Holdfast had, under her husband's settlements, the sole interest in Yokieshill.   Inquiries were instituted on her behalf by the Maryland authorities; but if Elspeth Cheyne left any issue, no trace of them was recovered.   So she reached the goal of her ambition; Eppie Holdfast was Mistress of Yokieshill.

I do not know that she was unhappy.   She looked keen and bright, and active and healthy, to the end.   She was very good to her poor cottars, very kind to children and beggars and wayfarers.   Her hair, it was said, had turned grey in a single night; but it had needed more, I daresay, than the mad misery of an hour to humble the pride of her heart, and soften the hardness of her ambition.   No—she was not unhappy.   She had contrived to live down (and it is done somehow) the exquisite bliss and the exquisite torture she had tasted in the Year One.

VI.

LISETTE'S DREAM.

IN an old story-book I told how Nancy had kept her tryste. A voice imploring help had come to her out of the dark while she slept. It was the voice of her lover, who, miles away, was in mortal peril. But in *Lisette's Dream* it was a Vision, not a Voice. I had heard the story long ago; only the other day, fishing a remote and secluded loch in Assynt, while the thunder rolled and the lightning flashed among the corries of Quinag, my gillie said to me suddenly—*It was here that the tinker's body was found.* They seldom speak of the tragedy on that wild coast; the shame of it is still felt by a community which in its seclusion does not readily forget; and the lad became studiously reticent when he realised that I had gathered the import of his half-involuntary exclamation. But I did not need his help; for, as I have said, the story was well known to me from of old. I need not add that *Lisette's Dream* is only an *adaptation* of the central incident of a strange history.

I.

BALMAWHAPPLE is at its best, I think, during that season which is called by some the late summer, and by others the early autumn. The season has a touch of both. The air is crisp yet mellow. The summer heat is over; but though the stars begin to light up the sky after dark, there is no frost at night to blacken flower or fern. It is during this pause in the year—which is only broken by the winds and rains of the autumnal equinox—that the Balmawhapple farmer harvests his grain.

It is at this season also that the bays and coves along our rocky coast are at their best. And at their best they are, I venture to think, as perfect in their way as Venetian lagoon or the olive-crowned wall of the Riviera. The crisp sea-sand —the crimson sea-weeds—the beaten sward with its hardy flowers—the fields of yellow oats which have been sown along the steep brae-sides, and which half-clad hinds are now reaping with the sickle which they and their fathers have used since the days of the Danes and Norsemen! The tarrock skims lightly along, and screams as the skua comes prowling round the cape; high up, the gannet watches its prey, and arresting its flight in mid-air, dives with prodigious force, straight as an arrow, below the surface; the terns, like handfuls of feathers, are blown about the sky, or, balanced upon the breakers, weave their wings swiftly together.

This August day, for example, has been one of those red-letter days whose charm is none the less exquisite because there are no words fit to arrest and accentuate its fugitive loveliness. Hour after hour the waves broke upon the sandy beach with the same monotonous roll, though a perceptible change of tone might be detected by the practised ear as the tide retreated from the land and again returned. The boat of a solitary fisherman and a lustrously white bird—a gannet or one of the larger gulls—lay the whole morning together near the centre of the bay. About noon, a large ship with every inch of canvas spread dropt lazily along to the south. As the day waned and the tide ebbed, the gull and the fisher left their stations; small flocks of ducks beat in quickly towards the shoal water in single file; and once a pair of red-throated divers, in their petulant coquettish way, chased each other round the margin of the bay. High up upon the downs the lights began to twinkle—a red lurid glow showed where the village blacksmith plied his craft—voices muffled by the twilight came down upon the shore—and a wary heron flapped its unwieldy wings as it passed along to the pool where, until the grey of the morning, it will watch the retreating tide. And now, while the voice of the restless ocean rises up to them for ever, silently, one by one, the stars come out above the hills.

The bay I have been describing—our North Bay, as we call it—stretches from the Ronheads to the estuary of the Whapple. On the other side of the placid stream lie the white sands and wavy bents of St Abbs—a long low belt between sea and sky, often struck into sudden radiance by the sunset. All this is visible from the door of the Cottage on the cliff, the only dwelling now in sight—or at least *was* visible before the sun went down.

As the evening fell, the door of the cottage opened, and a girl dressed, as the fisher-girls dress, in white wrapper and short blue petticoat came out. Putting her hand over her eyes, she gazed out to sea; but nothing was visible through the grey mist that had gathered since sunset. The moon had not yet risen, but from the ruddy glow in the upper sky it was evident that it was not far below the horizon. The girl sat down on the wooden bench in front of the window and waited. The silence over sea and land was intense, and for a time unbroken; but by-and-by the measured beat of oars outside became audible. Then—still later—when from out of the mist and the twilight the sound of voices was carried to where she sat, she rose and ran lightly down the winding footpath that led to the water. Just as she reached the beach, the boat entered the cove,—its black mast cutting in two—as it seemed from where she stood—the blood-red disc of the newly risen moon.

Three men were on board,—the girl's father and cousin, and one other—Allan Park. They had been a week away at the deep‑sea fishing, somewhere beside the Dogger Bank. The heavy boat laboured in; and as it touched the jetty, the eldest of the three exclaimed—

"Is that you, Lisette?"

Our fisher-girls, as a rule, are not pretty, but Lisette would have been considered a beauty anywhere. The pure classic outline of her head and neck would have satisfied a Greek; a Parisian would have been charmed by her sauciness, her petulance, the mockery of her smiling mouth, her elfin and bewildering prettiness. She was a born coquette — now reserved and demure, now arch and caressing—but a coquette who had yet at times her dreamy and incalculable moods. Lisette was, or professed to be, the daughter, the only daughter, of honest John Buchan, a simple fisherman of the Ronheads (the unsavoury suburb of Balmawhapple where the fishers live); but if we had been told that this child of the sea had been cast ashore in a wild winter gale, or caught in a salmon-net in whose meshes she had got entangled, and from which she could not escape in time, the tale would not have seemed strange or incredible. There were those at least who had seen her sitting upon the rocks of summer nights while she sang a beguiling song and combed her flaxen hair. The mermaiden—if such indeed she was—had been taken from her native element; but, even in the dingy surroundings of the Ronheads, she remembered, like the sea-shell, her august abode; and the murmur of the sea, of the vast and fickle and mischievous sea, was around her.

I do not know where Lisette got her Southern coquetry, or the deft fingers, and the native taste and refinement which could give her simple Shetland shawl the graceful fold of a mantilla, and turn her coarse homespun petticoat into the tunic that a duchess or a Greek nymph might have worn. These fishers are mostly Danes or Norsemen—genial giants with the blue eyes and the yellow hair of the Scandinavian colonists; but mixed with them we find another race, where the gipsy or Spanish blood shows itself in coal-black eyes and hair, and swarthy olive skins, and voices which are low and musical indeed, but through which the force and violence of

ungovernable passion can find an outlet when needed. Some
of this gipsy blood was in Lisette; probably it came from her
mother, who belonged to a fishing village beside which one of
the great war-vessels of the Armada had been wrecked,—the
hull, of a windless day, when the water is limpid and serene,
is still visible, they say. Some score or so of the crew had
been saved, and their black beards and swarthy cheeks had
proved attractive to the blue-eyed daughters of the village.
Whether the strain of alien blood was thus sufficiently
accounted for, I am not prepared to say; but the fact of two
typical races living side by side in these remote and secluded
communities is not to be gainsaid. Allan Park, for instance,
was Norse or Scandinavian to the tips of his fingers—a mighty,
modest, blue-eyed Goliath; whereas Lewie Gordon was dark
and slim, with eyes that, though furtive at times, could blaze
with passion, and a voice that might wile the bird from the
tree. For Lewie, as for Lisette, one had to go back to the
time when Philip's ships were driven by stress of weather
beyond the farthest Hebrides. The contrast between the two
races is perhaps most noticeable in their manner. The blue-
eyed are bluff and hearty, and even their women look you
straight in the face, as a hawk does without winking; the
black-eyed—the girls at least—are petulant and caressing,
while the men are instinctively courteous, deferential, and
refined. The blue-eyed are gentlemen; the black-eyed,
courtiers.

Lisette was not always gay; she was a daughter of the sea
indeed; but the sea which she had known all her life was the
Mare Tenebrosum. Her sea had little leisure for the multi-
tudinous laughter in which elsewhere it is said to indulge;
hers was the sea of the black fogs, and the white breakers,
and the fierce winds, and the driven rain, and the blinding
sleet, and the ghostly winter twilights, in which men and
boats are lost to sight and never return. When the rain
streamed down the window-panes, and the storm howled
down the chimney, while father and brother were outside
the white line of surf, which grew whiter as the wind rose
and the darkness gathered, she would leave her bed and peer

out into the night, and listen in dreary solitude to the raving of the storm and the muffled thunder of the waves. She was not afraid—there was no room for fear in her stout little heart; but she felt very lonely; and the poised head and pure profile, against a background of cottage wall grimy and black with smoke, were as wan and pallid and statuesque as if indeed ages ago they had been cut from the solid marble by a Greek.

We are presently, however, in our Indian summer, and Lisette's spirit is not touched by any winter gloom. She is apparently, however, in one of her tricky, defiant, impish, mischievous moods; and the mood has been on her for days. Only the most ardent of the many lovers of this adorable vixen, whose smile is as sweet as her tongue is bitter, have not been put to flight. But Allan Park and Lewie Gordon are not easily discouraged. It is true that at times these big, stalwart fellows are mortally afraid of this slight slip of a girl; daunted by her scorn and bewildered by her caprice; but all the same, the sea-witch has "cuist the glamour o'er them," and they cannot leave her. Nor is she always hard; she melts, she relents at times; and then one or other of them— it is a toss-up which—is in Paradise for the day. For though she likes both, she is in real, earnest, downright love with neither.

At least, so it was till the other month; we shall see immediately how it was now.

I have said that John Buchan lived in the Ronheads; but, in point of fact, his cottage stood by itself—an outlying cottage, one hundred yards beyond its nearest neighbour. So that it had its own seclusion, its own sea and sky, and its own lawn, studded with primroses in spring,—a lawn of close, crisp grass, such as golfers love, that ran right down through the centre of the rocky cove—where the boats are drawn up in winter—to the very lip of the water.

I don't know that it would be fair to say that Lisette had played the one lover against the other so as to prevent the suit of either of them pressing too closely, and so becoming embarrassing. The truth is, that she did not know her own

mind. Neither dominated her; she was not the sort of girl
who would surrender at the first assault. She was too critical;
had she been in a higher station, people would have said too
cynical. A pair of very observant black eyes looked out from
under heavy eyebrows, which reminded me of Mary Stuart's
in her picture at the Castle, and gave the eyes themselves the
same languid yet obstinately masterful expression.

Lisette would often blaze out at both: the lazy strength
of the blue-eyed giant would irritate her one day; while on
another the crisp, sleek, almost cat-like comeliness of Lewie
Gordon would have a like effect upon her nerves, and she
would turn with a sense of relief and repose to the heavier
but more open and candid face of his rival. Allan, as we
know, was a fisherman; Lewie was one of a fraternity that
has almost died out, the travelling merchant or pedlar. At
the time of which I am writing, when communication with the
outer world was slow and uncertain, the packman was a personage of some importance: it was on his periodical visits
that the country people relied for their hardware and cutlery
—knives, forks, spoons, and suchlike articles of household
use; and one corner of his pack was sometimes reserved for
daintier trifles which, when stealthily exhibited to the laird's
sister or the farmer's daughters, excited emotions in their
chaste rustic bosoms similar, or at least not widely dissimilar,
to those with which a petted beauty regards a masterpiece of
art in a Bond Street jeweller's. Lewie had more than once
endeavoured to persuade Lisette to accept one or other of the
really rather pretty knick-knacks (for his taste was good)—
locket, or brooch, or bracelet—which he had picked up in
the South; but after trying on his whole stock, fastening
them all over her dress, so that she dazzled them like a
queen—

—"Lollia Paulina,
When she came in like star-light hid with jewels,"—

she would make him a mocking curtsey, and point-blank refuse to have any. The dull tarnished silver chain and cross
which she wore round her neck, and which when closely

examined proved to be a piece of really rare workmanship, had been given to her by Allan when she was a child. They had been fishing—he and his brother—at the Heughs, not far from the spot where the Spanish vessel had foundered. They had shot their lines, and were anchored near the shore while they waited to draw them. (The "long lines" are paid out from the boat, which is kept in motion, and with a bladder at either end are left for an hour or so under water, near the bottom.)   The water in the bay was of limpid clearness, so that they could see the pink shells and the crimson sea-weeds on the sand, and brown and green crabs walking leisurely about, fifteen or twenty feet below the surface.   A gleam of metal caught Allan's eye as he looked idly over the boat's side.   He was the strongest swimmer and diver in Balmawhapple (where the boys take to the water like ducks); and as it was one of the hottest days of a hot summer (such as we used to have before the storm-cloud of the nineteenth century darkened our skies), he had rapidly undressed and plunged overboard.   When after his long deep dive he returned to the surface, he held the prize in his hand,—the silver chain and cross which Lisette had worn ever since, and on which some letters of the maker's name could still be read. It was that of a famous jeweller of Seville who had in his time worked for Philip and Don John.   So the expert in gems from the British Museum, who came to Balmawhapple for change of air, told us.   He told us, too, that they were still worn by the Spanish women as charms or amulets.   If a girl wore hers during the day, it would keep her from harm, for they had power to drive evil spirits (whether in or out of the body) away; if she wore it at night, she would dream of her lover.   But we did not know of these queer old Spanish monkish tomfooleries (if they were tomfooleries; but the orthodox belief of one age is the superstition of the next) till afterwards.

I rather think Allan had an obscure hope, somewhere in his heart of hearts, that so long as Lisette wore his cross he had a chance some time of winning her.   *That* was *his* superstition; and curiously enough, it was shared by Lewie

Gordon, who on most other subjects was rather inclined to scoff.
Lewie had more than once tried to induce the girl to part
with it or put it away—without success; for even to her
unpractised eye the tempting baubles of his wallet, pretty as
they were, seemed tawdry in comparison with this sea-worn
charm.

Gordon had been absent with his pack for the last month;
but on the evening of which I am writing he had returned,
and while they still lingered in the cottage kitchen (supper
being over), the door opened noiselessly and he entered.
There was gloom on his brow, and the black eyes blazed
rather viciously when he found that Allan (who lived at the
other end of the village) made one of the party which were
now gathered round the peat-embers which smouldered on
the hearth.   The men were smoking; Lisette, who had
washed and put away the coarse earthenware dishes, was
knitting one of those gossamer trifles—fine as a spider's web
—which we buy at Lerwick, but which may be had anywhere
along the coast where the native wool is sufficiently delicate.
Lewie was hospitably welcomed by the old man; Allan
nodded to him; Lisette, with something between a blush
and a laugh (for she was visibly embarrassed), inquired where
he had been so long.

He sat down among them; but his answers were curt and
sullen.   Something ailed him,—that was clear even to the
unsophisticated and unsuspicious Allan.   Lewie was commonly a bright and lively companion; his calling made him
sociable; and his jests and stories, when he was in the
humour, kept Hodge's supper-table in a roar—the jolly red-
faced Hodge in whose house he lodged for the night; he was
a favourite with the women, too, for his natural courtesy
(handed down possibly from some remote courtly Hidalgo?)
made him behave to them with a deference to which they were
unaccustomed.   But when the black fit was on him, his gloom
was excessive.   And for some months now the gloom had
been gathering.   Rumour had been busy, as usual; but no
one ever knew if Lisette had actually rejected him; it was
more probable that, with his keen vision, quickened as it was

by love and jealousy, he had silently observed a change in her which had not been noticed by the others. Although he had not given up the pursuit, he was wellnigh persuaded, I fancy, that within the past two months she had made her choice, and that her heart—which had swung like a pendulum between them—had at last settled on the other.

He did not remain long, and Allan left with him. He was to start in the grey of the morning on his usual autumn expedition,—a protracted tramp along the Atlantic seaboard from Loch Broom to the wild highlands of Assynt; a district which at that time was thickly peopled, and where the packman drove a thriving trade with the clansmen who had not yet been disbanded and cast adrift by their chiefs. Curiously enough, these East Coast fisher folks were familiar with the other side of the Island, where among the salt-water lochs of the Western Highlands they fished twice a-year—in spring and autumn. Lisette herself had been once in Assynt. Her aunt had married a Mac who had a croft on the shoulder of Ben More; and a year or two before, she had paid Mrs Mac a visit at her Highland home. But hemmed in all round by mighty mountains, the sea-maid had pined for the sea; and she was glad to go back to Balmawhapple and breathe freely again. Lisette needed a wide horizon.

Allan parted from Lewie at the corner of the Ronheads. "We'll be at Lochinver for the cod before the month is out, and you'll be passing that way," Allan had said as they parted. To which the other, who had barely opened his lips, responded by a savage grunt. "What ails him?" Allan asked himself, as he took a last look at the broad expanse of sea before turning in. The modest giant had no inkling of the truth.

For the truth was, as Lewie had guessed, that Lisette's heart had gone out that summer to Allan. This was how it came about.

All her life till now Lisette had regarded Allan as she might have regarded a good-natured Polar bear. He might be bland and benevolent; but he was big and uncouth; and he made a poor show at the festivities of dance or wedding, of "Clyack" or New Year,—at least when compared with

Lewie, who was as refined and high-bred as the Duke himself.
(So Lisette thought; had she known the Duke, she would
have said that Lewie was the finer gentleman of the two.)
But one memorable Monday night in July of this same year
—not yet forgotten, nor like to be forgotten on our rock-
bound coast—she had suddenly a vision of quite another
Allan.

The July evening had been fine, and more than five
hundred boats had gone out to the fishing-ground. Gulls
of every kind had been seen the day before in immense flocks
upon a bank at some distance to the north, and the clamour
they made as they hung with quivering wings over the water
where the shoal of herring lay, had been heard miles off. So
the crews had started in good time, looking forward to a
heavy fishing, and little dreaming of what was in store for
them. Allan was almost the only man in the fleet who was
dull and depressed; Lisette had been teasing him in mere
wantonness all the morning. He had left her at last with a
heavy heart. The parting had been cold and formal; and
Lisette, repenting too late of her wicked petulance, had shed
a tear or two after he left. "If he wasn't just such a big
bear!" she had said to herself, as she wiped them away.

The twilight had deepened into night when Lisette barred
the door, and went up to her little cot among the rafters.
She was vaguely disquieted. Though the sea was smooth
and glassy as oil, its roar was loud and menacing,—as sometimes happens when a storm has swept down the Norwegian
fiords, and spent itself *at sea*. There was hardly a breath of
wind; what there was came direct from the east, and felt cold
and chill for the season. Lisette was weather-wise, as all
fisherwomen are; but even now, though she said to herself
that there would be more wind ere morning, she did not
believe that a great gale was in the offing. Before she slipt
into bed, she gave one last look across the wide expanse of
water. The mist was rising from the land; yet she saw, or
fancied that she saw, the lights on board the fleet twinkling in
the distance many miles to the nor'ard.

She slept soundly—the sleep of the young—till nearly

three, when she wakened with a start. The wind was shrieking down the chimney. She knew at once that a great gale was blowing—blowing dead inshore. Dressing herself hurriedly, she went out to the cliff, where she barely managed to keep her feet; and from there, by the uncertain light of the dawn, she could see that the sea was already fiercely agitated. Huge white breakers roared in hoarsely, and dashed themselves against the rocks below—the spray blinding her where she stood. Here and there among the waves a scrap of sail was visible,—the brown sail of a boat in awful peril. Already the St Abbs shore was black with wreck, —the wreck of yawls which had just managed to weather Rattray Briggs, but could not venture again to face the full force of the gale in the open sea. Some half-dozen boats, however, whose crews had shot their nets farther south than the rest, were running under nearly bare poles for the harbour.

Lisette, wrapping a shawl round her head, hurried down to the shore. There was an excited crowd on the pier,—women mostly, whose *men* were outside in the storm. But it was not a noisy crowd; the wives and daughters of fishermen could measure the danger; and but for a muffled scream, when a luckless boat hugging the rocks of the Keith Inch too closely was sucked in and swamped among the breakers, they waited in absolute silence. For they were well aware from past experience that the most imminent peril was at the harbour-mouth—within fifty yards of where they stood. Between the breakwater on the weather side of the harbour where the coastguard were stationed, and the Black Rock immediately below the house occupied by Miss Christian and Miss Anne, on which the breakers burst with a noise like thunder, there ran a narrow lane of smooth dark water, and along this lane the path to safety lay. The utmost skill of the crew was required here. The protecting jetty needed to be fairly rounded, and sufficient "way" left on the boat to carry it *against the wind* into the inner harbour. All depended upon the dexterity with which the sail was lowered at the exact moment; if it was caught by the wind as the jetty was rounded, the boat lost the necessary impetus, and was driven back upon the sharp saw-like ridge of the fatal reef. When this happened—and it had already happened more than once —Lisette shut her eyes, and a stifled murmur went up from the crowd. For it was instant death,—in that seething whirlpool there could be no escape—no deliverance for man or boat. The misery of it was, that from where she stood (the rain in her eyes, the wind in her hair), the faces of the crews who were hurried past to destruction could be plainly seen. They were friends, neighbours, kinsmen ; and now at last, rushing in at tremendous speed on the back of a mighty wave which threatened every instant to break, and overwhelm it, came her father's boat. Old John Buchan was at the helm ; Allan, sitting on the weather gunwale, had the sheet in his hand—the rope which held the thrice-reefed foresail. Lisette could see him as plainly as if he stood at her side, and for the first time her heart told her that her modest lover had the soul of a hero. Cool, steadfast, ready for life or death, his mouth firm, his eye calm and confident, holding the sheet in one hand while with the other he signalled to John—how indeed could she have been so blind as not to know that this was a man of whom any woman might be proud ? "If he wun through," she inwardly vowed, "I will never tease him any more." He held on—even with a smile on his comely face, as it seemed to her—till the right moment ; then the sail fell sheer, and another crew were safe.

This was the vision which had sobered and steadied Lisette. Thenceforth the current of her wayward fancy set steadily towards Allan.

Yet the honest young fisherman did not fare much better than before, when in the course of the evening he appeared at the cottage. Lisette indeed was even more unapproachable than usual. She had not forgotten her vow ; but she was incensed at her own weakness. She resented what she held to be an ignominious capitulation. She !—to lose her heart to a man who was too modest (or stupid) to see that he had won it. All the arrogance of her nature, all the exclusiveness of her maiden reserve, rebelled against being thus led away—

a captive victim who hugged her chain. It was too humili-
ating. It was indeed past bearing.

This contradictory mood, in which pure passion struggled
with morbid pride, lasted more or less into the autumn; so
that Allan departed for the West Highland fishing early in
September, without any suspicion of the conquest he had
made.

II.

BOTH her lovers, and half the young men in the village, were
now absent; and as she sat and knitted mechanically in front
of the cottage, her eyes would wander away to the Rattray
Skerries, round which the boats had to return. A local
distich, known to every seaman on these coasts, ran—

> " Keep Mormond Hill a handspike high,
> And Rattray Briggs you'll not come nigh ; "

and day and night, with the obstinate persistency of fever, the
refrain rang in her ears. Allan had taught her the lines when
she trotted after him in her childhood—a tiny mite, whose
great round eyes, as black as jet, were often clouded by
fits of childish passion, which were more than childish in
their intensity; and it was Allan they recalled. Her waking
thoughts were of her lover, and, with the amulet in her hand
or under her pillow, she dreamt of him at night.

Lisette had always been a dreamer; her thronging fancies
took form when she was asleep; and her dreams were often
so vivid (especially when she was left alone in the cottage for
weeks without a break) that she would sometimes ask herself
with an amused sense of bewilderment, Which was the dream?
and, Which the sober fact?

But never had she dreamt as she dreamt now; and one
dream—one dream from which she tried in vain to escape—
began to repeat itself with dreary persistency. In this dream
she did not see Allan's face; but all the time she was uneasily
conscious that he was somehow present.

Those of us who are familiar with the great moors round

Loch Assynt know what a bare and miserable and God-for-gotten country it is—what a stony wilderness. But an oc-casional oasis is to be met with by burnside or mountain tarn, where wild roses bloom in the watery sunshine, and the rare ferns flourish in not uncongenial fogs. The burns are pure and sparkling, for they come from the live rock ; but a black tarn in the middle of a black peat-hag on a black winter day is one of the gloomiest combinations to be found out of the *Inferno*.

It was beside such a tarn as this that Lisette beheld two men in her dream. The only bit of colour was a mountain-ash (with a profusion of scarlet berries) that grew out of the precipitous rock which on one side overhung this stagnant pool.

After a time Lisette began to recognise the place. It was a lochan not far from her aunt's cottage on the Ben More Moor. The scarlet berries, after which she had scrambled, first re-called it to her mind. A path, little frequented, except by tramps and gipsies, passed close beside it, and led to the Lochinver road.

One of the men whose face was always averted wore the blue jacket and the blue bonnet of a sailor. She seemed to know him perfectly, and yet in the strange perversity of her dream his name persistently escaped her. The other, slight and slim, with black eyes and an olive skin, was — Lewie Gordon. Of that the dreamer had no doubt.

There had been a hot altercation between the two—so much also was clear. But how it came about that on a sudden they should be wrestling desperately for dear life on the edge of the precipice was not so clear to the dreamer. Lewie had bent forward ; there had been a flash of steel and a rush of blood ; and then the larger-limbed of the two, the wounded man, had recovered sufficiently to throw himself upon his would-be assassin. The struggle lasted some time ; no cry escaped from either ; but it began to be plain that Lewie was overmatched. Yet he clung to the other with the ferocity of a wolf, and what he meant to do became plain to the dreamer. She read it in his eye—the eye of a maniac—from which all expression except that of mortal hate was banished. He would take the other with him over the cliff; they would go down,—go down together. He nearly succeeded; but on the very brink his strength seemed suddenly to fail; his grasp relaxed; his eyes closed; a deadly pallor spread over his face; and he fell back into the loch, clutching instinctively at the branches of the rowan-tree as he fell. The other had fainted.

Here on the first night the dream broke off. On the following night the story was resumed.

The man whose face was always in shadow lay for hours insensible. Then life began painfully to return. He sat up and looked around him. The moon was on the wane. It threw a wan light on the moor; but the tarn was black and inscrutable. There was no living creature in sight; no sound except the croak of a heron in a pool near by. The man had obviously no idea where he was until a dark object lying beside him attracted his attention. It was the pedlar's pack. Then he remembered—remembered vaguely—what had taken place. It came back upon him gradually with a lurid horror that, in his weakened state, for he had lost much blood, was more than he could bear. Was he a murderer, or was he not? His brain grew giddy again, and he fell back upon the heather. At length he rose, and lifting the pack with what strength remained, dropt it over the rock. He heard it plunge into the water. His jacket was torn, his shirt was wet with blood, his head was bare. He groped about—trying to find his cap; but he failed. Then he hurried away, bareheaded, across the moor.

Beyond this the dream did not go.

The autumn closed in; the crews returned—Allan, her father, and the rest; but even when winter was at hand, there came no news of Lewie Gordon. It was well on to Christmas before rumours of foul play began to spread through the town.

Then Lisette could keep her dreadful secret no longer. She had never as yet mentioned her dream; for she had a haunting dread, for which she could not account, that it would bring trouble to them all. And as yet, too, she had never been able to identify, so to speak, the man who had gone away bareheaded across the moor.

Now, however, she told her father; and old John Buchan, though attaching no importance to it, mentioned it casually to the Fiscal,—a brisk, kindly, good-humoured official, who had done John a good turn more than once. The Fiscal looked grave, and intimated that he would come and see Lisette. He came the same night. Allan was with them—looking delicate and haggard. He had had brain fever when he was away; he had been found wandering in a half-crazy condition across the moor below Suilven; and some gipsies, after rifling his pockets, had brought him to Lochinver, where he had been nursed in a cottage built by the Duke for the sick poor on his estate. He must have injured himself seriously when out of his mind; his clothes were in shreds; he was covered with bruises; there was a deep gash in his neck. But he recovered with amazing rapidity, and was able to return in his own boat when the fishing was over.

The Fiscal was urgent, and Lisette, somewhat against her inclination, told him briefly the main incidents of her dream. Whereabouts was Lochan Dhu? Not a mile, she replied, from her aunt's house; both aunt and uncle knew it well; the path by it was a short cut to the kirk. He put a score of questions—most of them shrewd and to the point; then he left, with a kindly greeting all round, though he looked thoughtful and preoccupied.

Allan had been sitting in a dark corner, and no one except Lisette had noticed the startled expression of his face while he listened to her story. The mists which had clouded his mind since his illness seemed to melt away. The whole terrible scene which he had so utterly forgotten came back upon him. A deep groan startled the other two. Allan rose and staggered to the door. Lisette followed him.

"It's God's truth," he said, looking pitifully into her eyes. "I mind it now." Then he went out into the darkness.

The veil fell from Lisette's eyes. This was indeed the "other man" she had seen in her dream. How could she have been so blind? What infatuation could have possessed her? The blue jacket—the sailor's cap—the broad shoulders—"I was clean wud," said poor Lisette as she crept into her bed.

But during a sleepless night she had determined what course to take. Some families of fisher-people from a neighbouring village had gone to Sweden on the invitation of Thomas Erskine—an Erskine of the old St Abbs stock which had stuck by Queen Mary, and traced its pedigree back to King Robert—half of Balmawhapple belonged to them at one time—who was then consul at Gottenburg, as his grandfather had been before him, where he had extensive works. A flourishing colony of Scotch-speaking people had there grown up under his eye, and many an invitation had been sent by them to their kinsmen on this side the water. Allan among others had been pressed to go; but as yet he had returned no answer. Why should he not go while there was yet time, and leave all this trouble behind him? That was the question Lisette put to herself as she tossed sleeplessly in bed.

A girl has little difficulty in finding her lover. Allan was engaged in putting a final coat of tar on the summer boat, which was now laid up for the winter, when he heard her voice calling to him from the beach. He was very pale— the lines under the candid blue eyes had grown darker than it was good to see. He too had spent a sleepless night. He came at her bidding; but the expression of his face was not that of an alert lover—it was grave and sad.

With gentle persistency Lisette urged him to go; but he was immovable. No; he had meant no harm to Lewie Gordon; but if he had been the unwitting cause of his death, he was sorry for it, would be sorry all his life. He could not quit the country, he could not leave Balmawhapple while a possible charge of murder hung over his head, until either his guilt or his innocence had been made plain. "How could he prove that he was innocent?" she asked, and he could make no reply. But his obstinate simplicity was beyond the reach of argument. "I maun dree my weird." To that sublime fatalism, that blind submission to an inscrutable decree, the serene composure which enables these humble heroes to meet danger and death every winter night is due.

Then Lisette broke down. "You will break my heart," she sobbed.

Allan looked at her with mild astonishment in his honest eyes. The truth, the astonishing truth, was beginning to dawn upon him; but he could not yet put it in words. It was not possible that she could love him?

But now Lisette could restrain herself no longer. She was shaken by her sobs; she gasped for breath; her face was dabbled with tears. "I will go with you mysel', Allan," she murmured at last.

Was he dreaming? Was this great, this incredible happiness really within his reach?

"I will go with you, Allan,—Oh, man," she added hastily, with a touch of the old petulant impatience, "do ye no' ken that I lo'e ye—lo'e ye better than mysel'?"

Then at last Allan understood. He folded her in his arms; that moment repaid him for much that was past and much that was to come. But even in that moment of supreme happiness he was immovable. "I maun dree my weird."

It fell out as Lisette had foreseen that it would. The Black Lochan—Lochan Dhu—was dragged, and Gordon's body was found. The pack also was dragged up, and along with them—the sailor's cap that Allan had worn. His initials were on it; they had been worked by Lisette. That he had been at the Macs on or about the day of the murder was also clearly established.

Allan was apprehended, and lodged in the Balmawhapple jail. When examined before the Sheriff, he said only that he was innocent. The Sheriff's duty was quickly performed; he had simply to remit a prisoner charged with murder to the Court of Justiciary, which twice a-year held sittings at Balmawhapple. The indictment, as it is called, was served in March; then Allan learnt that he was to be tried at the Spring sittings. The 20th of April was the day named.

All Balmawhapple was in Court that day. There were Corbies, and Caldcails, and Buchans, and Meldrums, and Skinners, and Hackets, and Holdfasts among the audience, which not only filled the spacious Town Hall, but overflowed into the High Street. Much sympathy was felt for the brave and simple lad whose life was in hazard, but Lisette's dream was the engrossing topic. Lord Oronsay, the President of the High Court, was on the bench, having good-naturedly taken the place of one of his colleagues who was in poor health. Lord Oronsay was one of those judges of whom it is almost impossible to speak too highly; serene, luminous, equable; never swayed by passion, never warped by prejudice; an orderly and abstemious reasoner, disinclined though not unfitted to deal with principles and abstract propositions, and clinging to fact with characteristic tenacity. Orderly—for the manner in which he grouped the leading facts of a case was so admirable that when the conclusion to which he had all along been cautiously working was at length disclosed, it seemed that no other was possible, and that argument was superfluous; abstemious—never throwing away a word, or a scrap of logic, or a grain of sense; always equal to the occasion, never below it, and (a common infirmity with men of great powers) never *above* it.

A smart and clever young counsel, Charles Newell by name, who later on attained celebrity as an incisive logician and a brilliant wit, conducted the prosecution as Advocate-Depute with exemplary fairness and moderation.

Allan's counsel had not been long at the bar; but he had already made his mark. He became afterwards, as we all know, a great advocate; his speech in a *cause célèbre*, of which the world has heard, is one of the masterpieces of our time—symmetrical in arrangement, and executed with a consummate knowledge of strategy and effect. For pure, lucid, intellectual force John Carstairs had no peer at either bar. But the moral force of his character was even more impressive. He was neither witty nor sarcastic; but the haughty scorn of his virtue, the intense bitterness of his integrity, crushed its victim to pieces. His presence was imposing, and he knew how to use it to perfection. He folded his black stuff gown about him with the austere dignity of a Chatham. The contemptuous curl of his nether lip was deadly. His manner was singularly still and restrained until the victim was fairly in his toils, when he came down upon him like a thunderclap.

The audience rose as Lord Oronsay, accompanied by Admiral Holdfast (whose notes made at the time I have been permitted to read), entered and took his seat; he bowed rather stiffly in response, and the business began. It is not my intention to describe what took place at any length: the legal discussions will be found in the authorised reports; the evidence in the newspapers of the day. Allan pleaded not guilty in a steady voice, and with an accent of sincerity that favourably impressed his hearers. There was very little dispute about the facts; the forensic battle raged round Lisette. When she entered the witness-box she was as white as a sheet; she was almost inaudible when she swore, as she would answer to God at the great day of judgment, that she would tell the truth, the whole truth, and nothing but the truth; but she rapidly regained her composure. Lisette was quick-witted, as we know, and she had come to understand that much depended upon the manner in which her evidence, if admitted, was given. So, though her heart continued to beat painfully whenever her eye involuntarily turned to Allan, she pulled herself together for the ordeal that was before her.

But it was doubtful for long whether her evidence would be admitted at all. She was no sooner in the box than the argument began. Allan's junior counsel professed to be convinced that what she would say must be irrelevant. He understood from his learned friend's statement that she knew nothing directly of what had taken place. She was brought, it was admitted, with quite another object in view. She was brought to speak of a dream she had had! A dream, forsooth! This was the first time in his recollection, and he dared say in his lordship's, that it was proposed to produce a dream as evidence in a court of law. But the Advocate-Depute cleverly evaded the destructive effect of the ridicule by declaring that he had called the girl with the object of showing only how it was that the inquiry had taken a particular direction. It was merely, so to speak, as a link in the chain of investigation that she was there. He did not, indeed, propose to examine her at any length, if at all, on the substance of her dream.

Here Carstairs sprang to his feet. He had got the admission he desired. What did the other side mean? Was the girl's evidence to be mangled and mutilated to suit the convenience of the prosecution? It must either be rejected altogether or admitted without reserve.

The counsel on either side continued to bob up and down for some time; but the President ultimately decided that no part of Lisette's evidence need necessarily be excluded. The audience were unable to follow the argument, and they listened to it with impatience. What was the good of all this fencing? They were not aware that the first move for the defence had been more or less of a feint, the object being to secure an uninterrupted hearing for Lisette. Carstairs was persuaded that if she was permitted without constant challenge to tell her story in her own simple and expressive language, as it had been told to himself the night before, the effect on the jury would be powerful, and upon the whole, though this line of defence was attended with a certain risk, advantageous for his client.

So Lisette was permitted to tell her story in her own way; and she told it well—with grace and modesty—at times with a touch even of the old vivacity.

It was thought by the onlookers that Mr Carstairs would have succeeded in gaining a verdict for his client—so persuasive and strenuous was his appeal—had it not been for the tell-tale cap. If Allan was innocent, how came his cap to be in the loch? That was how the jury would reason, they said.

Lord Oronsay summed up with the perfect impartiality for which he was renowned. No consideration that could tell either for or against Allan was overlooked. If Lisette's narrative was credible, or rather if it correctly represented what had taken place at the Black Loch, murder had not been

committed, for the death of Gordon was, according to her
account, due to an accident. The prisoner had no doubt
caused Gordon's death; but he had acted in self-defence, as
he was entitled to do. But what in law was the worth of her
evidence? She had not been present; she had not been a
spectator, except in her dream. He admitted the force of Mr
Carstairs's contention that the case was one of the most excep-
tional that had ever been tried in a court of justice. It was
undoubtedly through this girl's instrumentality—through her
dream, in short—that the criminal authorities had been enabled
to show that Gordon had met with a violent death. This they
admitted, although they refused to go a step further, and
accept her version of what had occurred at Lochan Dhu. He
was not a metaphysician; he could not explain those obscure
conditions of the consciousness in sleep or in the second-sight
with which, from the earliest times, a marvellous power of
vision had been associated. He himself was a Highlander,
and Highlanders were held to be more credulous than their
Lowland neighbours. He had himself known cases in which
the bodily or the spiritual ear had been so keenly on the alert,
so morbidly active, that the last words of one dearly loved,
though dying at a distance, had been distinctly audible. Only
the other day he had heard of a shepherd who was drowned
in Yarrow, and whose wife, at the door of their cottage miles
away, had caught his parting sob, "O Ailie, Ailie!" But
while, as a Highlander, he might believe in what one of their
bards had said—(here he gave the Gaelic with immense gut-
tural inflection; the passage was subsequently translated by a
living poet—

> " Star to star vibrates light ; may soul to soul
> Strike through a finer element of her own?"—

or more literally, " As messages are sent through the starry
spaces by invisible couriers, so through the magic of love
those far distant from each other in body may be brought
together in spirit ")—he could not, as a judge, advise them
that it was safe or prudent in a court of law to attach any
weight to intimations that had been made through so ques-

tionable a medium. Let him not be misunderstood; when he spoke of a questionable medium he meant the dream, not the dreamer, who had given her evidence, he was bound to say, with perfect simplicity and candour, and yet with a force and vivacity which were rare anywhere, and in a court of law were generally conspicuous by their absence.

With these words the President concluded his charge, and the jury retired to consider their verdict.

While they were absent Carstairs rose, looked round, and catching her eye, beckoned to Lisette. They met at the door.

"Go home now," he said to her. "I rather suspect the jury are not at one,—they can't get over Allan's cap—some of them anyway. But don't be afraid; I give you my word of honour that, whatever the verdict is, Allan will be a free man in a week. The dream will save him; good or bad as evidence, it supplies the one credible explanation of all that took place. I make no doubt whatever that Gordon had divined that his rival had won the prize—if you will allow me to say so,—and that, mad with jealousy, he had struck as a maniac strikes. Take my word,—the Home Secretary will send Allan a free pardon before the week is out."

It was a speech dictated by true kindness, for Carstairs had felt that he had failed to convince Boghall, the obstinate farmer who acted as foreman, and he instinctively apprehended what the issue would be. It was not well, he thought, that this spirited but delicate girl should be present at the last scene of all. So Lisette went home with her father—her eyes moist, but her heart wonderfully light.

The jury were absent until the dim tallow candles of the period were brought in. So that their verdict was delivered in comparative obscurity, or rather in a darkness that might be felt. By a majority of seven to six they found Allan Park guilty of MURDER. The verdict, however, was accompanied by a unanimous recommendation to mercy.

Well, it was over; and Allan had been sentenced to be taken from the prison of Balmawhapple to the place of execution, and there hanged by the neck until he was dead.

But Balmawhapple had inwardly resolved that these cruel and barbarous words were relics of a cruel and barbarous age, unworthy of an enlightened Balmawhapple, and that the sentence should not be carried out. The fiery cross was sent round the coast, and from a score of villages interested in the credit of their craft there was a ready response. From Buchanness to the Pentland Skerries a thousand stalwart fishermen had sworn that if Allan was not released by the law, he should be rescued by themselves.

The day was drawing near, and no reprieve had come. The outlying fishermen had begun to arrive, and both harbours were crowded with their boats. They had come ostensibly to make their bargain with the curers, but the authorities had been privately warned that this was not the real object. The Sheriff had ostentatiously pooh-poohed the warning; the Fiscal had smiled placidly, as he could afford to do, having been confidentially assured from headquarters that a reprieve was being prepared. Of this, however, he could say nothing,—although he had gone quietly along to the cottage one evening when the citizens were mostly in bed, and told Lisette to be of good courage and cheer—as indeed, to the surprise of the village gossips, she had been all along.

The jail of Balmawhapple was an old-fashioned building which had at one time been used as an inn. The Home Secretary, though warned of the risk of disturbance, had refused to give the governor—an elderly gentleman with silky white hair, and the manners of the last century—a single policeman or a single trooper; and on the night for which the rescue had been provisionally fixed, Captain Keith had been invited by Miss Christian and Miss Anne (I am afraid the worthy ladies on this occasion were not so innocent as they looked) to make a fourth at their nightly rubber. The old gentleman was passionately fond of whist, and of course he went, taking his wife with him. Thus only a turnkey was left to look after the "inmates"—*rari nantes in gurgite vasto* —and a collection had been judiciously made to pay *his* expenses. The fishermen were marshalled noiselessly on the

Keith Inch shore behind the breakwater; and whenever nine
struck—nine was the hour that had been agreed on—they
marched in perfect order and silence, three abreast, from the
Keith Inch past the harbours and along the High Street to
the front gate of the jail. The turnkey having been duly
summoned, protested loudly that he only yielded to superior
force, and thereupon handed over his prisoner. Allan was
quickly brought down amid smothered cheers to the north
harbour, where a long light whaling-boat, manned by eight
stalwart seamen, was waiting to take him off to the sloop in
the offing. There had been much restrained jubilation; the
hero of the night had been nearly shaken to pieces by his too
ardent admirers; and he was just stepping on board the skiff
when the undaunted Fiscal, elbowing his way through the
threatening crowd, appeared on the scene. There was such
an angry murmur as precedes a storm; but he was known to
many of them, and his good-nature and good-humour were
proverbial. So they listened to him as they would probably
have listened to no one else. "Men, men, what are you
after?" he exclaimed, addressing those nearest at hand, but
raising his voice as he proceeded. He seemed stern, but
there was a twinkle in his eye. "You are doing Allan an
ill turn. Prison-breaking is an ugly business. Have none of
you heard the news? A special messenger arrived a quarter
of an hour ago with a reprieve" — here there were frantic
cheers—"a free pardon is on the road"—here the cheers
became deafening—"and the sooner you have Allan safely
locked up again, the better it will be for him and for us all."
The leaders looked blankly at each other; their labour had
been for nought; but the advice was so obviously sound,
that, hoisting the Fiscal (much to the worthy man's disgust),
as well as Allan, shoulder-high, the crowd surged up the High
Street as it had done an hour before, and paused again before
the great gate of the jail. Here, however, they encountered
an unlooked-for obstacle. They found to their dismay that
the gates were securely barred against them. They had got
the prisoner out easily enough, but how were they to get him
in? The turnkey had thought it prudent to take French leave

of his masters, and the prison was actually deserted. There was not a soul at least within the walls who could unbar the outer gate; and it almost seemed at one time as if Allan, with or without his consent, must still submit to be rescued. At this crisis it happily occurred to some one to suggest that the Provost had the keys in duplicate—which proved to be the case; and in the nick of time Allan was restored to his cell and securely locked up. Just in the nick of time, for the key had barely been turned when the Sheriff arrived. That dignitary was either judicially or judiciously blind, or he was too much engrossed otherwise to notice that anything was amiss. The letter from the Home Office was in his hand, and turning to Allan, he read it aloud. The cheers with which it was greeted by the bystanders were taken up outside, and Balmawhapple will not soon forget the roar like thunder that came from a thousand throats, and that startled the sleeping sea-gulls a mile off in the bay.

When he had finished reading the letter, which concluded with the intimation that it would be followed immediately by a free pardon, the Sheriff—he had the reputation of being a humourist, and his jokes from the bench, although he shared the proverbial "deeeiculty" of his countrymen, were always received with respect by the Bar—shook hands with the prisoner, and added, with more than judicial gravity (this was supposed to give the jokes their point), that though he dared say it was against the rules approved by the Commissioners, yet as the dream and the use that had been made of the dream were innovations for which no precedents could be found in the series of Reports so meritoriously conducted by Mr Cowpen of that Ilk (afterwards Lord Drumsaddle), he would, in the language of the poet, "for this night only" make bold to disregard them.

And then, with a proud and happy smile on her face, Lisette entered the condemned cell.

VII.

AFTER CULLODEN.

I HAVE said in an earlier chapter that the records of
Balmawhapple during the last century are meagre.
I had hoped to find in the charter-room at the Cleuch
many references to "the King across the water," and
the risings of the '15 and the '45. But I was disap-
pointed. It was probably considered safer to "read
and burn." But the other day I came upon a scrap
in cipher of old letter or journal—journal most likely
—without beginning or end, which had, however,
plainly been written a month or two after Culloden.
Sir Gilbert Holdfast himself—the then laird of the
Cleuch—was, as we know, a stout Hanoverian,—like
most of the Balmawhapple townsfolk; but, in spite
of warning and remonstrance, young Walter Holdfast
of the Heughs—the Holdfasts of the Heughs were a
younger branch of the house—had joined the Prince.
He came back after Culloden in sorry plight, and was
more than once in dire peril from the red-coats, who
swarmed, like angry wasps in a hot summer, all over

the country-side.   His most vigilant and pertinacious
enemy was the contemporary Corbie; whereas the
great-great-grandfather of my veteran ally Dr Jackson
was mainly instrumental in aiding him to escape.   I
am not positive, but I fancy that the parish minister
of the day was an Evergreen; for, in the Kirk of
Balmawhapple, son has followed father in unbroken
succession from beyond the memory of man.   The
letter, which was discovered quite lately within the
covers of an old family Bible, is incomplete and un-
signed; but its writer (whoever he was) must have
had a decided literary aptitude, for its drift is clear
enough.   A captious critic indeed might be tempted
to opine that it is even modern in its realism,—
which however is partly due, no doubt, to the fact
that the cipher is obscure, and the decipher more or
less tentative and provisional.   Throughout this volume, as the reader will have observed, I have carefully avoided the archaic.   It needs a great master
of "our English" to make the obsolete vital.   Did
even Thackeray quite succeed?

"It was late on the Friday night—a Friday night towards
the middle of September.

"I was about to undress when I heard a soft tap on the
window.   My room is on the ground-floor, and looks into the
garden.   It was nearly midnight, but the yellow hunter's moon
had risen, and a long lane of light lay upon the unquiet plain
of water that stretched away to the horizon.

"'Are you up, Mr James?' said the Doctor, peering in at
me through the open window.   'We must get this foolish boy
out of the way.   Corbie is off for the red-coats.   The Shirra
is a good fellow, who does not love Corbie, and he gave me a

hint. I have got Watty to the Old Manse, where our good friend the D.D. is taking charge of him till we come. One of the whaling brigs is in the bay; she sails with the first light; and I want you to have a boat ready to take him on board. Get old Peter Buchan if you can—he would do anything for Watty—Watty used to go with him to the deep-sea fishing years ago when a bairn. Meantime I shall try to get the lad's belongings together—if I can manage it quietly.'

"The Doctor darted off into the darkness, and, putting out the light, I went down to the fishers' quarter of the town, where Peter lived. The unsavoury suburb was all astir; the lines were being baited in the flickering lamp-light; the fleet were to leave with the first flow of the tide. I sought out Peter, who was yet barely awake; but he brightened up presently when I told him my errand, and he promised that his yawl would be lying under the sea-wall of the Old Manse at one sharp. It was now midnight.

"The townspeople were fast asleep, and the oil-lamp at the Provost's door was economically turned out, as I made my way along the shore to the Old Manse. Only the blue and red lights of the smacks were burning in the bay, though further off, near the point of the promontory, a star-like flash from the brilliant lamp which the Laird keeps in the Tower showed that the inmates of the Cleuch were still up.

"The door of the Manse stood open, and I entered quietly. The evening devotions had been delayed by the arrival of the unexpected guest; but the household were now gathered in the parlour, and I could follow more or less distinctly the tremulous voice of the old man praying the Lord to guard those who had wandered from the fold, and to guide their feet into the way of peace. They were singing a verse from a good old Scottish hymn,—

> ' To an inheritance divine
>   He taught our hearts to rise ;
> 'Tis uncorrupted, undefil'd,
>   Unfading in the skies,'[1]—

---

[1] I had fancied that this version was of later date.

when I heard the Doctor's feet on the gravel. 'We must hurry up,' he whispered. 'Corbie will be back in an hour—there are red-coats at Ardallie—they will take the short cut across the hill. We can't wait.'

"The old man laid his withered hands upon Watty's head, and gave him a last blessing. 'Be a good lad,' he said; 'be a good lad.'

"We went down noiselessly to the beach. The moon was high in heaven, and it was clear as day. The black shadows of the hedges lay across the path—cut sharply as by a knife. Cautiously we opened the wicket-gate in the sea-wall of the garden, and looked out. The sands lay white before us. Black sails were beginning to leave the harbour. At the little pier beneath our feet a boat was drawn up. I whistled softly; there was a low whistle in reply: the coast was clear. We glided down the steep path—the three of us—the Doctor, Watty, and myself. When we reached the pier no time was lost; the oars were already in the water; Peter stood with one foot on the jetty, with one on the gunwale of the boat, ready to shove off. I grasped Watty's hand, bidding him in a whisper to bear himself like a man, and all might yet be well; the Doctor bundled the valise into the bow; and in another second four strong oars were driving the heavy boat through the phosphorescent water.

"Even while we waited a shrill whistle came from the big ship. The sails were up; the anchor was in; she was eager to be off—to whale and iceberg. The boat glided alongside, and then after a moment's delay the two dark objects fell apart. Those on board the Orion—bound for the Faroes and the great whaling-grounds beyond—would not see England again for two years.

"The Doctor's gig was waiting for him at the corner of the Deacon's Wynd. 'There is a nip in the air,' he said, 'it must be near the dawn.' As he spoke we heard the big clock in the Tower strike two. The bells of Balmawhapple answered across the bay.

"Then in the moonlight silence that followed we heard the clatter of hoofs. It was the red-coats—Corbie with them—

riding down the Langgate. But we were in deep shadow, and they saw us not.

"'The bird has flown,' said the Doctor, with a chuckle, as he took the reins. 'I am bound for Cuddiestone—old Davie Dewar will not last the night—but I'll see the laird as I pass the Cleuch, and warn him that Watty is weel awa'. And the Prince too—thank God!—if this night's news be true.'"

I may add that Walter, a sea-bird like them all by birth and breeding, took to the sea, and lived to be an old man. My father used to tell us that he had had a client who was "out in the '45." Watty was the man.

* * *

Here in the meantime I put away the pen. But how about the struggle over Hector's body? It had been my intention, as you may have gathered, to conclude the First Book of the *Chronicles of Balma-whapple*—the historical series, if I may make bold to use the expression—with a true and particular account of the great election fight between Mark Holdfast, who represented the party of privilege and a creed as extinct as the Dodo (so Pat's rival editor remarked), and the great social and domestic reformer Mr Pigs-wash, who was in favour of the payment of members and purity all round. ("Pigswash and Purity!" indeed, during these days met us at every turn.) The whole forces of the ancient burgh were trotted out; here Bohemian sharpshooters, there the heavy cavalry of the Philistines; Corbie, and "G.G," and

"daft Davie Dewar," and the butter and egg merchant on the one side; and Pat, and the *Tomahawk*,
and the Doctor, and the Ronhead fisher-lads, and Miss
Christian and Miss Anne, and Lawrence and Dobbs
on the other. But the documents have been mislaid,
and if I write from memory only some considerate
critic will be sure to remind me that I am morbidly
inaccurate. Besides, though it took place only thirty
years ago, the vital spark is fled. The speeches have
grown vapid; the sting has gone out of them; the
pleasantries which evoked tumultuous "cheers and
laughter" are no longer intelligible. Oblivion scattereth her poppies. The honest yeoman who said in
the witness-box the other day that he had lived on
his land from time immemorial was not so far wrong
as the audience fancied when they laughed. The
pace grows more and more furious as we near the
goal, and the newspapers of 1860 are already further
away from us than Homer or Jeremiah.

And yet from another point of view I regret the
misadventure. Had I been privileged to bring this
opening series to a close with a vivid report of the
famous Balmawhapple "mill," the reader would have
been able to compare the Balmawhapple of a milder
and possibly happier age with the Balmawhapple
which burnt witches, and continued to regard with
wholesome respect the tail, the horns, and the cloven
hoof of the dreaded enemy of mankind. The report
not being forthcoming, I am haunted by an uneasy
suspicion that my record is more or less imperfect.

How, I ask myself, is the gap to be filled? How can I prove to you that we have travelled many miles, have entered indeed into another world altogether, since John Knox thundered in the High Street against the Witch at the other end of the Canongate? I can only comfort myself with the reflection that in the later Books of these veracious *Chronicles* an answer may possibly be found. Mark shall speak for himself,— shall take us with him to Summer Isles which look out upon the Atlantic, where the eider nests, and the solan dives, and the great seal basks upon the tangle; his daughter Madge, in an Idyll of Alpine Valleys, shall tell us, with not unbecoming freedom, let us hope, how among the mighty mountains which we have come to love, but which were so "monstrous" to our great-grandmothers and their beaus, her wooing sped; the impressions of an Impressionist shall not be unre-corded; and on the hillside, over above Balmawhapple, we shall listen, it may be, to animated discourse on the wits and critics and poets and painters and philoso-phers who in the autumn (or winter) of this Nineteenth Century have been falling as the leaves fall in October.

END OF THE FIRST VOLUME.

PRINTED BY WILLIAM BLACKWOOD AND SONS.

www.ingramcontent.com/pod-product-compliance
Lightning Source LLC
Chambersburg PA
CBHW031345020726
47499CB00005B/1400